MURDER, MY DEER

Berkley Prime Crime Books by Jaqueline Girdner

MURDER, MY DEER

JAQUELINE GIRDNER

BERKLEY PRIME CRIME, NEW YORK

MURDER, MY DEER

This is a work of fiction. Names, characters, places, and incidents are
either the product of the author's imagination or are used fictitiously,
and any resemblance to actual persons, living or dead, business
establishments, events or locales is entirely coincidental.

A Berkley Prime Crime Book
Published by the Berkley Publishing Group,
a division of Penguin Putnam Inc.,
375 Hudson Street
New York, New York 10014

The Penguin Putnam Inc. World Wide Web site address is
http://www.penguinputnam.com

First Edition: March 2000

Library of Congress Cataloging-in-Publication Data

Girdner, Jaqueline.
Murder, my deer / by Jaqueline Girdner
p.   cm.
ISBN 0-425-17328-3
I. Title.

PS3557.I718 M88 2000
813'.54—dc21
                                                            99-045137

Printed in the United States of America

10   9   8   7   6   5   4   3   2   1

To my own, sweet deer, Greg,
big brown eyes and all

ACKNOWLEDGMENTS

My thanks to Enid Schantz of the Rue Morgue and Susan Miller of Mystery Bookshop Bethesda for two of the best lines in the book.

CAST OF CHARACTERS
✿

MEMBERS OF THE DEER-ABUSED SUPPORT GROUP:

Avis Eldora: Owner of Eldora Nurseries, a former B-movie actress, and friend to Kate. She has daughter problems.

Dr. Searle Sandstrom: Ex-military, now a doctor in private practice. He'd like to napalm a few deer.

Dr. Reed Killian: Guest lecturer, a plastic surgeon of many distractions, including romantic ones.

Darcie Watkins: A thirteen-year-old girl with problems who adores her grandmother and hates her father.

Jean Watkins: Darcie's grandmother, an occasionally wise woman with her own set of ethics.

Lisa Orton: Support-group junkie and heiress. She doesn't like men much but adores her therapist.

Gilda Fitch: An ex-British postmistress who is both witty and observant, but is she "postal"?

Howie Damon: High school administrator. He's written a three-generation chronicle of California history and would like everyone to read it.

Natalie Miner: Realtor. She's more interested in the marital possibilities concerning Dr. Sandstrom than in deer tips.

Maxwell Yang: Talk-show host. Dr. Sandstrom thinks he talks too much.

Kate Jasper: Marin County's own, karmically impaired sleuth.

Wayne Caruso: Kate's sweetie and new husband.

Felix Byrne: Pit bull reporter, he's suffering a little karmic impairment himself.

OTHERS:

Barbara Chu: Felix's psychic sweetie and Kate's friend.

Captain Thorton: Head of the Abierto Police Department. He's having a pre-retirement nervous breakdown.

Lieutenant Perez: He's his captain's keeper.

Officers Ulric and Zenas: Loyal officers of the A.P.D.

Deer Count: A deer rights group.

Kevin Koffenburger: Kate's brother. He has a deal for you.

Xanthe: Kevin's girlfriend. She has the same deal.

Slammer: Kevin and Xanthe's friend, muscle-head for hire.

Various partners, friends, relatives, employees, lovers, police officials, and food servers.

PROLOGUE

✣

Ever so gently and delicately nibbling, savoring the moisture of the rosebud, exulting in the darkness and wind. Paradise. Bushes and bushes of paradise. Another munch. Ah, the second bud was just as succulent as the first. But then, an alien scent. A two-legged beast moving in the shadows. Nibbling is suddenly forgotten. Perhaps paradise might be better enjoyed in another yard? Hind legs tensed in readiness. Or was it too late? Something clicked in the beast's hand. And paradise exploded.

One

✶

"Just shoot 'em, I say—"

"Lighten up! Cripes, it's only March. You can't just shoot deer out of hunting season, or in your own backyard for that matter," Dr. Reed Killian tried to reason, bouncing on his heels and waving his hands. Reed had handsome, slightly fleshy features under his dark, exquisitely styled hair. I wondered if he'd sculpted those features himself. He was a plastic surgeon. And there was probably nothing he could do about the unfashionable fleshiness. Nothing but starve.

Reed looked frantically over his lectern, signaling the owner of the nursery for backup. After all, it was Avis Eldora who'd asked him to be tonight's speaker at the Eldora Nurseries Thursday evening Deer-Abused Support Group, or the Deerly Abused, as I was beginning to think of our fledgling membership. And there we were, all neatly arranged in a semicircle of metal folding chairs near the cash register to hear everything that Reed had to say on the subject of deer abuse.

But Avis didn't respond to Reed's signal for backup. She just pulled up a shoulder as if to hide behind it and turned her ageless, elegant profile away under her trademark wide-brimmed hat. I didn't blame her. Battling deer was one thing, but battling members of the group came under another category. Actually, it probably came under a lot of categories, beginning with Bad for Business.

"I don't care if it is illegal," Dr. Sandstrom resumed from his chair, two seats over from me, his voice loud enough to grab everyone's attention without even yelling. Now, Dr. Sandstrom couldn't have been called handsome. His features might have been even, but they were as long and narrow as a stalk of lupine. And the visual assault of his compressed, thin lips and the squint of his eyes under his aviator glasses was enough to make you want to turn your head away. That much anger in a face could turn a person to stone. Not to mention a deer. The back of my neck prickled. "I'm talking the laws of nature," he went on. "Nature isn't a moron. Haven't you noticed how small and sick the deer are these days? Nature doesn't want 'em. Now, a simple coffee-can Claymore mine, that's the ticket. You have to do what's necessary. Bam-bam-Bambi, I say."

Yuck. I hoped Dr. Sandstrom, as he insisted on being addressed, wasn't going to tell us any more about land mines. I looked over at Wayne's sweet, homely face, catching his large hand in mine and squeezing it. *Wayne*, I cooed inwardly, a coo I would have never repeated aloud. How embarrassing. Wayne, my husband. Even more embarrassing was the giddiness I felt when I said the word "husband," even in the privacy of my own mind. Wayne and I had finally gotten married, secretly, at the Marin County Clerk's office two days ago. I remembered his whispered vows—

"Hey, you lay off, you wickety-wack old man," Darcie Watkins broke in from my other side. She was only thirteen years old. Still, she looked almost as angry as Dr. Sandstrom. Her square face was flushed under her baseball cap and her prominent teeth were bared under dark brown lipstick as she leaned forward in her seat. "You're as messed up as my dad, and that's saying a whole effing lot. Deer are just animals. Nice animals. And you're just a jack—"

"Now, Darcie," her grandmother, Jean Watkins, intervened, her jaw just as square as her granddaughter's under a face very like Darcie's despite the generations between them. She put a hand on Darcie's shoulder, a hand that seemed more loving than reprimanding in intent.

"Aw, Gramma," Darcie whined. But she leaned into her grandmother's hand despite the whine.

"Listen," Reed suggested, forcing a cheery smile. "Let's just keep this discussion upbeat—"

Too late.

"Yeah, Darcie," Lisa Orton put in. This battle wasn't over yet. "Fathers! I thought the deer were abusive, but you're worse, *Doctor* Sandstrom. You should be sorry—"

"Lisa," Reed interrupted gently, though there was impatience underlying his mild tone. He bounced on his heels some more.

Lisa looked up at our speaker. She must have been twenty years older than Darcie, but at that moment she looked like a child herself, with her round dark eyes wide open. Or maybe it was her freckles and ponytail. She sucked in her lower lip and pulled on her fingers like a chastened schoolgirl.

"Let's have fun with this," Reed tried again. "We're all here to talk about protecting our gardens from deer—"

But Dr. Sandstrom still had a few of his own licks to get in.

"You," he accused, pointing at Lisa. "Darcie is only a child. Her behavior is excusable. But aren't you old enough to engage in reasonable discussion without bringing up your father? Are you one of those fools who blames their parents for your own problems? Grow up . . ."

I looked back at Wayne. His rough cheeks were pink now. I traveled inward to a world of silent coos and left behind the angry voices surrounding me, breathing deeply of the scents of rosemary and wet potting soil drifting in the doorway. Did my new husband know what I was thinking as I sat next to him? Wayne, my sweet Wayne, one of the homeliest men I'd ever met, with a face dominated by a cauliflower nose and brows so low you had to be below him to look up into his vulnerable, brown eyes. Of course, looking up at him was easy since he was tall and muscular below that gargoyle's face. A gentle giant. An intelligent giant. A loving and sensitive giant. And now my husband. I realized I was getting giddy again and shook my head to clear it. We'd come to tonight's support group because our garden had been mauled by the local deer. And because neither of us had time for a honeymoon. I told myself I should at least listen. I might learn something.

". . . to read my manuscript," Howie Damon was finishing up as I tuned back in. I looked over at Howie's undistinguished round face. A little blob of a nose, a small mouth, and even smaller eyes looked back. His manuscript?

"What does your manuscript have to do with killing deer?" Dr. Sandstrom cut back in.

"Not *killing* deer!" Reed insisted, his voice shrill now as he rolled his eyes in their handsome sockets. "Controlling deer. Come on, get real! There are lots of ways to control deer that don't involve claymore mines—"

"Look, I say what I mean," Sandstrom cut back in. " 'Controlling deer,' " he mimicked, his voice unnaturally high. Then he snorted. "No euphemisms for me. Now, maybe you don't want to get your yuppie hands dirty to deal with the critters. Maybe that's what you're afraid of. Yeah, and I'll bet you didn't go to Vietnam either." He sat back in his chair triumphantly.

Reed closed his eyes and took a deep breath.

"Actually, I did, Dr. Sandstrom," he replied, lowering his voice with an obvious effort. "And *I* did not have fun. But we are here tonight to talk about deer management. Maybe we've gotten off to a bad start, but I think we ought to keep rolling. Since there are many of us here who obviously have some feelings on this subject, let's all introduce ourselves and talk about those feelings, okay?"

Wow, Deer Anonymous.

"Capital idea, my dear chap," the black, thirty-something woman from the end of the row put in. I blinked in surprise and hoped no one noticed. Somehow, I hadn't expected to hear the high, nasal twang of the British upper classes coming from the membership of the Deerly Abused. The woman had laughing eyes in a face the color of true maple syrup. She reached up to twiddle one of the curls in her topknot and smiled, her teeth sparkling white. "Deer are nasty little blighters, it's true. But even as a postmistress of your fair county, *I* wouldn't go postal on the poor creatures, what?"

A silence descended on our group. I realized I wasn't the only one surprised by the woman's manner of speech.

"Oh, what a nuisance," the woman added with another sparkling smile. "Forgot to introduce myself, what? Gilda Fitch, late of Great Britain, now an American citizen." Then she saluted. "Rah-rah."

Ah, Gilda was having fun. Good. I was glad someone was. She winked my way as though she'd heard my thought. Or seen me smiling back, most likely.

"Well, *I've* already introduced myself," Howie Damon finally put in. "I'm a high school administrator. I garden. And I write. In fact, I've just finished a manuscript detailing three generations of Californians—"

"Any California *deer* in it?" Maxwell Yang drawled from Howie's side. Maxwell Yang didn't need any introduction. Anyone in the San Francisco Bay area had seen his well-groomed impish Asian features on TV's *Everyone's Talking*. Even those of us without TVs had seen his face in the newspaper or heard him interviewed on the radio. Our local answer to Oprah.

"Well, yes, Mr. Yang," Howie squeaked enthusiastically. "Man and deer, their fates entwined. In fact, I hoped you might take a look at my manuscript tonight," he added raising about four inches of paper from his lap. I wondered how many pages four inches made. Too many, I guessed from Maxwell's momentarily unguarded blink of annoyance.

"*Will* you keep your idiotic manuscript out of this discussion?" Dr. Sandstrom demanded.

Howie ducked his head as if to look down at the doctor's olive-drab hiking boots, but there was hurt in his movement.

"Well, I'm Maxwell Yang," our TV host interposed quickly. That was kind of him. Or maybe he was just tired of the squabbling. "And I, too, have a deer problem. In the animal world, my appeal seems to extend to does as well as stags, not to mention fawns." He waved his hand, smiling that attractive self-deprecating smile that had probably charmed many a man, if not a few women. "But in this case their attention is unwelcome—"

"Deer, folks," Dr. Sandstrom interrupted again. "We are not here to talk about fathers or manuscripts or sexual proclivities. We're here to talk about deer."

Maxwell merely smiled at the interruption, with a faint arching of his eyebrows. Dr. Sandstrom might have been flirting with Maxwell for his response.

"I think the doctor's right," a woman sitting next to Dr. Sandstrom cooed. *Ugh.* I didn't like hearing my inner coos aloud. Except that hers had a raspy, Southern accent. She had a nice makeup job on her postmenopausal baby face, and her blond hair twirled from her head like a spray of extra-long rotini pasta. She turned to Sandstrom. "I'm Natalie Miner, and I must say that the good Lord knows we're all here because deer are decimating our gardens. Surely you folks ought to appreciate that. I'm sure I do." Then she tilted her head and threw the doctor a sympathetic glance.

Dr. Sandstrom flinched. What all the yelling and reasoning could not do, a little Southern coquetry had accomplished. Sandstrom was quiet. He crossed his arms and turned his head away from Natalie.

"Jeez, what an airhead," Darcie commented in a stage whisper.

"Darcie!" Jean Watkins rapped out. This time, she didn't put a comforting hand on her granddaughter's shoulder.

"Sorry, Gramma," Darcie said quietly. The thirteen-year-old was wearing an awful lot of makeup under her baseball cap, but it couldn't hide her blush. "Sorry, Ms. Miner."

"Why don't you introduce yourself, Darcie?" Reed suggested cautiously.

"Um," Darcie answered. "I'm, like, Darcie Watkins. I'm here 'cause Gramma's got deer in her garden, and they eat her roses, and she feels bad." She paused, then added, "I live with my gramma 'cause my dad is all messed up like Dr. Sand—"

"Darcie lives with me because I love her," Jean Watkins intervened. "And she's right about my garden. I'm afraid I have very high standards for my blooms, and I get upset when the deer eat them. But I do believe we should act responsibly and reasonably to discourage the animals. The way we treat a species such as deer affects the way we treat our entire planet. And each other."

"Good point," Reed chirped, beaming.

"Well, you're not alone, Darcie," Lisa Orton added. "I can understand your feelings. My father was a doctor—"

Dr. Sandstrom started to open his mouth, but Lisa got back on track before he could cut in.

"I have trouble with deer, too. I've been trying to grow vegetables and a nice border. Then I heard about this group. I love support groups." She brought her palm to her face and popped something in her mouth before continuing. "See, it works out great. I have my survivors' group on Tuesday, and Women Without Partners on Wednesday, and on Thursdays I see my therapist at six o'clock, so eight o'clock is perfect for the deer group."

"Kate?" Reed asked quickly, before Lisa could go on.

"Huh?" I said, briefly startled. Then I caught up and identified myself and my trouble with deer. It took a while to cover every kind of plant they'd eaten, from chrysanthemums and roses to tomatoes and strawberries, but everyone seemed to nod at the mention of each. When I had finally exhausted my complaints, Reed's eyes traveled to my side.

"Wayne Caruso," my sweetie—my husband—jumped in without further prompting. "Same garden, same worries." Rank, name, and serial number. Groups have that effect on him.

We all looked around. Reed had introduced himself when he took the podium. Who was left?

"Well, you all know me—Avis," came the hesitant but clear

voice of Eldora Nurseries' owner. For a moment I glimpsed
the beauty of her aging face under her hat and scarf. Avis
obsessed about skin cancer and kept each and every one of
her body parts protected from the sun. Or maybe from questioning glances. Her elegant profile, almond-shaped green
eyes, and sensual lips were hard to forget once sighted. How
many years ago had she been in her prime as an actress?
Thirty? Forty? "Lots of you have asked what to do about the
deer over the years, and I just thought it would be nice to get
together and discuss solutions. And Dr. Reed Killian has stud-
ied the subject extensively. Shall we go on?" She turned her
head toward Reed.

Reed looked toward Dr. Sandstrom, inviting him with
sculpted eyes to formally introduce himself. The doctor got
up, pushed his chair back, and then stomped from the room
out the front door to join the flats and pots of plants resting
silently behind iron gates. Deer-proof iron gates.

Reed sighed loudly, looked at our group, and then followed
Dr. Sandstrom out the door.

"Well, shall we have a little break?" Avis suggested shyly.
"Maybe we can just mingle informally for a while. Enjoy the
evening. Feel free to look around the nursery. It's really pretty
this time of evening."

"Righto," Gilda Fitch agreed, popping out of her chair. "Just
the thing." She exited the front door too. This time, I caught
a glimpse of twilight-blue sky and the fragrance of narcissus.

Metal chairs clattered as the remaining members of the
Deerly Abused stood.

I vacated my chair simultaneously with Wayne.

"Walk outside?" he asked, and I nodded silently, internal-
izing my romantic sigh. Flowers, magical twilight, Wayne.
You betcha.

He took my hand, and we made our way to the door. But
not out of it.

"Surely you appreciate the fact that the man is just trying
to help," I heard Natalie Miner say to Avis.

Avis stood cornered, her panicked eyes just visible under her hat.

But before I could think of any words of defense to offer Avis, Lisa Orton was already speaking, her freckled face earnest.

"My therapist would say that a man with that much anger is suffering from estrogen deprivation," she told Natalie.

"But he—"

"My therapist is great, she hypnotizes me and everything. If anyone can get me through the abuse I suffered as a child—"

"Gramma sent me to a therapist too," Darcie interrupted. "But then I stopped going. The old wackhead wanted me to say I did dirty things with my father."

"There are other forms of abuse besides sexual," Darcie's grandmother put in. "But this young man didn't seem to understand that physical and verbal abuse can wound too, wound very deeply." She sighed. "All this insistence upon sex as the root of all evil forgets the basic human need for compassion and love."

"Yeah," Lisa agreed, with what I wasn't sure. "Wounded, that's it. *My* therapist has even uncovered memories—"

Reed blew back in the door, chatting with Gilda.

We all turned his way.

"Dr. Sandstrom is ranting out there," he told us. "God, I'd hate to be a deer in his gunsight."

"Or a human," Maxwell added, laughing easily. "He's quite a character, isn't he?"

"A character!" Lisa objected. "He's worse than a character. He's real. And nasty. And abusive!"

I was really getting tired of the word "abusive." And so, apparently, was Natalie Miner.

"Hon," she whispered, grabbing Lisa's hand in hers. "Y'all just don't understand what the man's been through. You've got to appreciate—"

But Lisa yanked her hand back and was next out the door before Natalie could even finish.

And now I was curious. Just what had Dr. Sandstrom been through? What abuse had he suffered?

I worked on formulating the question. But not quickly enough.

"He wasn't even interested in my manuscript," Howie Damon piped up before my thoughts could become words.

"Mr. Yang," Howie pleaded, "you're interested in my manuscript, aren't you?" Grasping his four-inch stack of paper in both hands, he thrust it in Maxwell's direction.

Maxwell Yang must have spent years controlling his facial expression. He maintained his smile as he spoke to Howie.

"Call my secretary, and we'll see what we can arrange," he suggested.

"Oh, thank you," Howie breathed, never asking the secretary's phone number. I had a feeling Maxwell was counting on that.

Avis stuck her gloved arm in the crook of mine. Even at night, her fair skin was covered, head to foot.

"It's beautiful outdoors, Kate," she told me. "Maybe we could walk for a minute?"

I turned to Wayne, longing for his arm tucked into mine, his hand holding mine, but Avis sounded shaky.

Wayne just nodded. I left with Avis out the front door.

The sky *was* magical, a shimmering blue over the rows of plants. No wonder Avis ran a nursery for a living. What a beautiful way to live. If it weren't for customers.

"Dr. Sandstrom is usually okay, Kate," she confided as we passed the flats of late primroses. "Courteous, doesn't argue over prices. I don't know what's come over him tonight. This deer thing has him all churned up." She sighed. "I just wish people would get along."

"They do, mostly," I answered inadequately, looking at this women swathed in layers of cloth and a straw hat. How much of the swathing was a protection from the incivilities of life? Plants were easier than people, that was for sure.

We continued our short stroll, arm in arm. At the end of a row of sweet alyssum six-packs, I stumbled over something.

Something substantial. I looked down and blinked, hoping I wasn't seeing what I was seeing.

Was that Dr. Sandstrom crumpled on the ground, a dark sticky patch on the back of his head?

And was that a bronze deer statuette lying beside him?

If it was, the deer had clearly won.

Two

🜨

I sucked in a big breath of sweet alyssum and locked my lungs around it, unable to take my gaze from Dr. Sandstrom's body. My muscles stiffened till they felt as rigid as the bronze that formed the deer statuette. Still, I doubted that the statuette's shoulders hurt like mine did. Or its head. Or its stomach. Or its conscience. Because here I was again, on the scene of homicidal violence, the Typhoid Mary of Murder. Here I was in a small group of people, and . . . and . . . It couldn't have been a mistake. It couldn't—

"Stupid morons," Dr. Sandstrom's body erupted.

I looked down, really looked, delivered from my self-absorption by the sound. Since when did dead men speak? Since when did they move? The doctor was rolling over now onto his back. Then he groaned and clutched his head.

Dead men spoke when they weren't dead, I answered myself. The relief unlocked my lungs long enough for a long gush of outgoing breath and loosened my muscles. In fact, my muscles couldn't seem to stop loosening. Was I going to end up on the ground like Dr. Sandstrom?

I couldn't have joined the doctor anyway. He stood before I had the chance and brushed off his clothing with his hands, making dust clouds in the twilight.

Avis jerked, her arm still linked with mine.

"You're alive," I told him. My words sounded strange in

my ears. Maybe the sound had something to do with the dryness of my mouth.

"Don't be a complete fool," he snapped back. "Of course I'm alive."

"But your head," I objected. Because standing or not, the doctor's head was still sticky with blood.

"It'll be fine," he assured me. "The clown who hit me didn't hit me hard enough."

"What clown?" I asked.

The doctor stared at me, his long, pinched features in thought.

"I never saw him," he admitted. "Coward snuck up behind me. Could have been anyone—"

"What happened?" asked a voice somewhere in back of me. Reed Killian's voice. And then his voice was joined by Lisa Orton's, and Darcie Watkins's, and Gilda Fitch's. Each voice seemed louder than the one before, each asking questions. And then Howie Damon and Maxwell Yang joined the chorus along with Jean Watkins and Natalie Miner. It was getting mighty noisy. Still, Avis remained mute, though she gently extracted her arm from mine.

"Some sneaky jackass hit me over the head," the doctor broke in. "I didn't see him, but I'll figure out who it was." He paused, eyeing the Deerly Abused. "That's a promise."

Wayne's hand grasped mine as Reed offered medical assistance, which Sandstrom of course refused.

"Doctor, you really need to have that attended to," Jean Watkins insisted.

"Oh, Lord, yes," Natalie Miner chimed in. "That's a really nasty—"

"I am a doctor, okay!" Sandstrom cut her off. "I'll find out what imbecile pulled this stunt, and I'll feel much better, trust me." Then he actually smiled in the descending darkness. It was not a pretty sight.

"We need to call the police," I began. "Let them find out who did—"

"No!" he bellowed. "Will you folks get it through your thick skulls that I can deal with this?" Then he winced. Ow, it must have hurt to bellow with a head like that.

"Fine," Avis whispered next to me. I jumped. I'd almost forgotten her.

Gilda broke the ensuing silence. "Were there any deer hoof-prints?" she asked.

I actually looked back at the ground for a giveaway clue left by a representative of the species. But all I could see was the bronze statuette, soil, plant detritus, and a mint-green capsule that the doctor picked up and shoved in his jacket pocket.

I looked back up at Gilda and saw the sparkle of her smile. Hoofprints. A joke. Ha, bloody ha.

"So who—"

"So what—"

"So do you think—"

The iron gate at the end of the parking lot rattled and all of us started. Was a deer rebellion in progress?

"Holy moly," a familiar voice boomed. But not one I'd expected here. "This place is locked tighter than the President's corset. Where's the friggin' class?"

I told myself it couldn't be, not my friend Barbara's sweetie, pit bull reporter, annoyance of annoyances. Felix? Why would Felix come to a deer-abused support group? And precisely when I'd found an undead body? My brain was fritzing like an elderly TV set about to die. I hit the side of my head with the heel of my hand. Percussive maintenance. It didn't work.

"Hey, man," the familiar voice came again. "How do you get into this friggin' mausoleum?"

Avis stared at the gates. Wayne looked down at me just as I looked up at him. Dr. Sandstrom eyed the crowd, and then strode off in the direction of the shed behind the main building, where the nursery wheelbarrows, tools, smocks, and gloves were stored. And more importantly, the restrooms. Presumably he wanted to clean his head wound.

Reed took over. "Cripes," he muttered, looking down at the statuette. No one seemed to want to touch it. "I guess the show goes on. Avis, you gonna open the gate?"

Avis turned slowly to look at Reed. She could have been an extra for *The Night of the Living Dead.* Actually, she really might have been one, I realized. She'd probably been a working actress when it was filmed.

"Oh, of course," Avis murmured and pulled a large bunch of keys from a pocket beneath one of her many scarves.

"Did someone hit the ole dude?" Darcie Watkins asked as Avis opened the iron gate with a great clanging noise.

"It looks like—" I began.

"Here comes the bride," the voice from outside the gate sang. Then it came in the gate, getting louder. "So stout and wide. Here comes the groom, all full of—"

"Stop that!" I shouted, my brain suddenly clearing. It *was* Felix. Even though it was nearly dark, it was still easy to make out his small, slender body, luxurious mustache, and dark, soulful eyes. Not to mention his smile, Cheshire cat-wide. But he was singing about weddings. How could he know? Barbara, my friend and our witness, had promised not to tell, especially not to tell her sweetie, Felix.

"Hey, musta been some whiz-bang nup-che-al," Felix went on, teasing out the syllables of the word so that it sounded obscene. Then he went into falsetto mode. "This inquiring mind wants to know what the bride wore."

"Ask Barbara," I responded angrily. But still, I didn't really believe that my friend would have told Felix, even if she did care for him for some irrational reason that I had never quite understood. I felt Wayne's hand on my shoulder. Was there a message in that hand?

"Why ask Barbara?" Felix replied, glaring. "My honeybun didn't tell me a friggin' thing. Doo-doo. Nada. Nooo. Not a word to her sweet tiger-muffin—"

"Then how'd you find out?" I demanded.

"Ever hear of public records?" he returned my question.

So that's why Felix had come to the first meeting of the Deerly Abused. He'd come to torture me. It had nothing to do with Dr. Sandstrom's un-demise. And I knew why Wayne was squeezing my shoulder too. The trick with Felix was to refuse to interact with him in any way. No matter what I said, I'd get entangled. I'd forgotten that trick.

I'd also forgotten the group behind us.

"Who is this guy?" Reed asked. But before he could get an answer, Dr. Sandstrom walked back on the scene, holding a soaked paper towel to his head.

"Hon," Natalie said to the doctor. "Are you sure you're all right? God knows you're a doctor and all, but a blow to the head—"

"A blow to the head?" Felix chimed in, his soulful eyes lighting up like headlights.

Dr. Sandstrom squinted through his aviator glasses. "And just who are you?" he asked.

"Felix Byrne," Barbara's sweetie replied.

"Ace reporter," I added, just to keep things clear.

Felix shot me a venomous look.

"Reporter!" Dr. Sandstrom yelped. "What fool called a reporter?"

"Why?" Felix inquired innocently. "Did someone attack you?" Felix was annoying, weaselly, and sneaky, but he wasn't slow.

"Just a bop on the head," the doctor said dismissively. "And none of your business in any case. Why are you here?"

"I think he wants to join the group," Avis interjected softly. She turned to Felix.

"Sure," Felix agreed earnestly. "Deer, gardens—"

"But you live in an apartment," I objected, my voice whining without my permission. "You don't even have a garden." Wayne squeezed my shoulder again. "But he doesn't," I insisted, looking up at Wayne. Wayne's eyebrows were lowered, his features impassive. The granite gargoyle was in place.

"I might get a house," Felix told us. Then he turned to Avis and smiled ingratiatingly. "And my mother has a garden."

Wayne was right. His hand on my shoulder was right. I had to ignore Felix. I clamped my lips shut and tried to look like Wayne, thinking granite. At least Dr. Sandstrom hadn't been murdered. So what did it matter if Felix was here? He knew we were married, that's what it mattered. And if Felix knew, he'd spread the word just for spite's sake. And we'd wanted to keep it secret for too many reasons to even keep track of. Of course, Felix wanted to stay for the last half of the meeting. He hadn't tortured us nearly enough yet.

Felix smiled in the near-darkness. My hands curled into fists.

"Shall we go back inside?" Avis asked quietly.

"But what hap—" Darcie Watkins tried.

"Nothing," Dr. Sandstrom interrupted her. And then he led the way back into the building with the military gait of a general leading his troops. Everyone glanced around, then each of us followed, including Felix.

Within minutes, we were all sitting in a semicircle around the podium again, plus one chair. One chair with one grinning, nosy reporter.

I tried not to think about Felix as Reed spoke. But as soon as I stopped thinking about Felix, I started worrying about Dr. Sandstrom again. It was true he was alive, but had his attacker intended him to be alive? The blow to his head hadn't been a minor one. I certainly didn't know how hard to hit someone in order to kill them. Maybe Dr. Sandstrom's attacker hadn't either. I brought my mind back to focus on Reed's words of wisdom. Deer, I told myself. I was here to learn about deer.

". . . to try safe plants. Lavender, oleander, rosemary, lantana, foxglove, yarrow, daffodils, iris, jasmine, wisteria, zinnias . . ."

The doctor certainly hadn't made any friends in class. Thinking about it, I could imagine almost any one of the Deerly Abused clobbering him with a deer statuette. Or a deer clobbering him, for that matter. Maybe Gilda hadn't been kidding with her "hoofprints" question. Ghostly deer spirits danced through my mind, their brown eyes suddenly intelligent, focused . . . deadly. I shook my head and tried to listen to Reed again.

"Some of the best deer repellents are actually plants," he was saying.

Or Felix, I thought. Felix could probably repel deer or just about anything. Maybe I should just nail his feet to our front gate. That was a cheery thought. Upside down would be especially nice.

". . . mothballs, soap, Tabasco sauce, monofilament line, sprinklers . . ."

And if I nailed Felix up by his heels, he wouldn't be able to tell everyone that Wayne and I were married. Fantasy is a wonderful place to dwell.

". . . of course, and then, there's always fencing. Fencing can be expensive, but it's highly effective . . ."

At least Dr. Sandstrom was quiet now. Maybe that knock on the head had done him some good, after all. As soon as the thought went through my mind, I felt guilty. What if the man was really hurt? I glanced over at him. He didn't look hurt. He looked alert. Alert . . . and angry.

". . . the double fence is really cool . . ."

I kept my eyes on Dr. Sandstrom. His face was reddening, his thin lips tightening.

"It can actually be fun to foil the deer," Reed went on. "These animals aren't evil. They're gentle. In fact, Native Americans—"

"If you were a rosebud, you wouldn't think the deer were so gentle, you dunce!" Dr. Sandstrom bellowed. In the ensuing moment of silence I wondered how many of us were thinking that the good doctor hadn't been hit hard *enough* on the head.

Reed's handsome mouth gaped open.

"Native Americans didn't grow rosebushes," Dr. Sandstrom bulldozed on. "And don't tell me they never heard of venison."

"Excuse me, Doctor," Howie Damon said quietly. "I think Reed was talking about the historical relationship between man and deer, their natural alliance."

Now it was time for my mouth to drop open. Howie Damon was braver than I'd given him credit for. His round face looked more distinguished now, as if it was taking shape under an artist's pen, the blobby nose and small mouth suddenly sharper, clearer. Being a high school administrator probably gave him a lot of practice in dealing with bullies.

"Well, yes, right." Reed recovered, his mouth moving again, but his eyes still glazed. "Um, thank you, Howie—"

"In fact, in my manuscript," Howie said, hefting his stack of paper, "I speak of the history of man and nature in California—"

"Your manuscript is—" Sandstrom cut in angrily.

"I treat the deer that visit my house with respect," Howie cut back in quietly but surely. "Just as generations of Californians have. I set out a bucket of water, a salt lick and vegetables and fruits that the grocery store would throw out—"

"You knucklehead!" Dr. Sandstrom overrode him by pure volume. "Don't you know that you're just inviting them into your own neighborhood? I bet your neighbors love you. Inviting the whole nation of gentle deer to your street. Hah!"

Nope, the doctor hadn't been knocked on the head nearly hard enough.

"But deer and humans can live in peace," Howie insisted, undaunted.

"They are animals!" Dr. Sandstrom yelled back. Then he looked Howie straight in the eye and asked, "Do you eat beef?"

Howie's features seemed to blur again. "Well, a little lean meat occasionally—"

"Hah!" the doctor crowed. "And what do you think the difference is between a cow and a deer?"

"Well I—"

I thought I heard Maxwell Yang sigh.

"Oh, come on, stop picking on him," Lisa Orton put in. I assumed she was talking to the doctor, not Howie.

"Antlers, perhaps?" Gilda guessed. "At least for the male deer, all that testosterone, don'cha know."

"Huh?" Howie and Sandstrom said simultaneously.

"The difference between deer and cows, gentlemen," she reminded them. "Antlers."

Dr. Sandstrom glared Gilda's way, but Howie just looked

confused. Apparently he'd never had anyone as formidable as Gilda Fitch at his school. Or Dr. Sandstrom.

"*You* don't kill the cow," the doctor belatedly answered his own question. "Someone does it for you. Don't you realize that it's the same thing? You're killing our 'gentle friends' either way. Eating lean beef from Safeway is the coward's way out—"

"Freezerful of venison, perhaps?" Gilda inquired innocently.

The doctor had to acknowledge Gilda's presence now.

"Wouldn't that be better," he began, his volume back to normal. "We all eat meat. Maybe we'd have a more 'natural alliance' if we were real about its source."

"I don't eat meat," I pointed out. Not that the idea of fresh venison hadn't had its appeal after seeing my rose stalks. But something made me want to argue with this man.

He turned to me, squinting. On second thought, maybe I didn't want to argue with this man.

"I don't eat meat, and I don't kill deer," I expanded, in case he hadn't taken my point.

"Do you get plenty of plant protein?" he asked. He didn't seem to be yelling anymore. In fact, his tone was almost sympathetic. Paternal.

"Well, yeah," I answered, shifting uncomfortably in my chair. I wasn't sure where all this was leading. "Tofu, beans, seitan—"

"You look all right," he told me, and he really was examining me, at least with his eyes. But his gaze was no longer frightening. I realized it was *concerned*. He truly was a doctor.

"Not anemic?" he prodded. Yep, a doctor all right.

I shook my head. Not that I actually knew the answer. I just wanted him off my case.

"Well, your diet's probably okay," he pronounced. "But if you feel any unusual fatigue, you might want to have your blood tested for protein levels."

"Or try a little venison, my dear," Gilda added with a sparkling smile. "The doctor chappie here has a freezerful to share with you."

Dr. Sandstrom's head swiveled.

Reed tried a cheery preemptive strike. "So, we have three possible approaches to invading deer," he summarized. "Resistant plants, repellents, and fencing. Can anyone think of any other approaches?"

"Hah!" the doctor answered. "Guns, bows and arrows, land mines, poisons, booby traps, explosives . . ."

Dr. Sandstrom was gone. General Sandstrom had returned. I went back to worrying about Felix while the doctor made verbal, military mincemeat of our gentle allies. I lost track of the voices that argued, objected, and otherwise tried to derail him. I could have told them. It would take a land mine at least to derail the man. Maybe a coffee-can claymore mine.

At least Felix had stopped staring at me. He was staring at the doctor now, fascinated. Felix had probably told half the known world of our new marital status by now. I looked up at Wayne. His face was no longer granite, but there was worry in its shape. About Felix? I gave Wayne's thigh a surreptitious squeeze. We were on honeymoon, after all. He smiled and reached for my hand.

I mimed a kiss his way.

"Well, that's all we have time for tonight," Reed broke in. "It's been fun. Let's keep it upbeat next time, enjoy ourselves." I pulled my hand back guiltily, wondering what I'd missed.

I had a feeling I hadn't missed anything pleasant. There was relief in the air as people popped out of their metal chairs. You could hear it in the big breaths they exhaled and the lilt of social voices. But there was anger too. I could almost smell it. Was it coming from Dr. Sandstrom? But he lumbered out the doorway before I could sniff out my answer, just as I saw Felix jogging my way, his finger pointed and his mouth opening for attack.

Then Avis put a gloved hand on my arm.

I turned to my old acquaintance, hearing but not seeing the door open and close again after the doctor. Maybe it was just my imagination, but it seemed to me that all of the remaining members of the Deerly Abused were watching and waiting to hear what Avis and Felix had to say to me. The suspense didn't build for long.

"Why didn't you tell me you were married, dear?" Avis asked, hurt inflected in her soft voice. My heart sank all the way to my toes. I'd been afraid that's what she was going to ask.

"We haven't told anyone," I explained, wondering how many times I would have this conversation after Felix told the other half of the known world our news. "We wanted to keep it secret till we had a more formal wedding—"

The hand on my other arm wasn't nearly as gentle.

"Thought you could bury the scoop from your old friend, huh?" Felix rasped. "Your own compadre, your old amigo, and do I hear diddly?"

"Felix," I tried, "it's a secret. Thanks to you, a few people know, but let's leave it at that, all right?"

He smiled. I kept forgetting the trick. Don't interact with a pit bull.

"I'll be glad to keep your secret," Avis said from my other side and patted my arm.

I waited for Felix to follow verbal suit. A few seconds was all it took to realize how futile that hope was. So I turned and hugged Avis. She couldn't stop the firestorm, but at least she'd sprinkled it a little.

We were mid-hug when Reed appeared next to us. Had he been listening as attentively as everyone else?

"We'll have to open the gate, Avis," he told her. "People need to get their cars out."

That's right, I remembered, the iron gate had locked us in as effectively as it had locked the deer out. And with Felix! He was still spouting about our betrayal as Avis and Reed ventured through the doorway into the cool night air to unlock our iron prison.

Once the gate was open, Avis flitted back inside and gave Wayne a hug too. Then she sang, "Happy trails to you," in a lilting whisper. And finally, Wayne and I left the building, waving goodbye to Avis.

Wayne and I walked quickly toward our car. But not quickly enough. Felix joined us within a few steps, still grousing.

"So, Big Guy," he addressed Wayne, "any last words for the press? Time to share a little poop on the big day—"

"Felix," Wayne warned, his voice heavy with menace.

But then Felix stumbled. Neither of us had pushed him. At least I didn't think so. Wayne and I glanced at each other questioningly as Felix looked down at the ground.

"What the hey?" Felix breathed.

Then Felix, the fearless pit bull of reporting pointed where he was looking, his soulful eyes widened, and he fainted dead away.

THREE

✗

I looked down at the spot where Felix had pointed just before he fainted. Actually, we weren't far from the bumper of
his own, precious, vintage '57 Chevy. Only Felix wasn't in
his car. He was on the ground. And he wasn't alone.

Felix had landed face down, his feet across another pair of
feet. Was that why he'd stumbled? Had those feet tripped him?
I didn't want to look any closer, but as usual, my eyes had
their own agenda. They traveled up from the entangled feet to
the top of Dr. Sandstrom's prone body. Déjà vu, I thought as
my lungs locked and my muscles stiffened. No, that wasn't
the right word, my brain informed me coldly. Déjà vu wasn't
supposed to be worse. It was supposed to be the same. The
air seemed to shimmer around the bodies. A part of my brain
may have been playing linguistics, but the rest of my body
wasn't. Maybe if I breathed? I forced some air out of my lungs
and drew some new air in. It didn't help. Because this wasn't
just worse, it was much worse.

This time, Dr. Sandstrom didn't moan from the ground. He
didn't stand up and brush off his clothes. He couldn't. His
head was battered in. It was clear that he hadn't just been hit
once this time. Only repeated blows could have produced the
dark hole in the side of his head; blood, bone, and worse
splattered from that hole. The doctor's aviator glasses lay

crushed next to his head, along with the bronze deer statuette. And, incongruously, the whole mess was topped with a branch of rosemary, as if a mad chef had added the finishing touch.

But deer didn't eat rosemary, I thought. No, rosemary was definitely not on the deer's favorite-foods list. This seemed very important to the side of my brain that had provided linguistic support earlier. More important than the shimmering light and floating sensation that tugged at me, trying to lift me up off my feet. More important than the gruesome reality lying in front of me. More important than—

Wayne! I'd forgotten Wayne. I turned to him, and instantly felt my senses thud back into my body, bringing awareness of cool air, my aching face and muscles and lungs, traffic sounds in the distance, the mixed smell of flowering plants and gasoline, and Wayne's face.

I looked up into his eyes. I knew they were asking if I was okay. I nodded, and my eyes returned the question. We continued our facial conversation for a matter of seconds, a conversation that would have taken hours verbally. After our mutual concern, we shared the shock over Dr. Sandstrom's obvious demise. Then Wayne's questioning eyes wanted to know if I was going to get involved in this murder, if I would want to find out who did it. I shrugged, too dazed to know the answer. His mouth seemed to sigh its resignation, but then he reached out and ran his hand over my cheek with a touch that assured me he would love me no matter what I did or didn't do. I grabbed his hand and held on, remembering why I'd married the man.

"Felix needs—" he began.

But before he got any further, a car started in the parking lot. Both of us jumped.

Our next shared look was urgent. There was a murderer in this place. And maybe there was evidence of the murderer's guilt on their body or in their belongings. No one should leave.

"Hey!" I shouted. Even with a car running, my voice seemed loud enough to wake the dead. Not the dead, I reminded myself. But maybe Felix.

At least I was loud enough to attract the driver's attention. Gilda Fitch turned to me. The top was down on her old Fiat.

"Stop!" I shouted again, waving my hands in the universal symbol of panic.

Gilda turned off her engine. I closed my eyes and sighed my relief. I'd forgive Gilda her jokes from now on.

"Cripes," a voice boomed from behind us. "What are you—"

Wayne and I whirled around simultaneously, arms rising automatically.

Reed Killian froze. Did he know he was seeing Wayne's karate and my own tai chi in motion? Or was it just the expressions on our faces?

"Excuse me," he said more softly, "but what—"

Then he spotted Felix and Dr. Sandstrom on the ground. His eyes widened. He turned, poised to run.

"Someone killed Dr. Sandstrom," Wayne said quietly.

Maybe it was the quiet tone. Reed stopped, mid-flight, and turned back to us.

"Not you guys?" he asked, his voice too high. I caught a whiff of acrid perspiration. Reed was a frightened man.

We both shook our heads.

"What about the other guy?" he inquired. I had no idea what he meant until he pointed at Felix.

"Fainted," Wayne supplied.

"Right," Reed murmured, apparently considering the option himself.

"Listen, Reed," I cut in hastily. I didn't want another body on the ground. "We gotta stop everyone from leaving."

"Why?" he asked, his voice lazy with shock.

"Murder, crime scene," Wayne answered.

Felix chose this moment to moan from the ground.

"Felix?" I ventured.

And another car started up in the lot. The smell of exhaust wafted our way.

"The entrance," Wayne suggested quickly. "Can we close the gate?"

Reed nodded, and then he and Wayne rushed to the entrance, just as a Saab backed out of its space and headed their way. They beat the Saab, and cut off its exit. And as they closed the iron gate with a clang, I saw eyes looking in from outside. Deer eyes, three sets each. I shivered. I knew that deer were the reason for the high gate and fences that surrounded us. A good deer feast can eat a mighty big hole in a nursery owner's profits. But still, there was a spark of intelligence there. Did the deer know that a man who had declared war on its species had been murdered? The air was getting shimmery again. It was too weird. Too spooky.

Felix groaned, louder this time.

I forgot about the deer and bent over to help Barbara's sweetie up. I'd grabbed one of his arms when he made the mistake of looking where he'd landed the first time and fell over again.

"Felix, are you okay?" I asked.

Nothing happened on the ground. Though I heard another car start up. I told myself they wouldn't get very far now.

"Felix," I tried. "Shall I call Barbara?"

Nada from Felix. Though someone honked their horn.

I thought about slapping Felix. It might not revive him, but at least it would give me some pleasure. Then I closed my eyes and told myself to be a good human being. And a creative one.

"Felix," I cooed. "You've got a scoop."

"*Mrmph?*" came his voice from the ground.

A car door slammed nearby.

"There's a fresh stiff here, just for you," I offered. "So don't ever tell me I've never given you diddly."

More doors slammed and I heard the sound of voices, argumentative voices.

"Kate," Felix murmured, rolling away from Dr. Sandstrom. "Thanks."

Was he joking?

I never got a chance to ask.

"What is going on?" Howie Damon demanded, coming

upon the scene. "Why is the gate—" Then he looked down at the doctor. "He's—"

"Dead," I supplied.

"Under the lilies, man," Felix piped up, as if I hadn't been clear enough.

"But, he . . . can't . . . be . . ."

Felix stood up as Howie Damon fell down.

"Howie!" I yelled in frustration. We needed a nurse out here. We needed a whole MASH unit out here.

"Holy moly, what a geek," Felix commented.

I just glared at him. Then I saw the damage on his face from his fall.

"You've got blood and dirt on your face, Felix," I informed him coolly.

"Doin' better than the doc," he replied, but he turned away in spite of his snappy comeback. Would he ever admit he'd fainted? "Gonna fix my friggin' face," he told me and sauntered off to the restrooms. But the saunter looked a little forced. Was Felix limping?

Howie muttered from the ground, and I forgot about Felix. I knelt down, gently patting Howie's hands, a method that would have been inconceivable for use on Felix. It worked on Howie, though. The high school administrator's eyes opened.

"You all right?" I asked.

"Be . . . okay," he assured me. "Give me a minute."

I saw Gilda coming our way. I just hoped she wouldn't faint.

"Spot of trouble, m'dear?" she asked, smiling. Then she saw the doctor's body. Her face stiffened. "Is he really dead?" she asked, her voice almost accentless now.

I just nodded, suddenly very tired. Why was I standing here with Dr. Sandstrom's dead body? Bad luck? Karmic impairment? A deer stunned in the headlights?

"What happened to Howie, then?" she asked.

"Fainted," I whispered. I had a feeling he might be embarrassed.

"Howie, old bean," Gilda offered sympathetically. "Need a hand up?"

Howie accepted and Gilda helped him to his feet, slowly and carefully.

"Kate?" a frail voice whispered at my side. Avis, finally.

But one look at Avis told me she was not riding in to save the situation like the Mounties. If anything, she might be on the ground next. She wavered before my eyes. I put my arm around her quickly, feeling how birdlike her body was under all those layers of clothing. If she fainted, she might break.

"Kate?" Avis said once more. I got ready for the obvious question, but it didn't come. "I suppose we should call the police, offer our cooperation."

"Of course," I answered with relief. The police. At this point, I'd be happy to see them. Maybe they'd bring some nurses for all the fainters.

"Can you manage the call?" I asked her. Despite myself, I wanted to stay near the body. Maybe I was protecting evidence. Maybe I was just being foolish. But it seemed like the right thing to do. And Dr. Sandstrom had been a human being after all. He had. And I hadn't even considered his humanity since I'd seen his body lying there. Did he have a family? Did he have people who loved him? I remembered the concern with which he'd interrogated me about my diet. And tears moistened my eyes. Damn.

"I'll stay with Kate," Gilda offered, her tone condolent, and I realized she was offering me my turn now. My turn for shock and horror. I was ready. Maybe *I'd* collapse. "Bit of a shock, finding the poor old thing—" she began.

"Oh, dear God," Natalie Miner broke in. My turn was over. "Is that the doctor? This can't be. What happened? The poor, poor man—"

"Avis is ringing up the constabulary," Gilda put in. Natalie looked at her without comprehension. "Calling the police," Gilda translated with a little sigh.

"The police?" Natalie murmured. "You mean—"

"He must have been murdered," Jean Watkins broke in. Was everyone here now? "This is not right. No matter how insensitive the man was, there was no reason to kill him—"

"Someone thought there was," Lisa Orton pointed out. Yep, the gang was all here.

"Wow, the ole dude really got it, didn't he?" Darcie said, her voice frightened and excited at the same time. She pulled her baseball cap lower on her forehead. "Gramma, you all right?"

"Oh, honey," Jean said. "I'm so sorry you had to see this thing." She surveyed our group, her square jaw set with resolve. "Who did this?" she demanded.

No one answered. But the silence tingled with unspoken fear, guilt, even anger.

Jean glared.

Gilda shook her head, as if in sudden disbelief.

Lisa stared at the doctor's body, frowning; her head jutted forward. At least she didn't look like she was going to faint.

"Well, the ole dude probably deserved it," Darcie commented, her voice trembling.

"No, Darcie," Jean corrected her granddaughter. "No one deserves a death like this. It is irresponsible. The man had no chance to redeem himself, no chance to correct his actions—"

"Was it Tennyson?" Maxwell Yang began, his voice serious for the first time that night, maybe even tearful. "Yes, Tennyson, I think. He said, 'Death closes all: but something ere the end. Some work of noble note, may yet be done. Not unbecoming men that strove with Gods.' "

"Thank you," Jean Watkins murmured. "Thank you."

I was glad the words provided comfort to Jean. I was still trying to figure out what they meant. Maybe Gilda could translate for me.

"Do we really have to stay?" Reed asked. I looked at him in surprise. He'd been quick enough to close the gate. But now his handsome features looked seasick. And the smell of fear was even stronger on him than before. "I have things to do."

"There's been a death, here," Jean reminded him reprovingly. There was no smell of fear on her.

"But still, can't they talk to us later?" Reed asked, his voice whining.

"Evidence," I said briefly and saw Avis approaching.

Reed looked unconvinced.

"Please stay, Reed," Avis implored. "The police are on their way."

Reed folded immediately. "Of course," he sighed, taking Avis's hand.

"I don't feel well," Howie objected.

"I still don't understand why we have to stay," Lisa put in. She curled her hands into fists. "I want to go home."

We had a rebellion on our hands. But Wayne was back. I felt his presence without even turning around. When I did turn, he rose to his full height and glared at the membership of the Deerly Abused, putting a full gargoyle into the look. "If you leave, you will be suspect," he pointed out.

There was a long silence. I could almost hear the neurons leaping in everyone's brains. Were they just now realizing that they would be suspect no matter what?

And then we heard the first siren.

Avis and Reed opened the gates for the incoming, uniformed police.

"Officer Ulric," a man with a tilted nose informed us.

"Officer Zenas," added a woman with a sheet of dark hair and the doleful countenance of Greek tragedy.

"Where's the body?" Ulric asked.

I pointed downward.

Officer Zenas squatted down and touched Dr. Sandstrom carefully. Her face seemed even more tragic when she stood. She nodded at Ulric.

"Did any of you see who killed this man?" he asked.

Silence was his answer. I doubt if he was expecting more.

"Do any of you have any special information pertaining to his death?"

More silence.

"Is there a place where we can all sit down?"

"Inside the building," Avis suggested. At last, a question with an answer.

Officer Zenas nodded toward the body, indicating that she would stand guard. Good. I was tired of the job.

Officer Ulric shepherded us back into the building, where we all sat in our semicircle, an extra chair added for Reed, who didn't seem inclined to lecture anymore. Then Officer Ulric stationed himself at the door.

"When can we go?" Lisa Orton demanded.

"After you have each been questioned," Ulric answered, his voice as cool as my limbs were now. Funny, now that we were inside where it should have been warmer, I was freezing.

"So ask," Lisa ordered. "You're the Gestapo."

"We need to wait for the chief," Ulric answered without blinking.

It seemed an eternity that we sat and waited. No one joked. No one even talked. The enormity of the situation seemed to be sinking in. I was just glad that I didn't have to call home. Wayne knew where I was, for once. Though I would have bet that my cat, C.C., was spitting mad.

"Wayne," I began, remembering suddenly. "I saw a bunch of deer peeking in the—"

"No talking, please," Ulric commanded.

After another eternity, two men in suits finally arrived. The first man in the door was seriously handsome, with olive skin, curly black hair, and dark eyes. But something about him didn't carry off the look. He seemed nervous. I wondered how many murders they had in Abierto.

The second man in was wrinkled all over, from his clothes to his face. There were deep pockets under his wide eyes. His eyebrows were raised in a look of perpetual surprise. And he walked with the gait of an awkward teenager, though he looked as old as you could get without falling over. But he had a big smile. A big, goofy smile.

The handsome, younger man introduced himself as Lieutenant Perez and the rumpled man as Captain Thorton, and began to fill us in on the procedures we would be following for the next few hours. First, he told us, we would all be interviewed separately. We were not to discuss the case among ourselves. We were not to—

The captain began to hum a show tune. I took a closer look at him. He seemed familiar, but I couldn't place him.

I did place the show tune, though. It was "Hello, Dolly!"

Perez started in on his litany again. "You will all be fingerprinted. Is there anything important any of you have to tell us?" He surveyed our crowd. I psychicly urged the murderer to confess. "Then we will—" he began

Captain Thorton cleared his throat, smiled, and spoke for the first time.

"Well, it seems we've had a little accident here," he offered cheerfully.

Four

✢

Accident? Did Captain Thorton really think Dr. Sandstrom's death was an accident? I tried to make sense of this explanation. Could Dr. Sandstrom have tripped and hit his head on the deer statuette, maybe twenty times or so? Or maybe an actual deer really had sneaked into the parking lot and trampled him. Or—

Abruptly, I realized who Captain Thorton reminded me of: Bobby McSweeny, a mental patient who'd been under my care when I'd worked at a psychiatric facility some twenty-five years before. And it wasn't just the physical resemblance between the two men, the similarity of their awkward gaits, or the show tunes. Bobby had hummed show tunes too. It was the expression, that goofy, cheerful expression both men shared. Now, Bobby had definitely been a few rosebushes short of a garden. The question was whether Captain Thorton's likeness to my ex-patient stretched that far.

The captain began humming "Tonight," and simulating dancers with his hands. The likeness seemed to be stretching and holding.

"And why would you think Dr. Sandstrom's death was an accident?" I asked the captain in my best humor-the-patient voice.

"Accident?" he questioned, tilting his face and giving his hands a dance break.

"The dead man in the parking lot," I reminded him.

"Oh, right," he answered, beaming. "Very simple, young lady. The victim must have fallen from his apartment window."

Well, I hadn't thought of that explanation. The fact that there were no apartment buildings near to the Eldora Nurseries parking lot didn't preclude this explanation, of course. At least not for Captain Thorton. The building could have hippity-hopped over to dump Dr. Sandstrom—

"Is this some kind of joke?" Howie Damon demanded.

"It's probably a trick," Lisa Orton offered. "Cops try to trick suspects all the time—"

"Lord, can't you see the poor man is . . . is . . . distressed," Natalie Miner cut in.

Captain Thorton winked at me as if to share a little joke, and then his hands began to dance to "I Feel Pretty."

"Captain," I tried again, "did you take a look at the dead man?"

"No," he answered succinctly. "Wanna see something really neat?" He pulled some string from his pocket.

But before the captain could show me his string trick, Lieutenant Perez had cautioned the members of the Deerly Abused to silence and pulled his superior aside. But not far enough. I could still hear his whisper.

"Sir?" he asked, his tone respectful. "Have you taken your evening medication?"

Yep, another Bobby McSweeny. And head of the Abierto Police Department. I had a feeling it was going to be a long night.

I looked at Wayne. *Nuts?* I mouthed.

Alzheimer's? he mouthed back.

And we weren't the only ones. All around us, people were looking at each other with raised eyebrows. Darcie sketched the age-old circle-around-the-ear that represented the reality-challenged. It was nice to see that some things don't change from generation to generation.

"Holy socks, this'll make a whiz-bang lead story," I heard

Felix tell Maxwell Yang. He tittered. "Scotty, the captain is not logged on—"

Unfortunately for Felix, Lieutenant Perez heard him too. The lieutenant whirled around and found the source of the voice.

"You!" he boomed, pointing. "Who are you?"

"Hey, man—" Felix began, then seemed to reconsider. "Felix Byrne," he said sullenly.

"He's a reporter," I added. It was petty, but then so was Felix. Anyway, I was beginning to feel a little protective of Captain Thorton. He was a sweet man, even if his elevator didn't go all the way up.

Felix turned to scream at me, but Perez didn't give him a chance.

"You're the one that found the body," Perez told Felix. I wondered how he'd found out. Had someone spilled the beans to one of his officers? Avis, maybe? "Primary suspect material."

"Hey, man—" Felix started up again. "You can't pull this gonzo cop trip on me—"

"You did find the body?" Perez interrupted.

"Well, yeah, I suppose so. But, my amigos Kate and Wayne were with—"

"I'd be careful what kind of stories I thought of writing if I were a top suspect for murder," Perez suggested, coldly courteous.

"Hey!" Felix objected, his voice still loud but his face losing color. "This is friggin' America, man, not some third-world tsardom. I can say what I like."

"Fine," the lieutenant agreed. "Then we'll question you first."

"Look, I'm not going to write anything about your nutso—"

"Ms. Eldora," Lieutenant Perez interrupted, nodding toward Avis, and grabbing a couple of extra chairs, "if I may?"

"Oh, of course," Avis murmured. Avis had to be the lieutenant's source of information. She'd called the incident into the police.

"Ulric, call the coroner and the crime-scene techs," Perez ordered and started dragging chairs down an aisle in the back of the building, the furthest one from our group. A couple of clattering trips and he had arranged Interrogation Central, somewhere behind the snail pellets and bug sprays and other pesticides, the organic and the politically incorrect. Captain Thorton, Lieutenant Perez, and Felix all took their seats. I could hear their descent into the metal folding chairs. And I could swear I flashed on Felix's panic at the same time. But as hard as I strained my ears, I couldn't hear anything but a general buzz once they began to talk. A buzz and a humming. A loud humming. "Some Enchanted Evening" maybe. If Captain Thorton was trying to blot out the words being exchanged, he was doing a good job. That was nice. He had a role in the interrogation. Because even if I couldn't hear the words, I could hear the speakers: Felix and Lieutenant Perez. No Captain Thorton. And from the lieutenant's tone, I was fairly certain that he wasn't just taunting Felix with the word "murder"—almost sure, in fact, that the lieutenant didn't consider Dr. Sandstrom's death an accident, unlike his superior officer.

I tried not to think of time, and immediately I could hear a clock ticking away in the relative silence. Then traffic noises, and the sounds of people uncomfortable in their chairs: squeaking, rattling, shifting. In fact, I was uncomfortable in my metal folding chair, too. I hadn't really noticed it before, but I did now. It was hard and not shaped to the contours of my short, dark, A-line body. Not anywhere near.

"I didn't friggin' faint!" burst out behind the bug spray as I slid forward to make myself more comfortable in my chair. But that's all I could make out for the next twenty minutes.

Waiting is always hard. Waiting in a grocery line is bad. Waiting for a dentist is even worse, but at least they have magazines. Waiting in a nursery near the indoor-plants-and-smaller-gardening-implements section might have been all right. But we had Officer Ulric keeping an eye on all of us. And there were no magazines within reach. And I wanted to talk to Wayne. Actually, I wanted to talk to anyone. I would have even talked to Felix. Instead, I looked at an orchid and tried to guess what it cost. That took a few minutes. Then I looked at the newest and greatest in hand-spade technology. A few more minutes. Finally, I began to focus on the members of the Deerly Beloved.

Avis sat as unmoving as a mummy. Though it was dark now, she still wore her trademark wide-brimmed hat, scarves, and gloves. I wondered about her skin cancer obsession. I'd never questioned the eccentricity of her dress before. It hadn't seemed important. But with nothing else to do, I questioned it now. Maybe she was making up for her years of acting, the years in which she'd been forced to wear ... what? Silk sheaths and rhinestone earrings? Feather boas and high heels? Her elegant profile, beautiful then, remained so to this day. I'd only seen Avis Eldora on screen a few times, but she'd always been cast as an alluring vamp. Never as a good girl.

Avis's green eyes moved ever so slightly, looking at Reed Killian. *Dr.* Reed Killian, I corrected myself. He was a plastic surgeon, an M.D. by any other name. Had he known Dr. Sandstrom professionally? Both men were medical doctors and interested in gardening. Were there any more similarities?

Reed returned Avis's glance even as he fidgeted in his chair. He rolled his eyes at her. Somehow, they were looking like a couple. Avis may have been Reed's senior by a few decades, but still ... Was that why Reed was teaching us about deer in the first place? Reed tapped his fingers on his chair. I remembered Avis's plea to him. Friendship ... or more?

"I gotta pee," Darcie Watkins announced. My bottom jumped in my chair. *Ow.* "Gramma—"

"Officer?" Jean Watkins said, addressing Ulric. "Perhaps I might accompany my grandchild to the restroom?"

Officer Ulric looked as if he could use some urinary respite himself. And as a matter of fact, I was feeling fairly squirmy too. But Darcie had beat me to the request.

"Ulric, you may escort the girl to the bathroom," came Lieutenant Perez's voice from beyond the wall of pesticides. He sounded irritated. But then, he was interrogating Felix.

"Me next," put in Lisa Orton. She pulled on her fingers and looked around as if daring someone to challenge her.

"Then me," I threw in my order. I only wished I had been as fast as Lisa.

And I wished Darcie hadn't spoken up. My bladder began to take on a weightier significance in the balance of the universe as Officer Ulric led Darcie around back to the shed that housed the restrooms. I looked over at Gilda, hoping her face would keep my mind off the subject of ever-expanding liquids. She smiled at me, as if reading my mind. I couldn't decide if there was something evil in that smile, or something genuinely friendly. Genuine didn't seem the right word for Gilda, with her phony British accent. Or was it necessarily phony? And even if it was, she had helped me with Howie, I remembered. There was something to be said for that. I stared at her. She did have rather patrician features. Was there British aristocracy lurking beneath her lovely, maple-colored skin? Yes, I thought. It was there in the long nose and slightly buck teeth. And in her attitude. Maybe I could take lessons. Gilda looked at Howie, her face concerned. Noblesse oblige?

Howie looked better than he had earlier, which was pretty much a slam dunk since he'd been in a dead faint before. Still, his color was good. He held his precious manuscript to his chest, his eyes half closed. He seemed to have this waiting routine down. Maybe being a high-school administrator had something to do with it. All those bad teenagers waiting to see him may have set him a good example. Or maybe just taught him to fake a good example.

Natalie Miner, on the other hand, did not look good. Her nose was red from repeated blowing, her blond pasta curls bunched to one side, and her makeup a wreck. Every few minutes she sniffled. Had she had a relationship with Dr. Sandstrom? Or maybe just hoped for one? Or was she merely sensitive? It was too painful to look at her. I let my eyes travel on to Maxwell Yang.

Maxwell's face was curiously blank, devoid of his usual

impish smile. Was this how he looked before he went on camera? Like a robot waiting for the On switch? It must be hard to be "on" all the time. Or maybe this was his face of grief. What had he quoted from Tennyson? Now that I had a chance to order my thoughts, I couldn't seem to remember anything clearly. Only the pressure on my bladder was real. And the metal chair. And the smell of dirt and flowers and pesticides. Maxwell breathed in and out rhythmically. Was he meditating?

Darcie came back in the building, escorted by a harried-looking Officer Ulric. I wondered how long Lisa Orton would take.

"My turn?" Lisa demanded.

"Have her wait a minute" came from the pesticide wall. Lisa's minute was my minute, I realized, and turned to look at Wayne in desperation.

But Wayne's features had turned to stone. There was nothing there to be seen, though I could smell the anxiety on him. I resisted the urge to sniff myself. Amusing as it might have been to the others, it was beyond even my level of appropriate behavior. I could feel the dampness of my body, though. Good. If I sweated enough, maybe I'd have to pee less. Stone. I liked that idea.

I took a big breath and told myself it was time for a stone meditation. Stones didn't have bladders. Stones didn't feel panic. Stones didn't get interrogated by the police. While there was actually no way of knowing if Captain Thorton was capable of interrogating a stone, it seemed a safe assumption. And there was something to be learned from stones: accepting the warmth of sunlight and the feel of rain, and the occasional housing relocation. A stone's life might be simple—

"You can go," I heard, and Felix came stumbling out from behind the pesticides. He didn't look well. A fleeting moment of sympathy engaged me.

"Lieutenant told you, you can go," Ulric reiterated as Felix sprawled back into his chair.

"Waiting for my amigos, man," he explained. "Kate and Wayne."

Oh, joy—

Lisa stood and eyed Officer Ulric.

He put up his hand in the halt position.

"Kate Jasper, would you please join the captain and me?" Lieutenant Perez called out. Damn. The restroom was going to have to wait even longer than I thought.

Lisa fumed aloud as I made the long walk down the aisle behind the pesticides.

"Hi, Captain Thorton, Lieutenant Perez," I said, smiling to make a good impression once I'd reached the settlement of folding chairs.

The captain smiled back. The lieutenant didn't.

"You were with Mr. Byrne when he stumbled over Dr. Sandstrom's body, weren't you?" Perez accused, gesturing brusquely toward a seat.

"Um, yeah," I replied, looking into his eyes and wondering if he knew I was the Typhoid Mary of Murder. Then I sat down in a chair that was a clone of the uncomfortable one I'd been sitting in before.

"Along with Mr. Caruso," he added for the record.

I nodded, hoping they couldn't hear my heart beat. I certainly could. The captain could have danced his hands to the rhythm. He started humming again instead. I found the sound oddly soothing. "Camelot," I guessed subvocally.

"And you found Dr. Sandstrom unconscious earlier?" he prodded.

"Yes," I said, telling myself I wouldn't try to explain, wouldn't even try to excuse myself. I had a feeling that karmic impairment wasn't going to be exculpatory in Lieutenant Perez's eyes. I tried not to squirm.

"Did you know the doctor previously?" he pushed.

I shook my head.

"Did his comments about deer anger you?"

"Not really." I tried to be truthful. "I wondered what made him so angry, but—"

"You're a vegetarian, aren't you?" he accused, jutting forward in his seat.

"Huh?" I said.

"And the doctor threatened to kill animals," he expanded.

"Now, wait a minute," I told him. "I don't kill people who eat hamburgers, and I don't kill—"

"But you were there both times."

Lieutenant Perez had a theme and he stuck to it. Over and over. The captain's humming was much better. At least he changed tunes every once in a while.

After about the thirtieth time, Perez tried a new tack.

"Did your friend Mr. Byrne faint?" he asked.

I hesitated. Whether it was the lieutenant's characterization of Felix as my "friend," or an actual concern for my "friend" that stalled me, I wasn't sure.

But the lieutenant noticed my hesitation.

"Well?" he demanded, staring into my eyes.

"Of course, he did," I whispered. "But he's embarrassed. Howie Damon fainted too."

"Could Mr. Byrne have been feigning his faint in order to interfere with the evidence?" he asked.

Damn, I hadn't even thought of that.

I just shook my head. "Mr. Byrne is not an easy person to know," I answered finally. "Or to like. But I honestly don't think he's a murderer."

The lieutenant asked me a lot more questions before I left: about Avis, about Wayne, about everyone else, about every interaction, every detail of the Deerly Abused. Nope, he definitely didn't think Dr. Sandstrom's demise was an accident.

And then he let me go, and called Wayne to the aisle of interrogation. We passed midway and gripped hands.

Once I was back into the land of indoor-plants-and-smaller-gardening-implements, I begged Officer Ulric to escort me to the restroom.

Very few pleasures in life compare to the emptying of an overfull bladder. I won't even try to list them. But I was feeling mildly euphoric when I returned to my metal folding chair.

When Wayne was finally released, and we were free to leave the building, I was even more than mildly euphoric. The only drawback was Felix's accompanying us to the parking lot.

"Jeez, the potato brains," he muttered once we were out the door into the night air. "And that nutcase. He was gonzo, man, friggin' gonzo. Holy Godzilla, man, if he's in charge, what are the rest of the inmates doing?"

"A good job, judging by Lieutenant Perez," Wayne answered seriously.

"Hey, man, that Gestapo-grad is a friggin' menace. Me, he accused me—"

And then Felix stumbled again.

Wayne and I dived for him and heard an unholy screech that reverberated though the parking lot.

My heart leapt into the darkness as I looked for demons, but saw only the tail end of one of the nursery cats scurrying away.

It was my turn to faint. But I didn't.

"You're okay, kiddo," came a familiar voice before I could complete my swoon. Barbara Chu, my psychic friend. Who else?

"But how did you know—" Felix began.

Barbara just grinned, her elegant Asian features as cheery as usual.

"Yeah, right," Felix grumbled. "Presto-pronto time. But you're not going to tell us who the friggin' murderer is, are you?"

She just laughed.

"You know these things fritz me, honeybun," Barbara whispered intimately. *Ugh*. How my friend could love a man like Felix defied all reason. But then so did Barbara.

She had just *known* to be in the parking lot. And Felix was right. If past experience counted for anything, the only thing she couldn't intuit was whodunit. We left the pair in each other's arms and quickly climbed into Wayne's aging Jaguar.

Wayne drove home. I nestled into the politically incorrect leather of my car seat, unable to resist a favorable comparison to the metal chairs we were leaving behind, and let the warmth and comfort of the car seep into my bones. I closed my eyes and breathed. Really breathed.

"Rosemary for remembrance," Wayne whispered. My eyes popped open.

"Did someone put it there on purpose?" I asked, not expecting an answer. "But why? Did someone really remember the doctor? Or is it a symbol we don't understand . . . ?"

My theories stretched out as endlessly as the drive home.

"Do you know who did it?" I asked finally.

"No," Wayne answered. "Do you?"

I shook my head.

"Kate, is this our business?" Wayne asked.

I shook my head again.

"But I have a feeling it will become our business," I added truthfully. These things always did.

And then there were a few blessed moments of silence before we pulled into our driveway, popping gravel.

"We can't just leave Felix out to dry," Wayne said as he came to a stop. I stared at my new husband in shock. Wayne had never shown any fondness for Felix before. Teeth-grinding irritation was more like it. But Wayne was a fair man. A good man. I put my hand gently on his thigh and gazed toward our house, misty-eyed.

My eyes traveled up the stairs to the deck, where two figures stood spotlighted under the deck light against the redwood shingling of the house.

Wayne must have heard my gasp.

"Felix?" he demanded.

"No," I said. "Worse."

"Worse than Felix?"

FIVE

It was hard to believe that there was anyone worse than Felix Byrne in this world, anyone more irritating, anyone more capable of stirring up trouble, but there was. Or maybe I should say, "there were." I shivered in the warm embrace of the Jaguar.

"Who?" Wayne whispered, his eyes following the trail mine had blazed to the two figures spotlighted on the deck.

"My brother, Kevin," I whispered back, wondering if we should just return to Eldora Nurseries for police abuse. Or maybe go to a motel. "And," I lowered my voice even further, "his girlfriend, Xanthe."

"Worse than Felix?" Wayne repeated. I took a good look at my new husband, the love of my life, and saw that he was poleaxed. His shoulders slumped. His eyes were glazed like doughnuts under his heavy brows, his pupils wide as the doughnut holes. And he was repeating himself. Wayne didn't repeat himself. I thought of his stone act at the nursery. How much had that taken out of him?

"Everything will be fine," I lied, and stroked his thigh, hoping to wish my lie into truth.

"Okay," he murmured and pulled up the Jaguar's hand brake. He reached for the ignition key.

My hand shot out instinctively, blocking his larger one.

"Wayne," I whispered urgently. "Can you just back the car up real quietly?"

"You mean back . . . out . . . of the driveway?" he returned my question. Yep, he was poleaxed. And why was I surprised after tonight's events? Wayne was so rock-solid, so easy to lean on, that it was easy to forget the vulnerability that lay under the stratum of rock.

"Yes, back out the way we came," I ordered, forming my words carefully and making little pointing gestures behind us in case illustration was necessary. Because I was really worried about my sweetie now, and he didn't need Kevin and Xanthe to make his life more complicated. And Kevin and Xanthe always made life more complicated.

Slowly, Wayne nodded his understanding, and even more slowly, he released the hand brake and put the car in gear. Too slowly.

In the seconds that Wayne and I had talked, Kevin and Xanthe had spotted us and hopped down the stairs like wind-up toys. And while Wayne had sought to follow orders, they'd reached the bottom of the stairs and run down the gravel driveway. We were trapped in the Jaguar before we'd even had a chance to roll. Kevin and Xanthe were always fast. A virtue to anyone else, except their prey.

I sighed and gave Wayne's hand a quick squeeze before we got out of the car to make formal driveway introductions.

I identified the man who looked like a Wookie with dark glasses as my brother, Kevin Koffenburger, and the woman with the large, mascara-laden eyes, long nose, and Mae West body as his girlfriend, Xanthe.

"Wayne Caruso," my new husband grunted and stuck out his hand.

"So, this is the hot honey?" Kevin commented, ignoring Wayne's hand and slapping his shoulder instead. "Great eyebrows!"

"Wayne's a black belt in karate, Kevin," I informed my brother coolly.

Kevin jumped back and smiled ingratiatingly, his close-set

Koffenburger eyes mercifully covered by the dark glasses, and the rest of him pretty much engulfed by his masses of curly, dark hair. My brother looked too much like me, it was true. But at least I had a better haircut.

"Hah!" Xanthe snorted, pushing out her impressive chest under her tight golden sweater. Was it really spun with gold? I wondered, watching the starlight glint off its threads. "Mere martial arts have no effect on the Goddess."

"Kevin's a goddess?" I inquired innocently. It was bad of me, but Xanthe was going to be angry at me within minutes anyway. I just thought I'd move the schedule up a little.

"The Goddess heard that," Xanthe told me.

"Oh, wow," I whispered, letting my mouth drop open and looking up at the heavens above. A part of me waited for a blast from the stars, but none was forthcoming from that direction.

Xanthe was a different story. She sent me a fiery glare when I brought my eyes back down, and I put up my mental shields, ready for her screed.

"Shall we go inside?" Wayne suggested an instant before impact.

Xanthe made a snarling sound, a sound that would have been acceptable from a small animal but not from a woman's lips. Even Wayne's head popped back at the sound. Not that Kevin was bothered. He'd listened to years of Xanthe's non-human utterances. Kevin would probably chat up a werewolf if he met one, which he might with that hair.

"Yeah, inside," Kevin replied enthusiastically. "So Wayne, you into holistic financial planning?"

Luckily, "holistic what?" was all Wayne was able to say before we walked in the front door, since the phone rang the moment I put my foot down onto the few yards of parquet flooring that constitute the entryway to my house and my living room. Then I heard my own voice on the answering machine's outgoing tape from my home office on the other side of the entryway, full of tinny, forced cheer announcing that I wasn't home, etc. etc.

"Hey, kiddo," came my friend Barbara's voice on the incoming tape. "Pick up."

I looked at Wayne. It was no use screening my calls when Barbara was on the line. She was psychic. But could my sweetie handle Kevin and Xanthe?

He mouthed *Okay* my way, and I sprinted to the machine, shutting it off as I picked up the phone.

"Thanks, kiddo," Barbara cooed, before I even had time for a Hi, hello. "Felix is really bummed."

"By tonight?" I whispered.

"Yes, Kate," Barbara answered, her voice tinged with amusement. I could almost see her Buddha-smile over the phone. "Unlike you, he hasn't stumbled over any dead bodies before."

"Well, now he knows what it feels like," I stated ungraciously. I plopped down in the comfy chair at the side of my desk as the nausea I'd kept at bay all night roiled my innards.

"Yeah, now he does," Barbara agreed seriously. "All of a sudden, he's not so eager for details about the 'stiff.' He never got what it felt like to see death up close. He never got why it upset you to be asked for details. Now he understands, in spades."

I wish she hadn't said "spades." It reminded me of the nursery. And I was beginning to feel ashamed of myself. Poor Felix. Poor Felix? Barbara had done this to me. Barbara, my psychic friend . . . and master manipulator.

"What does he want from me?" I asked finally, though I was afraid I already knew the answer.

"Help in solving the case, of course," Barbara answered cheerfully. "I told him I'd call you, kiddo. He's too busy being all macho and trying not to throw up." Her voice went down a notch. "But he really is scared."

"Me too," I told her. "For good reason. I'm staying out of it. All right? I've got my own problems."

"Yeah, ain't relatives a bitch?" she said, her laughter tinkling over the line.

"Especially their girlfriends," I whispered back, not even

bothering to ask how she knew about my relatives. It was useless to try to figure out how Barbara's brain worked. She knew more things than anyone ought to about stuff you'd rather she didn't, but she always froze on the big stuff, the important stuff.

"Yeah, I'm sorry, kiddo," she answered my thought. "I don't have a clue about this murder. You can help Felix find out who did it. I know you will."

The hair went up on the back of my neck. Barbara saying she "knew" something was not like other people saying they knew things. If she knew I would, I would. And I didn't want to. I remembered Dr. Sandstrom's battered head all too clearly.

"But—" I tried.

"Thanks, Kate," she said, made a kissy-kissy noise, and hung up.

I climbed out of my comfy chair and approached the living room.

Wayne sat in one of the chairs suspended from the rafters, swinging. Kevin and Xanthe sat side by side on the handmade wood-and-denim couch that was in the center of the room, a room that overflowed with bookshelves and plants and mismatched pillows. Not to mention the pinball machines, covered in papers and more books. But I hadn't been expecting company.

"Kevin's name is synonymous with integrity," Xanthe announced before I had a chance to get self-conscious about the state of our housekeeping.

Maybe she didn't know I was off the phone. To me, my brother's name was synonymous with things like bail and co-sign, not to mention scam and, worst of all, Xanthe.

"And these are real pyramids," Kevin took over. "A real paradigm shift, you know. We're really zoned in on it now."

"On what, Kevin?" I asked, putting my hands on my hips where I stood, reminding myself of the car I'd "co-signed" for Kevin, read "paid for," which he'd managed to total within two months.

"Hey, Katie," he enthused. "It's a cosmic multilevel-marketing thing, you know—"

"No, I don't know," I said, keeping my voice cool and level. I was getting better. I'd only lost three hundred bucks on his most recent, ozone generator scam. "And don't call me Katie."

"Okay," he said cheerfully, "All you gotta do is buy the pyramid kit and sell it to your friends. And then your friends sell it to their friends and—"

"Didn't we do this with herbal teas, already, Kevin?" I asked. I still had them somewhere. The tea bags had leaked, and the "herbs" had turned out to be flavored sawdust. I'd kept them as a reminder never to do business with my brother again.

"Yeah," he said. "But this is even cooler. Pyramids, Katie, real pyramids."

"Are you trying to sell me Egyptian pyramids?" I asked. "Because if you are, I'll trade you the Golden Gate Bridge."

Wayne swiveled around and stared at me, as if wondering who this rude woman was he'd married. I flinched. It was true that I hadn't fully disclosed the details of my family to Wayne. Kevin-disclosure takes an effort.

"So, we just thought we'd visit—" Kevin went on blithely.

"For how long?" I asked

Wayne didn't even have a chance to look at me this time. He was too busy staring at Xanthe. Because Xanthe's reaction to my words had been to hiss at me—a real hiss, like a snake. Her repertoire of animal sounds was expanding. She probably went to the zoo for lessons.

"Well, we need a copacetic business base, you know," Kevin began. "And you have a business license and all—"

The phone rang again. I felt like a boxer. End of round two.

This time it was Avis who wanted to talk to me. She sounded as if she were calling from another planet, a very slow, confused planet. I wondered if she'd been drinking.

". . . all so unreal, Kate," she was saying. "I keep wanting to ask if it was real. It was, wasn't it?"

"It was, Avis," I told her, worried now. If she doubted that what she saw was real, she was at least in good company. Captain Thorton's company.

"It was supposed to be nice, you see," she rambled on. "Nice. People talking, sharing ideas. Harmonious, positive . . . but . . ." Her voice faltered. Not drink, I decided, shock.

"Are the police still there, Avis?" I asked.

"Oh, they are," she answered, "but I'm not. I'm at home. It was too weird there. At least now I'm with my things . . ." I heard a sob.

"Avis, it'll probably turn out all right," I soothed desperately. Okay, lied. Unlike Barbara, I didn't "know" it was going to be all right. I just hoped so.

"Maybe," she sniffled. "Maybe. Reed thinks they'll figure out something forensically. There were all these technicians there when we left."

"You and *Reed* left?" I asked.

A short silence followed my words. I could hear Kevin's voice in the living room.

"Reed's been a big help," Avis said finally, but her voice was flat. Maybe I wasn't supposed to talk about Reed. That left talking about the murder. Or deer. I didn't want to talk about deer.

"Did the police give you any idea who they thought did it?" I asked as quietly as I could.

"No, no." I could almost see her shaking her head. I wondered if she was still wearing her hat. "That's why . . ."

"What?" I asked. "That's why what?"

"Well, I thought you might know, Kate."

The words tumbled into my brain separately and then arranged themselves into a sentence.

"Me?" I said.

"You find these things out, don't you?" she tried again, a trace of hope in her voice.

"Not really, I . . ." Now, *I* was faltering.

"I didn't mean to trouble you," she told me, her voice flat again.

"Oh, no," I squeaked. "No trouble."

"Maybe, you could try . . ."

"Um, maybe," I answered, hoping Avis would forget my words once her shock had worn off.

"Oh, thank you, Kate," she breathed. "Thank you."

As she hung up, I wondered what my "maybe" had encompassed in her mind. Too much, I was sure.

Back in the living room, Kevin and Xanthe were still on the couch, but now they were wearing pyramid caps. To get a pyramid cap you could take a baseball cap and remove the bill, then add a pyramid on the top. A gold, shining pyramid. Not that you'd want to, mind you. Though seeing Kevin in his pyramid cap brought back an instant of affection, remembering him in a birthday hat as a toddler. But then he started talking again.

"Cosmic," Kevin declared. "That's what I meant by holistic financial planning, you know. This is the leading edge—"

"Kevin Koffenburger," I ordered. "Take that cap off. You look silly." I couldn't help it. Kevin *was* my younger brother.

"But Katie," he whined, his voice suddenly nasal.

"You have no right to talk to your brother that way," Xanthe declared. Then she hissed again.

"Maybe, we can all—" Wayne began.

"Yeah, Katie," Kevin piped up. "And you haven't seen all the really cool stuff: earrings, T-shirts—"

"Kevin, neither Wayne nor I will be buying your pyramid kit, so give it up," I suggested, down to the bottom line now.

Xanthe made a low, growling noise in her throat.

My cat, C.C., scooted into the room to confront the giant animal on the couch, growling back.

Xanthe sketched the shape of a cat in the air and clapped her hands.

C.C. was not impressed by her magic. She arched her back and hissed.

"Cool cat," Xanthe commented, surprising me. She smiled at her soulmate. C.C. sauntered off, having made her point.

"Xanthe does the actual handcrafting," Kevin told me. "So the pyramids are sacred."

I looked at my brother. Did he actually believe that? Probably. It was hard to tell under the dark glasses.

"Kevin?" I asked. "Did you hear me say no?"

The phone rang again before he could answer

End of round three.

It was Felix. Of course it was Felix.

"Hey, Kate," he began. "I'm still tripping on tonight, man. Too weird."

"I'll agree to that," I said cautiously.

"So, my honeybun told me you'd help me—"

"I didn't say that," I cut him off. For all it was worth.

"Yeah, man, but Barbara did. And you know her presto-pronto act—if she said it, whiz-bang-boogaloo—it's true."

"Not necessarily," I tried. I might as well have been talking to the air. Actually a phone wasn't much more than air, especially with Felix attached.

"And I'm deep in doo-doo without a friggin' pooper-scooper, if you catch my meaning."

"Why do you think you're in so much trouble, Felix?" I objected. "All three of us found the body—"

"And I played the-emperor's-got-no-clothes with their nutso, potato-brain police chief," he reminded me.

"But still, Felix," I insisted, "they have plenty of suspects. They'll probably find out Dr. Sandstrom was connected with someone in the group—"

"Yeah, like your good buddy here," he interrupted.

"You *knew* Dr. Sandstrom?" I demanded. "Tell me you didn't."

"Hard to say I didn't know the stiff, he was my friggin' sawbones, man."

"Your doctor?" I translated hesitantly.

"Yeah, the doc poked and prodded me like I was a friggin' turkey. You wouldn't believe the mystical, medical hoo-haw that man put me through. All for a little case of gout, man. You remember my gout, don'cha? It wasn't my friggin' fault that we had the argument—"

"Argument?" I repeated.

"Well, the friggin' quack was driving me bananas over my diet. Like diet would cure my gout—"

"Diet does cure gout, Felix," I said, then remembered that his medical prognosis wasn't important now. "Did Perez ask you if you knew the doctor?" I demanded instead.

I didn't like Felix's sudden silence. A silent Felix is unnatural as the Pacific Ocean without waves.

"Felix?" I prodded.

"Holy socks, it was none of his friggin' business. So I told him no. It's not some kinda of Titanic crime—"

"Felix, it is a crime—"

"So, how's the potato-brain gonna find out, anyway?"

"Public record?" All right, I have to admit it. It felt good, using the words Felix had used earlier describing his discovery of my marriage to Wayne. Not some kind of Titanic crime, using his own words, right? My guilt button buzzed anyway.

"Can't be," Felix came back uncertainly. "All this geeky confidentiality stuff, man. Patient files gotta be confidential."

"But not patient names, I'll bet."

"Man, you gotta help me, Kate!" Felix moaned. "They got me all stitched up for this thing. I'm gonna take the fall. It's the big house for me. Maybe the chair—"

"Felix, stop. You sound like an old movie. You'll be all right." I was full of lies tonight. "Did anyone hear you argue with the doctor?"

"Just, um, the whoozit-receptionist and a couple of other poor saps in the waiting room, man. But I didn't kill him, Kate—"

"You just found the stiff," I finished for him, shaking my head.

"What—"

"Just found the stiff," I repeated, my voice rising. "Fun, isn't it, Felix?"

"Hey, man, this is your old amigo . . ."

Ten minutes later, my old amigo finally hung up. I'd tried to make it clear that I wasn't committing myself to helping him, but I had a feeling my lack of commitment was about as clear as a politician's promise. Still, I was off the telephone, a return to relative sanity. No, a return to Kevin and Xanthe.

Kevin and Xanthe had spread the contents of a pyramid kit on the floor and were demonstrating a wind-up, walking pyramid for Wayne. Wayne's face had shut down completely, his eyes invisible, his chin stiff. But his shoulders were trembling.

"Hey," Kevin greeted me. "Who was on the phone?"

"Just a friend," I answered coolly.

"In trouble with the police?" Xanthe asked. That's another thing I hated about Xanthe. Sometimes, she seemed to be as psychic as Barbara. But I assured myself that if she were really psychic, she'd know how I felt about her and just leave the house now. Fast.

"Hey," Kevin interjected. "A little jail time never hurts."

I locked eyes with Wayne, as if to say, See?

Then we looked at the ceiling together

"Listen, you two," I announced, tired now, way too tired for my brother and his girlfriend. "We have to go to bed. You can have the futon if you want it."

In half an hour, they had the futon, the bedding, magazines, and the leftovers from the dinner Wayne had prepared earlier. But they didn't have our money for a pyramid kit. I took my purse with me down the hall and into the bedroom, where Wayne and I lay on the mattress on the floor that served as our bed, side by side, fully clothed, staring out the twin skylights.

"Sorry," Wayne growled finally.

"Sorry?" I asked.

"The deer class, my idea," he explained.

"Oh, sweetie," I murmured and rolled over to hold him. "I love you. I'd love you even if Kevin was *your* brother."

He smiled, a little smile, but a smile nonetheless.

"Say, aren't we on our honeymoon?" I asked a few minutes later.

Wayne's smile deepened. He was my sweetie again, my husband.

I kissed his smiling mouth, and held him until the warmth

and strength and pulse of his body were my own. Kevin, Xan-the, Felix, even Dr. Sandstrom, disappeared.

Much later, we were almost asleep when a keening sound jolted us both back to alertness.

Six

"Wha . . . what?" mumbled Wayne, sitting up and swinging his legs off the mattress in a matter of seconds.

"No," I told him, placing my hand on his chest before he pushed himself out of bed. I could feel his rapid heartbeat beneath my fingertips.

"But—"

"It's only Xanthe," I assured him, keeping my voice low. Or maybe I should say, tried to assure him. "Only Xanthe" was something like "only a tidal wave," after all.

The keening escalated, a howl of grief and menace now. The hair went up on my arms even as I tried to downplay the phenomenon to Wayne.

"She's just putting a curse on me," I told him. "Xanthe always puts a curse on me. And she always makes sure I know."

"An actual curse?" Drowsiness and concern struggled in his tone.

"Only if I believe it," I replied, smiling to show I didn't. My smile was almost real. Just like not being afraid of a giant dog on a strong leash. Logically, there was nothing to be afraid of. Illogically . . . I lay back down and pulled a pillow over my head just as the keening stopped.

"Oh," Wayne said and lay back down beside me, instantly asleep, the musical portion of our evening's entertainment having ended. Wayne was practical that way. I wasn't. I wondered if Xanthe had just given voice to the curse that had already happened. The curse of finding Dr. Sandstrom's body. I wondered all night long.

The following Friday morning, Kevin and Xanthe were still snoring on the futon while Wayne and I had breakfast. It was actually comforting to hear Xanthe snore. It's harder to believe in a curse cast by a nasally challenged human being.

And they were still asleep after we'd showered and I'd begun my morning's paperwork on Jest Gifts, the business I owned and operated from my house and an old warehouse across the bay in Oakland. It might sound easy to own a gag-gift business, but it's no mean feat to sell the same gags to professionals year after year. Not to mention thinking up the new ideas. All right, I admitted to myself, it was fun thinking up the new ideas. I was working on a gardening and hardware line now in addition to my shark/attorney line, shrunken head/ therapist line, twisted spine/chiropractor line, and all the rest of the old standbys. Terra-cotta planter mugs, shovel, scythe, and pitchfork silverware took shape in my mind. I glanced across the entryway to my sleeping visitors and wondered if I would ever be able to explain the concept of enjoyable hard work as opposed to scheming as a business model. Nah, it would never fly. Kevin and Xanthe were free spirits. It would be too cruel to expose them to the realities of invoices and ledgers and order forms. The phone rang. I added employees to my list of harsh business realities.

"It's Jade," said my warehousewoman, announcing herself. I dragged the phone to the middle of my desk and dropped back into my office chair. "We've got that order for acupuncture earrings, but the box that says 'acupuncture earrings' has tai chi slipper earrings in it. Jeez, where do you think the acupuncture ones are?"

Another thing I'd never impose on my little brother: the long trail of crises in a continuing business. But I still wished he'd get a regular job. And cut his hair. Boy, was I getting old or what? But then, I'd always be older than Kevin.

"Have you tried the box labeled 'tai chi earrings'?" I suggested.

"Wait a minute," Jade ordered and slammed the phone down on a table. I pulled the receiver back from my ear too late. Someday, I'd learn to beat her to the slam. Until then, I could just rub my ear and—

"Morning, Katie," I heard from behind me. "Time to target our energies—"

"Time for you to take a shower," I interrupted.

My brother wasn't wearing his dark glasses, and his close-set eyes were bloodshot. And then there was his eau-de-snooze. I tried not to breathe too deeply. But Kevin had no idea what he looked or smelled like. He was ready to sell pyramid kits. I didn't have to be psychic to recognize that gleam in his eyes, the one he'd had in fifth grade when he talked me out of a hard-earned dollar to buy lemons for a lemonade stand that never materialized.

"Where's Wayne?" Kevin tried.

"At work," I answered succinctly.

"What does he do, Katie?" Kevin asked. "Something cool, I'll bet."

"He owns a restaurant combined with an art gallery," I replied cautiously. I would have liked to brag, to have mentioned how chic that restaurant/art gallery was, to have told Kevin that in fact Wayne owned more than one, but then Kevin might have figured out Wayne's financial status, which was triple A, also known as: ripe for sucking. No, that wouldn't do.

"La Fête à L'Oeil is its name," I said instead in a gloomy whisper. I shook my head sadly. "It's deep, deep in debt."

The last part was a lie, but if you can't lie to your relatives, who can you lie to?

Kevin's face fell. I could hear his fleet of inner salesmen regrouping. *Forget the boyfriend*, *go for your sister*, they were advising.

"Kate!" Jade screeched into my ear. "They're in the tai chi earring box. Jeez, you're smart sometimes."

I blushed. Maybe I wasn't such a bad detective after all. "Thanks," I told her. "So if there's nothing—"

"The guy who was supposed to make the new computer mouses called," she went on before I could delude myself that there would be no more bad news. "He's got a problem . . ."

Twenty minutes of crises later, I was off the phone and Kevin was still in the shower. So was Xanthe. Good, they'd save water.

I put aside the stack of bills I was paying and reached under the desk blotter for the notepad on which I'd begun a suspect-list. Maybe I should start manufacturing suspect-notepads. I wasn't sure who I was hiding the pad from anyway. Wayne? Kevin? Myself?

So far, I had a series of columns. It was easy to fill in the column for names, but the rest? MOTIVE? All question marks. MEANS? Anyone could have wielded the deer statuette. Opportunity? I couldn't even remember who had walked in and out of the main building. Did one of them have a better opportunity than another? I wondered if anyone else could remember. I added another column: KNEW DR. SANDSTROM BEFORE, and checked Felix's name.

Then I made a note to ask Avis how well she knew the victim. And another note to ask Avis what she thought about opportunity. Maybe she'd kept a closer eye on the Deerly Abused than I had. I was so engrossed in my notes that I never heard Xanthe walk up behind me.

"What're you working on?" she asked.

I quickly slid the notepad under the blotter again.

"Gag-gifts," I said, turning in my chair to look up at her.

She smiled at me. She looked good, her balloon of blond poodle hair clean, her eyes loaded with mascara again, and her magnificent chest covered in a pyramid T-shirt. But that smile . . . I hated it when Xanthe was nice to me.

"Kate, I guess you know I'm psychic, right?" she began.

"Aren't we all?" I answered, keeping my voice serious.

She narrowed her eyes, unsure if I was playing with her.

"I see a lot of things in the great cosmos," she continued, giving me the benefit of the doubt.

"Right," I concurred.

"Do you know you share a strong karmic bond with your brother, Kevin?"

I nodded seriously, then said, "I guess I must have done something pretty bad to him in a previous life, huh?"

"What?" she asked, halted for a moment in her script.

"Well, he's sure getting even with me in this life," I explained.

"Now, Kate," she reprimanded me gently and smiled again. Yow, she had big teeth. And she was even controlling her temper. This was getting scary. "Doesn't it strike you as more than serendipitous that you have a gag-gift business in place just at the time that Kevin is beginning a much more profound business, one that could have truly transcendent potential, but still, one that needs all of the resources that you already have—"

"A business license, a system, manufacturers—" Kevin cut in from behind her. He looked better too, his Wookie mane, beard, and mustache symmetrical and clean, his dark glasses on again. And he smelled clean too, like Wayne's soap and shampoo.

"Know-how, a warehouse—" Xanthe took over.

"Wait a minute!" I objected. "Jest Gifts has all of those things because of the years of work I've put into it. They are nontransferable assets."

Kevin and Xanthe just stared at me. I began to sweat under the pressure of their united need. I felt like an open can of beef stew within reach of a hungry bear. Well, even beef stew can fight back if it has to.

"Nontransferable," I repeated. "Get it?"

The phone rang and I dove for it, wondering if they would have hypnotized me otherwise.

"Hey, Kate," Felix greeted me. "The Big Guy around?"

"No," I told him. Nothing more, nothing less. I was still

reeling from the attack of the hairy people, both of whom were still watching me hungrily.

"Far friggin' out," Felix breathed. "No offense, but the Big Guy can be pricklier than a pit bull on steroids, sometimes."

"Felix—" I warned.

"But a friggin' great guy otherwise, a friggin' great guy."

Xanthe sighed and made an impatient, tapping gesture on her wrist as if to tell me time was up for my phone call.

"So, how's it going, Felix?" I asked leisurely, waving Xanthe and Kevin away with my hand, and turning in my chair so that my back was to them. I could still feel them, though. Maybe that much hunger generates heat or something.

"Huh?" Felix answered, blindsided by my friendliness. If I had known this approach could stop him, I would have used it years ago. But I had a feeling it would only work once. And not for long.

I listened as Kevin and Xanthe rustled behind me, and then left the room, Xanthe's feet managing to slap the carpet as she went.

"Man, let me tell ya, Kate, I'm not sailing so fine, you know," Felix confided sadly. I knew he was doing the soulful bit with his eyes even if I couldn't see it. "It's like nobody knows but Oz whodunit. If I was down at the cop shop, I'd pick your favorite reporter to pin this murder on. You gotta talk to people, Kate. Get the poop on 'em like you always do. Use your little gray cells or whatever—you know what I'm saying—"

"Felix, I don't solve these things," I told him in a whisper, hoping Kevin and Xanthe couldn't hear me. "I'm just there—"

"Yeah, but when you're there, presto-pronto, things happen, murderers confess."

"Felix, I—"

"Kate, come on," he begged. "We're a team, sleuth times two, boogaloo. We can do it . . ."

I couldn't avoid Xanthe and Kevin indefinitely, but I could hang up on Felix. And eventually, I did.

Kevin and Xanthe were back like sharks, the minute I was

off the phone. I turned to them, drawn unwillingly.

"So, Katie," Kevin summarized. "Jest Gifts and Pyramid Power are perfect partners—"

"Kevin, I will not buy a pyramid kit or have anything to do with your business—"

"But, Katie!" There was true distress in his cry. A cry I remembered from childhood, and never failed to respond to. I wanted to comfort him, to pat his back, even to tell him I still loved him, but it was too dangerous. Any affection would give him the edge he needed. And it wouldn't do either of us any good for me to get involved in his business. Past experience had taught me only too well. I felt the hint of tears behind my eyes. If only I could be kind to Kevin without reaping the rip-off.

"You can stay here for a very short time," I told him gently. "But you cannot live here, all right?"

I was glad I couldn't see his eyes under those dark glasses, because he knew I was serious. Unfortunately, so did Xanthe.

She drew herself up to her full, impressive height, her back straight as a broomstick, and began to speak in the voice of a prophet . . . or a madwoman.

"I call upon all the gods and goddesses, ancient and present, all unearthly and earthly beings—"

The phone rang again just as I began to feel a chill.

I picked it up, hoping it was a solicitor, one of those terriers who, for a worthy cause, bit your leg and wouldn't let go.

But it was my ex-husband, Craig Jasper. The man whose surname I'd kept rather than become a Koffenburger again. The man whose name I still kept, having used it too long to change it to Caruso.

"Kate, I heard," he intoned mournfully. For a moment, I thought he was talking about Dr. Sandstrom's death, but then I realized it was worse. He knew that Wayne and I were married. Craig had hoped that he and I could remarry after our divorce—he'd even spent an infinite amount of time re-wooing me—and he'd lost. Much as I never wanted to be married to the man again, my heart went out to him. And my stomach didn't feel so good either. A triple-guilt day.

"Who told you?" I asked softly.

"There was an article in the *Marin Mind*." Felix! The *Marin Mind* was the paper Felix wrote for. And now he wanted my help. Anger heated my blood.

"Craig, you had to know, eventually, but I'm sorry—"

"I love you, Kate," he interjected, his voice thick. And then his tearful voice took on a Groucho Marx accent. "Though there's always the divorce to look forward to."

"Craig!" I allowed mock horror into my voice.

"Just kidding, Kate," he told me, the mournful tone back. "You know me, always the kidder. If you ever want to hear a good joke, you know who to call."

"Oh, Craig—" I began. Then a thought hit me. "Was the article in today's *Marin Mind*?"

"Yeah," he answered. "Why?"

"Then Felix wrote it before—"

"Before what, Kate?" Craig asked.

"Nothing," I told him. "Nothing.

"Did you hear the one about the parrot and the freezer?"

"No," I said, my heart reaching a little further. "Why don't you tell me?"

So he did, and I laughed as heartily as someone with a lump in their throat can.

When I hung up I felt like Simon Legree, only meaner. Craig and I had been married fourteen years. He'd been a philanderer, it was true. But he was not a cruel man. Craig was more like a puppy who tinkles on your rug and is really, really sorry. Pant, pant, howl! Hitting him with a newspaper would have been kinder than letting him find out the news of my marriage. Then I realized he *had* been hit by a newspaper, figuratively speaking. And I also realized that Craig was not the last person I could expect to hear from on the subject. People feel excluded when you don't tell them little details like that. Friends. I felt my hands go clammy. Relatives—

On cue, Xanthe started up again. "I call on the spirit of fire, the spirit of earth, the spirit of water, and the spirit of air to teach this woman—"

The phone rang again. I cringed. Another friend who'd just read about my getting married?

But it was Maxwell Yang on the line this time. I wondered why he'd called me, of all people. I didn't have to wonder for long.

"My staff did a little research, Kate," he explained. "I understand you're a real winner in the whodunit field—"

I groaned. How come no one understood that there were no winners in the whodunit field?

"Sorry if I'm being insensitive," he put in immediately. "I know it must be hard to have found the body. But our goals may be aligned on this one. I want to know who killed Dr. Sandstrom. And I have a feeling the police aren't too . . . well—"

"Sane?" I offered.

He chuckled. "Well, let's just say, not too competent. Perhaps you could keep me informed?"

"Mr. Yang—" I began.

"Maxwell, remember?" he said.

"Maxwell," I began again, "I'm not an investigator. I just have very bad luck."

"You underestimate yourself, Ms. Jasper," he replied.

"Kate," I corrected him, unable to tell if I was being flattered or merely contradicted. Or both. "Really, I'm just karmically impaired—"

He chuckled again. "Very good," he pronounced.

He thought I was joking. I sighed.

"Well, if you do find something out, would you let me know?" he persisted.

"I . . . I . . . well, all right," I finally agreed.

"Thank you, Kate," he murmured politely. Then more loudly: "But I should let you get back to work."

And he did. As I hung up, I wondered why he wanted to be kept informed. Was the suave Maxwell Yang our murderer? Or was he really—

"Again, I call to you, all the forces of heaven and earth—" Xanthe resumed.

And the phone rang again. Maybe Xanthe was calling down the forces of the phone company. Gotta be careful where you direct your Goddess energy these days.

"Um, Kate?" a quiet voice asked. "Have you started investigating yet?"

"Avis?" I guessed.

"Oh, sorry, Kate," she apologized. "I should have said. It's me, Avis. I just wanted to see how you were doing."

"I haven't really done any investigating yet," I told her, wondering if it was possible for a person to explode from guilt. That person being me. Avis sounded so forlorn, and I wasn't keeping my promises. I put on a cheery voice. "Let's see what the police come up with first—"

"Oh, of course," she agreed. "I don't mean to pressure you. I'll talk to you again soon. Take care."

I squirmed in my chair. "Well, I'll see what I can—"

I was talking to a dial tone before I remembered the questions I'd wanted to ask Avis.

"Police?" Xanthe inquired. I turned to see her raising an eyebrow.

"Never mind," I ordered, fighting to keep my voice even.

"Have it your way," she snarled and straightened her back again. "Goddess, just get her, okay?" she cursed me quickly.

And she was smart to make it quick, because the minute her words were out, the doorbell rang.

I was ready to welcome anyone but Kevin and Xanthe, I told myself, and opened the door. Felix slipped past me faster than a wombat intent on chocolate biscuits.

Felix Byrne. My amigo, sleuth times two, boogaloo. Felix Byrne who'd written a recent article for the *Marin Mind* about my marriage to Wayne. But then, I *had* asked for anyone. And I'd gotten Felix.

"Hey, Kate, ready to sleuth the truth—" he began.

But then he stopped speaking and really looked at me. Too late.

I advanced on him, my face hot with anger, my lungs aching with the urge to scream.

SEVEN

❧

But my lungs continued to ache, unvented. Kevin and Xanthe were in the room. I curled my hands into fists and shoved them behind my back. If I screamed at Felix about his article, Kevin and Xanthe would be sure to ask what the article was about. Even a quick kick to the intrepid reporter's groin might bring up questions I didn't want to answer. My brain tried to take my rage and squeeze it into an acceptable outlet. All it did was make my face hotter. I wanted a therapist, a punch toy, maybe even a gun.

Felix's soulful eyes followed mine and he saw my brother and Xanthe. And sensed that they were the reason for his reprieve.

"Hey, man, Felix Byrne," he introduced himself. "You buds of Kate's or what?"

" 'What,' " Xanthe answered, practicing a withering stare on him. But Felix didn't wither. He just smiled as if Xanthe had uttered a friendly witticism. Xanthe remained unimpressed. She turned to Kevin. "Come on, let's go. Forget *her*," she commanded with a jerk of her head in my direction.

But Felix was not so easily deterred.

As the pair moved past him, Felix stuck out his hand in Kevin's direction and introduced himself one more time. Always open to a possible friend, or investor, Kevin opened his mouth to respond.

And the phone rang. I told myself I didn't want to watch the three meet anyway as I ran to answer it, my face cooling in the passing breeze. Observing them might be something like watching insects mate on public television: slightly disgusting, and not intellectually or even sexually stimulating.

"Kate, Barbara here," said my friend as I scooped the receiver up.

"You wanna talk to Felix?" I guessed, trying to outdo Barbara at her own psychic game.

Her laughter tinkled like rain on the roof at the suggestion.

"So what do you want?" I demanded. Rain just wasn't appealing right then. Especially considering her connection to Felix. Talk about disgusting insects.

"Felix isn't that bad, kiddo," she informed me seriously. "I wanted to talk to you about the Goddess."

"Oh, no. Not you too?"

She laughed again, then modulated her tone. "Kate, the Goddess doesn't curse people," she murmured gently.

"What?" I blurted. How did she know what Xanthe had been trying to do? Then I remembered. How could I have forgotten? I banged my forehead with my palm. Barbara knew everything, everything except the important stuff.

"The Goddess can only bless, kiddo," she finished up.

And then I heard the dial tone.

The Goddess can only bless? What kind of message was that? And then I got it. In Barbara's world, even Xanthe couldn't subvert a benign power. I was safe . . . at least from Xanthe's curses.

All right, sometimes Barbara is pretty cool, even if she can't tell whodunit.

I was still smiling when I headed back to the entry hall. For a moment, anyway. Kevin was waving his hands and telling Felix all about his pyramid kits. I wouldn't have minded Felix buying one. But Felix's countermove came out of the blue.

"So, betcha you're pretty friggin' excited about your sister and the Big Guy tying the knot," he put in.

"Tying what?" Kevin asked, stopped midpoint in his explanation of multilevel marketing, one hand still in the air.

"Trippin' down the aisle, man. I mean, holy socks, they finally did the deed."

"Like a mortgage?" Kevin asked, scrunching his face beneath his dark glasses.

"No man, legalizing the bouncy-bouncy, if you catch my drift—"

"Kate and Wayne are married?" Xanthe demanded, much sharper than my brother on this one. Actually, Xanthe was much sharper than my brother on most things, except for the curses.

"Katie?" Kevin asked, tossing back his Wookie mane. Hurt lurked in the timbre of his voice.

"Kevin," I cut in, "Wayne and I haven't told anyone yet. Felix only found out by accident—"

"By friggin' hard work—" Felix corrected me.

But Kevin didn't care about Felix anymore. "Didn't you even tell Mom?" he asked.

I cringed. I didn't want to even think about telling my mother. Secret, the wedding was supposed to have been a secret. I turned on Felix, my arms rising involuntarily as I walked toward him.

"You, you . . . insect," I growled.

"Hey, don't get your high-tops in a wad, man," Felix replied innocently, backstepping quickly. "Just spreading the word."

"Mom's gonna be really upset," Kevin murmured.

"Listen, Kevin. Mom doesn't have to know," I suggested, my voice mellow and soothing. Hypnotism was my only hope. "We'll wait and surprise her with a real, fancy, formal wedding—"

"Guess my curse worked, after all," Xanthe interjected, smiling smugly, her arms crossed atop her large chest.

"Goddesses can't be used to curse people," I informed her.

"Says who?" she replied.

"Says my friend Barbara," I snapped back.

She put her hands on her hips and began to circle me. Was

she going to curse me . . . or go right for a knockdown-dragout fight?

I centered my body in a tai chi stance, took a deep breath and willed myself to relax, then stepped carefully to the rear, turning with her, my arms in a ward-off position. That ought to take care of either a curse or a fight.

"Thought I'd come home for lunch . . ." A much-loved voice interrupted our dance, faltering on the last word.

Wayne. Wayne was home. What was he seeing? I was afraid to take my eyes off Xanthe to look at him. But I heard his quick footsteps and felt him at my side. Now my body really was relaxed, the way I had willed it to be earlier. Safe. I felt the warmth of relief filling my torso and spreading to my limbs.

"What . . ." he began, then finished up with, "Felix!" as if that explained everything. And in fact, it did, I remembered.

"Felix is here to spread the word of our marriage," I explained maliciously. I didn't have to swivel my head to see Wayne's face turn to stone.

"Hey . . . um . . . Big Guy," Felix greeted Wayne, his voice too high. He quickly moved behind Xanthe. A good choice in shields, as far as human shields went. But a shield wasn't going to be enough.

Wayne strode toward our pit bull reporter, and Xanthe stepped aside. Felix looked around him, as if for another hiding spot. And this man wanted our help finding a murderer?

"Whoa!" Felix yelped, "Holy moly. You going friggin' nutso or something?"

"I got a copy of today's *Marin Mind*, Felix," Wayne said, his voice deceptively soft. "My head chef gave it to me. Wanted to know why I hadn't told him about the marriage." Felix paled.

"Have fun, Kate," Xanthe cooed. "And you'll be hearing from 'Mom.' " Then she grabbed Kevin's hand and dragged him out the door, leaving it gaping open.

I could hear the clomp of their footsteps on the stairs as Wayne continued to advance on Felix, and Felix stepped backwards, stumbling over the futon that was still spread out as a bed in the middle of the living room floor. Supine, he looked up into Wayne's face.

Wayne pulled a folded copy of the *Marin Mind* from his pocket.

He looked down and read at random. " 'Former bodyguard and heir to a reputed drug fortune . . . Typhoid Mary of Murder'?"

"I wrote it before the doc bought the big one," Felix told us.

"Explain yourself," Wayne demanded.

"I . . . I—"

"Craig read it too," I put in.

Wayne winced. Much as he disliked my ex-husband, he had the imagination to know how it must have felt. Unlike Felix. "I'm sorry that he had to *read* about our marriage," Wayne said. Then he looked back down at Felix. "Aren't you sorry too? Do you understand the pain you've caused our friends and loved ones?"

"And family?" I added.

"Why, Felix?"

" 'Cause Kate didn't tell me," Felix whined. "My amigo, man, and nothing. Friggin' nothing. And Barbara didn't tell me either." His voice was getting higher, louder. "My own honeybun and zip, nada. D'ya know what that feels like, man? Everyone's in one big happy family, everyone but me. Noooo. Felix be part of the whole, whiz-bang secret? Noooo. Not Felix. He doesn't even friggin' count. Forget him—"

"Your feelings were hurt, so you took it out on us," Wayne summarized. I couldn't tell by his face whether he had any sympathy for Felix. But his shoulders had loosened. He wasn't going to kill the man. Even I was feeling a little sorry for Felix. It was true, we didn't consider him part of the family. We didn't even consider him part of the human race most of the time. There's nothing like being treated as an outsider to cause pain. And I was beginning to believe that Felix's pain was sincere. Well-deserved, maybe, but still sincere.

"The article can't hurt you," he told us.

"It already has, Felix," I murmured. "Craig's hurt. My brother's hurt. My mother's gonna be hurt. And my friends—"

"But I—"

"No more," Wayne commanded. "It's done." He walked slowly back to the swinging chair for two and sat down. I followed and sat beside him. I could still smell the tension on him, though. I searched his features and saw only misery beneath his all-stress facade.

"Maybe we should have a formal announcement printed up and send it to all our friends and family," I suggested. "I wonder how fast we could get it printed and sent—"

And then Felix spoke, so softly, I couldn't hear him.

"What?" I asked.

"I'm sorry," he muttered, looking at his lap. "I'm sorry. I didn't think."

I looked at Wayne. Wayne looked back at me. Forgiveness? Was it possible?

"I'll help with the announcements," Felix offered. "If you want me to."

"Thanks," Wayne muttered back. I looked at him in amazement.

Almost a whole minute went by before Felix spoke again.

"We gotta sleuth this Sandstrom massacre," he declared.

"Oh, do we?" I replied. How far could forgiveness stretch?

"Man, they got me sawed up like prime rib," Felix declaimed. "Perez waltzed in to drag me over the coals again this morning. Jeez Louise, hadn't even had my caffeine fix. He's hot for my blood—"

Wayne cleared his throat. Loud enough for C.C. to yowl back from the next room. "We were there too, Felix," he stated calmly. "Lieutenant Perez's a good man. He'll figure out who killed the doctor—"

"What doctor?" a voice asked from the entry hall.

I swiveled my head around. Xanthe and Kevin were back. I wondered how long they'd been standing there listening. I wondered if they'd left the front door open on purpose. But I didn't answer Xanthe's question. Nor did Wayne. Even Felix was quiet for a change.

"Is this what all the police stuff is about?" Xanthe demanded. "You guys involved in a murder?"

"Never mind—" I began.

But Wayne squeezed my hand. He looked into my eyes as if for permission, and then spoke without ever having obtained it.

"No more secrets," he announced.

I wanted to argue. But he was right. What good were secrets that would never remain secret?

Felix piped up then. "Your sister, the Typhoid Mary of—"

Wayne instantly stood up, anger vibrating from his pores. C.C. yowled again, then came sauntering in to help Wayne disembowel Felix.

Felix flinched and rephrased his sentence. "Your sister, the whiz-bang super sleuth found another stiff last night," he explained. "I was there too, and the friggin' Gestapo have the hots for me."

"Felix is not the only suspect," I said for the record as Wayne sat back down next to me.

"Yeah, but those potato brains at the cop shop wouldn't mind tightening the noose around my neck."

Kevin and Xanthe drifted in and took their seats on the floor near Felix, where he lounged on the futon.

"Listen, man," Felix implored, waving his hands in the air. I realized it could have been worse. Felix could have been a lawyer instead of a reporter. "I wasn't even there for the first act. Somebody bonked the old codger with a deer thingy—"

"Statuette," I supplied

"—while I was still outside. And that place is a friggin' fortress, man. You're in or you're out."

"Why was everybody there?" Kevin asked.

"Get this." Felix snickered. "They were all having a Marin experience at some kinda support group for geeks whose gardens have been defoliated by deer."

"Like us," I reminded him, a warning in my tone.

"Yeah, but that old lady who owns the nursery, man—" Felix kept on like a blender gone mad. Chop, chop, chop. "The friggin' creature from the crypt. She's my top contender for putting out the old doc's lights—"

"Why?" I asked, stung. Avis was my friend.

"The gloves, man," he answered, stretching out his hands in an elegant imitation of Avis. "She was the only one wearing gloves. Think there're any fingerprints on the friggin' deer thingy?"

I was too shocked to answer. Why was Felix worrying about the police suspecting him with Avis as a fellow candidate? My stomach danced uneasily with my brain. It was Avis's nursery, her deer statuette for sale, her group—

"And then that Mr. Bigshot, TV geek, Maxwell Yang, gay as a floral print frock, man—"

"But he doesn't hide it, Felix," I argued.

"He's not the only wacko. We are talking Disneyland for weirdos, here. That kid, Darcie, what a slob. And her hoity-toity grandmother—"

"Be nice, Felix," I interrupted.

"About the suspects?" he asked incredulously.

"You're a suspect," I reminded him.

"And that Lisa, whoa, man." Felix shook his head. I guess he hadn't gotten my point. "A man-biter, ready for action." He bared his teeth and made grinding noises with them.

C.C. tilted her head, watching him in fascination.

"And Howie what's-his-face—what a banana brain. Goes around holding his friggin' manuscript like a baby. Like anyone cared. Did you see Yang give him the brushoff?"

"How about Natalie Miner, Reed Killian, and Gilda Fitch?" Wayne asked quietly from my side. He must have had a list in his head. Mine was still under my desk blotter.

"I kinda like Reed," Felix offered.

"Why?" I asked in exasperation. I wanted equal-opportunity personality-shredding here.

"I don't know, man, but he's cool, you know." Felix took

a quick breath and finished up. "That Gilda is a graduate of some kinda Rule Britannia clown school, and Natalie Miner oughta look for men somewhere else than at a friggin' deer meeting."

"So, who do you suspect other than Avis?" Xanthe asked. There was real interest in her voice. Which scared me. Because I couldn't see any leverage in the situation for her. And the Xanthe I knew didn't do anything unless it had potential personal leverage. Well, she usually didn't, I corrected myself. Actually Xanthe had been nice to me more than once—all right, quite a few times . . . which in its own way was really scarier than her curses.

"I don't know yet, man," Felix admitted to Xanthe. "But I can do friggin' research. A lot better than the zucchini-heads from the Abierto Gestapo."

"Xanthe?" I asked, unable to keep my mouth shut. "Why do you care who Felix suspects?"

"Because I like you, Kate," she explained, her head jerking back as if surprised by my question. "And you're in some kinda trouble here." Did I believe her?

"But—" I began.

Then Felix directed his soulful gaze in my direction.

"See, Kate, that's the plan. I'm a whiz-bang researcher. You're a whiz-bang investigator—"

"I'd help," Xanthe offered.

"Thanks, Xanthe," I offered back in as friendly a voice as I could muster. Because by now, I did believe in her goodwill, however fleeting it might be. "But I'm not going to investigate and there's no need for you to, either—"

"We'll all friggin' sleuth the truth together, man," Felix told us, sitting up straight on the futon. "Barbara said Kate here would help me." He looked at me again. "You know you will." He was better at this hypnotism stuff than I was. My toes tingled.

"Who's Barbara?" Kevin asked.

"My honeybun, my little dim sum, my—"

"His girlfriend," I interrupted. Too many sweets can make a person throw up. "What does Barbara think?" I asked hopefully. Or maybe hopelessly.

"Nobody knows but Oz, man," Felix replied. "You know how this weirdball stuff fritzes her circuits. She doesn't know doo-doo."

I looked at Felix and thought: It was true, we always had treated him as an outsider. And it was also true that he had done everything in his power to make that happen. But still, I'd hate to see him charged with murder.

"I can't believe Dr. Sandstrom was your doctor, Felix," I murmured, shaking my head.

"His doctor?" Wayne put in from beside me.

I'd never told Wayne that part, I realized, in the chaos following Felix's confession to me.

"That's why you gotta do the Poirot thing, Kate," Felix whined. "Talk to these friggin' geeks. Get the scoop—"

"Felix," Wayne interrupted with another glance for permission my way. This time I nodded. "I think it's time for you to go. Kate is not for hire."

Felix did eventually go, but not without protest, and not without Kevin and Xanthe at his side. And that made me really nervous.

The three of them marched down the front stairs talking about sharing a meal at a nearby restaurant. I wondered who'd get stuck with the check. They were almost to the bottom step, when Felix asked Kevin if Koffenburger was my maiden name. All the hair on my body stood at attention, even my eyebrows. Was he planning on telling every single one of my relatives about the marriage?

Then, Wayne comforted me the best way he knew how. Well, the second best way, with food. He fixed me a quick risotto with portabello mushrooms and paired it with a nice garden salad topped with his homemade roasted peppers. Just the aroma was enough to make my tongue spasm.

I was just digging in, savoring the richness of the mushrooms, when Wayne asked if I was going to investigate.

"Felix could be a member of my family," I told him.

My sweetie . . . my husband, didn't smile.

"Joke," I explained.

"Are you investigating?" he asked again.

"I hope not," I told him. And then I filled him in on Avis's and Maxwell's phone calls to me.

Wayne ate in silence for a while.

"Motive," he finally declared.

"Motive?" I asked. "Who?"

"Don't know yet," he answered, and then with his sternest look, he pleaded, "Don't do a thing without me?"

I nodded, figuring I could at least hold off for the rest of the evening. Friday nights were important at Wayne's restaurant. I would hole up and work while he was gone.

"Thank you, Kate," he whispered and gave me a kiss to live for, a good strategy to keep me out of trouble.

After he'd gone, I practiced my tai chi. The flowing movements often calmed my mind to the point where I could see the important stuff that hid beneath the tumult that usually reigned in my brain. But that night, all I could think of was how cool the terra-cotta planter mug would look once it was done. I did a slow turn toward the back wall and saw it take shape.

And then the doorbell rang.

I ran to my office to peek out the window, promising myself I would not open the door to a suspect, not even Felix.

But then I saw who stood on my doorstep, Avis Eldora. My friend. And while I peered out the window, Felix's description of Avis seeped into my mind like water into drought-ridden soil.

Was Avis a friend? Or was she a suspect?

Eight

✶

Avis Eldora. My mind brought up her file. Owner of Eldora Nurseries. Former actress. Long time friend? I'd almost always seen Avis in the setting of her business except for those rare occasions when we'd met at parties, our own or someone else's. We'd talked at gossipy length, but we'd never been to lunch. Friend or acquaintance? Did the semantics matter? I saw her shoulders slump as I peeked out my office window. Avis, in high-top sneakers, jumpsuit, and wide-brimmed hat, was covered as always from head to toe so that not an inch of skin was exposed to the sun's rays. All in shades of green. Even her gloves were moss-green.

Gloves. My neuro-fibers stood on end. What had Felix said about her gloves? It didn't matter, I told myself. But the thought persisted. If Avis were to walk in and murder me, there would be no fingerprints.

I glimpsed her face from beneath the wide brim of her hat as she looked up at the door. Then she closed her green eyes for a moment. I couldn't hear her, but I could feel her sigh. She turned to go back down the stairs.

I rushed out of my office to the front door. Avis was my friend, lunch or no lunch. Could I keep her out of my house and let Felix in? There was only one verdict. No way. I flung open the door.

Avis was just stepping off the deck onto the stairs.

"Avis!" I yelled out.

She jumped, then turned to face me. There was worry in the lines of her face. And fear.

"Oh, Kate," she breathed. She raised a shoulder as if dislodging something. "I'm so glad you're home. I hope it's okay to visit you here. I just couldn't stop worrying. I know I should be more positive, but—"

"Come on in and talk to me," I ordered and hugged her as she stepped over the threshold, not too hard, not wanting to injure the body that felt so fragile as I put my arms around it.

Avis walked carefully into the living room and sat down on the denim couch. I wondered if her joints were hurting her. It was so easy to forget that Avis was older than I was, with the possibility of the infirmities common to her age. But however carefully she walked, she kept her back erect, her movements as graceful as those of the dancer she had once been.

"Tea?" I offered.

"No, no," she demurred, her hands rising to stop me and then folding themselves in her lap.

I lowered myself into one of the hanging chairs and watched her, impatience compelling me to push off with my feet and let myself swing in the chair. Avis seemed totally absorbed in some world I couldn't glimpse, her head bent so that I couldn't see her face beneath her hat, either.

"If not tea, then sympathy?" I asked finally.

"They think I did it," she answered quietly.

"Avis," I told her sincerely, "you're not the only one the police suspect. You're not the only one who's afraid. As long as you didn't kill Dr.—"

"No, no!" she cried, her words no longer soft. "You must believe me, Kate. I abhor violence. All I want is harmony, peace, a place to unite with nature!"

Suddenly, I was wondering what would happen if someone got between Avis and her unity with nature. Uneasiness quivered in my chest, making it hard to breathe. I pushed harder with my feet, my chair swinging so frantically that a breeze fanned my face. Avis might feel and look fragile, but she lifted sacks of potting soil and fertilizer daily that I couldn't lift without a few years of body building. Wielding a deer statuette would be nothing to her. And I had let her into my house.

Maybe it was the look on my face, or maybe the fact that I'd stopped talking, but Avis was staring at me now.

"You believe it too," she declared, her voice sad.

"No, Avis, I just—"

Avis whipped her hat off her head, revealing her boyishly, and expensively, cropped silver hair. And her lovely face: clear, milky-white skin; full lips that were still sensual; and those almond-shaped green eyes.

"Kate, look at me," she begged. "Do I look like a murderer?"

"You look nothing like a murderer," I told her honestly. I didn't add that she looked like an actress playing the part of a murderer convincing some poor sap she wasn't one. And I wished she'd taken off her gloves instead of her hat.

"You believed it for a minute, though," she said, and continued before I had time to argue. "That's why you must help me find the true culprit. Kate, they can't prove I killed Dr. Sandstrom, but they can make people believe I did. What would happen to Eldora Nurseries then?"

"I'm not sure it would hurt your business, Avis," I told her. "People are weird. They might like visiting a place with a suspected—"

Her widening eyes stopped me from finishing.

"It's not just business, Kate," she persisted. For a woman I'd always thought shy and unassuming, she was getting awfully assertive. Or was it aggressive? "I have to know. My nursery has been a refuge. Only the truth will bring peace there again."

I wanted to tell her she was being melodramatic. But then, that probably came naturally to her, after all her years of acting. So instead I asked her how she thought we could discover the murderer's identity.

"I don't know," she pronounced carefully, an undertone of impatience in *her* voice now. "That's why I've come to you."

"Well," I suggested brightly, "we could talk about the suspects. What do you know about the members of the Deerly Abused?"

"The Deerly Abused?" she asked, squinting my way.

"The Deer-Abused Support Group," I corrected myself. "You must know its members better than anyone."

"Well," she answered slyly, "I thought I knew you and Wayne. But I didn't know you were married."

I clenched my jaw.

"A little joke, Kate," she told me. "Who was that obnoxious man who came for the last half of the meeting?"

"Felix?" I said, as if there had been other obnoxious interlopers roaming the nursery.

She nodded.

"He's a reporter."

It was Avis's turn to clench her jaw.

"But I doubt that he's doing much reporting on this incident," I reassured her. "He thinks the police have *him* tagged for the murder."

Avis smiled, a genuine and beautiful smile.

"I know I shouldn't be happy," she apologized in advance. "But I'm glad to hear they suspect someone besides myself."

"Tell me about Reed Killian," I ordered.

Now Avis blushed. No wonder she wore that hat all the time. She needed the camouflage.

"He's, um, a doctor," she answered, her hands fluttering in her lap. "A plastic surgeon. But he has a garden too and was very interested in the deer problem. He was the one who came up with the idea for our little group."

"Did he know Dr. Sandstrom?" I asked, slowing my swinging chair to lean her way. The two doctors might have been connected. Reed could have concocted the idea of the common-interest group to get his victim there. Or Avis could have, I reminded myself.

"I . . . I don't know," she whispered. "I haven't asked him yet. I didn't want to seem to pry."

"Avis," I told her. "Pry."

She laughed a little, blushing again.

"How about—"

But before I could ask my next question, C.C. jumped up on my lap without warning. She stared up at me, her little black and white face seeming to strain to tell me something. Was it about Avis? Then C.C. put her nose in the sleeve of my sweatshirt, a game she'd rarely indulged in since her early days as an orphan cat.

"She's a sweetie," Avis cooed. "My daughter had a cat like yours growing up."

"You have a daughter?" I asked.

Avis grimaced.

"Olive," she said. She didn't sound happy.

"Olive?"

"Olive, my daughter." She sighed. "She's going through a rough time right now. She's staying with me. She's . . . I don't know—"

"Not harmonious?" I guessed.

"Right." Avis laughed again. It was good to hear.

"Listen, Avis, if you're serious about this, do you think you can arrange another meeting of the Deer Group?"

"How about Sunday?" she offered eagerly.

"Done," I accepted. Somewhere along the line, I'd stopped being afraid of Avis. "All right, back to suspects. Which of them do you know the best?"

"Well, Maxwell comes in fairly often," Avis answered. "I think he likes talking to an old relic like me."

I opened my mouth to object to "old relic." Avis was a vital woman, nowhere old enough to be a relic. But she put up a hand, forestalling my objection.

"Maxwell is very funny," she told me. "Maybe 'witty' is a better word. And kind, I think. Howie Damon comes in a lot too. A nice young man. And Lisa too, she's doing so well with her therapy. Now, Jean Watkins, she's great, taking care of her grandchild like that . . ."

Avis liked everyone, it seemed. The only information she was providing was enough to make her and Felix the best suspects, given the general saintliness of the rest of her customers. She was, however, a little concerned about Dr. Sandstrom's behavior on the last night of his life.

"He was usually so gentlemanly, but that night . . ." She clicked her tongue. "I think maybe it had something to do with his wife's—"

The phone rang, cutting her off.

I was about to let it ring, when I recognized the enthusiastic voice coming from the answering machine's tinny speaker.

"Hey, Kate, if I may call you that," he began. "This is Reed Killian. Any chance that Avis might be around? I just wanted to—"

I dislodged C.C. and picked up the phone, exchanged a few stilted words, and handed the receiver over to a blushing Avis. Then I went back to sit in my swinging chair.

I couldn't help overhearing, honestly. The living room is just too close to the office for a really private conversation. Especially if you hold your breath and keep very, very still.

"Fine," Avis kept saying. Then, "No, I am not in danger. Don't be silly."

A silence.

"Kate is helping me, Reed."

Another silence.

"I know you are."

C.C. popped back in my lap and I lost a little then. But I was beginning to get the gist of the conversation. Reed was worried that *I* was going to hurt Avis, that *I* was the murderer. Or at least he was pretending to. What better way to look innocent himself? Then an even nastier thought crept into my skull. What if Avis had arranged the phone call to make them both appear innocent? What if—

Avis set the phone back down before my mind could succumb completely to paranoia.

I stroked C.C. absently. And as I stroked her I came to a hole in her fur. An icky, bleeding hole in her fur on her left flank.

"C.C.!" I gasped. So this is what my little cat had been trying to tell me. She was hurt. Hurt.

"Kate?" Avis inquired gently.

"Look," I said, holding C.C. as tenderly as possible to expose the unfurred patch on her side.

"Oh, dear," Avis murmured, crouching cautiously next to the swinging chair. "Do you think it's a cat bite from one of her friends?"

"I don't know." I could hear the whine in my voice. It was time for the vet. Help for C.C., and maybe some sedatives for me.

My sweet little orphan cat, hurt, and I hadn't even noticed!

"Do you need my help, Kate?" Avis asked.

I calmed down, looking more closely. My cat wasn't dying. She just had a little piece missing. I hoped.

"No," I assured Avis. "But thanks.

"I'll let you go, then," Avis said briskly, tying her wide-brimmed hat back in place. "I've taken too much of your time as it is."

"Oh, no," I protested, politeness kicking in even in crisis. I would probably go to a firing squad apologizing. And joking.

"Avis," I called out as she reached the front door. "Tell Reed I promise not to hurt you."

Avis blushed once more, grabbed me for a quick hug and left the house giggling, closing the door softly behind her. The woman had class. Maybe she *was* a relic, a relic of a more courteous age.

But now I wasn't feeling funny anymore. Except funny as in dizzy. I locked the cat-door first. Then I went in search of the cat carrier.

I'd finally found the wood and wire carrier under a pile of blankets in the back room when the phone rang again. I told myself I wouldn't answer it under any circumstances. Nothing could be more important—

"Kate," the answering machine said. "This is your mother."

I froze. Mothers are psychic. She'd know I was really there

if I didn't pick up. But C.C. sighed as if to say, Get on with it, talk to her.

"Mom?" I answered tentatively.

Silence.

"Mom?" I tried again.

"Is it true what Kevin tells me? Are you married?"

"Well, I . . . uh . . ."

"A simple yes or no will do," she prompted. At least she didn't add "young lady," though I'm sure it was implied.

"Yes," I admitted.

"And you didn't see fit to invite your mother to the wedding?"

"Well, yes," I answered again.

"Do you know what this means to me, Katie?" she said.

And then she explained, at length. My ear was sizzling all the way to my toenails when I hung up. I deserved to be boiled in oil. To be dredged in flour and fried. To be popped into the microwave—

The phone rang again. This time it was Felix. I changed my mind. Felix tempura. Felix tacos. Felix steamed with broccoli.

"Felix, you creep," I said to him.

"Whoa, Kate," he objected. "Are you friggin' gonzo or what?"

"Friggin' gonzo, that's it, Felix," I told him. "And you are going to be fried and battered. Actually maybe I'll batter you before the frying. Actually—"

"You not so whiz-bang, today?" he asked.

"No, and it's all because of you," I said, taking one breath before I slammed the phone down. It felt good. But then I remembered C.C. I put the wood-and-wire cat carrier on the dining room table, then gathered C.C. into my arms, waiting for the great battle that was bound to ensue when I tried to fit her into the carrier. But she just closed her eyes and walked with a dignified limp into her cell. Now I really was worried.

The phone rang again.

Not this time, I told myself.

"It's Barbara," the machine said. "C.C. can wait a second longer. Pick up."

So I did.

"Help Felix," she ordered.

"After what he did to me, that creep—"

"Helping Felix will help yourself," she assured me.

I hated it when she made these pronouncements. Because she was usually right.

"Felix can be your backup," she went on. "He can take notes. He can keep you out of Wayne's way—"

"But—"

"I've already talked to him about what he did to you, Kate," Barbara insisted. "He's very sorry. He just doesn't know how to tell you. He really does consider you his friend."

I was weakening.

"Well . . ."

"It'll be okay, kiddo, really. And so will C.C. Her wound isn't serious."

"But, how did you—"

I stopped myself.

"Have you called the vet yet?" Barbara asked.

I called the vet. They told me to come down anytime. I looked at C.C. She blinked her eyes. And we were off.

I rushed out the door, cat carrier in hand, and collided with an all too solid body that began to fall backwards. I grabbed her hand to yank her back to an upright position before I even saw her face. It was Jean Watkins, grandmother extraordinaire.

"I have to explain to you about Darcie," she told me.

Nine

ϰ

My friend Barbara may have been a mind reader. My mother may have been a mind reader. Even Xanthe might have been a mind reader. But I was sure hoping that Jean Watkins wasn't one.

Because if she was, she might have been ready to slap me by now for my inner rage at people who got in the way of other people trying to take their sweet little wounded cat to the vet's. Not to mention my inner language. Mom would've killed me for that.

I looked at Jean Watkins and decided she was more the type to rap my knuckles with a ruler. It was something about the squareness of her jaw in that serious, round face. And the no-nonsense, short, curly gray hair. I wondered if she'd ever been a teacher. Or a nun. Or both.

"Kate, are you feeling well?" she asked, peering my way. Ah, good, not a mind reader.

"I'm fine," I answered, lifting my cat carrier to chest level. C.C. peeked out, looking as wan as possible for a cat. "But look at my cat, she's hurt."

Jean bent forward to take a look inside the cat carrier. And I got a closer view of her sturdily dressed ample body, and a whiff of apple shampoo. She and Avis might have been close in age, but physically, Jean Watkins was about as different from Avis Eldora as I could imagine. And yet there was something alike in the two women. Was it determination? I wouldn't have thought of Avis as determined, but she had just talked me into . . . what?

"Oh, dear, I see the wound," Jean announced before I could compare her to Avis anymore. "I won't take much of your time."

I looked at C.C. through the wire of the cage. None of our time would have been preferable, C.C. and I agreed silently. But Jean Watkins clearly wasn't a party to our agreement.

She started speaking thoughtfully, slowly, her eyes on mine. She didn't even ask to come in. And I didn't offer. Instead, I stood outside on the deck and listened, still holding onto C.C. in the cat carrier as Jean spoke.

"My granddaughter, Darcie, has problems," she began. "But she isn't totally irresponsible. Actually, under the circumstances, she's behaving quite reasonably."

"What circumstances?" my mouth asked, and C.C. glared at me, slitting her eyes. Asking questions wasn't going to get us to the vet's any quicker. I squirmed in place and then reminded myself of Barbara's prediction that C.C. would be okay.

"Darcie's mother died when Darcie was a child," Jean explained. She sighed and her eyes went out of focus for a second. But only a second. "She was a good woman. My son couldn't have asked for a better wife. She died when Darcie was eight years old."

My heart clutched. Eight years old? Suddenly, I appreciated my own mother, even her recent lecture. Well, maybe not the lecture—

"My son took his wife's death very hard. He seemed to forget that he had a child too. And when Darcie went to him for comfort he was cold, even verbally abusive. There are times I'm not proud to be his mother. But I know what's right and what's wrong. When my son told me to take Darcie if I was so"—Jean took a deep breath before finishing her sentence—" 'goddamned' worried about her, I did just that. I took her home. And I love her. No matter what's she's done."

This time I kept my mouth shut. No questions to slow us down. But I hoped Jean Watkins's "what" didn't include murder.

"Darcie got into a lot of trouble last year. Vandalism. Drinking. Joy-riding. It doesn't sound like much, but last year she was only twelve." Jean shook her head. "She's thirteen now. And since she's come to live with me, she hasn't been in any trouble. She's developing her own set of standards. She's a good girl. You can even ask Howie—"

"Howie?" I interjected. I needed to bite my tongue. I was pretty sure C.C. would have liked to bite it herself at this point.

"Howie Damon is the administrator of the school Darcie attends now. And he would be the first to tell you that Darcie's turned around. She would never do anything violent."

The grandmother doth protest too much, I thought, wondering why she'd brought this information to me. But I didn't ask. I kept my lips firmly locked and waited for Jean to finish.

"I read the papers," Jean announced.

Did that mean Felix *was* writing up Dr. Sandstrom's murder? I was beginning to feel as wan as C.C. looked.

"I know you've been instrumental in solving murders before, Ms. Jasper—"

"Kate," my mouth corrected her without permission.

"Kate," she went on, a slight smile recognizing my offer of familiarity. "I know you'll consider what I've told you and weigh it fairly."

Then she stuck out her hand. I shook it awkwardly with my left hand, my right hand still holding the cat carrier and beginning to cramp around its handle. Actually, my right hand was going numb. I switched the carrier to my other hand as soon as Jean let go.

"Well, I know you need to go, so I'll get out of your way," she finished and turned to stride down the stairs.

So, maybe she was a mind reader. But what had compelled her to confide in me? C.C. snarled me back to reality and I realized I hadn't even said good-bye. Of course, Jean Watkins hadn't actually given me a chance to say good-bye.

I stuck C.C. on the passenger's seat in my old Toyota, buckling up the carrier. Then I got in on my side, the comforting smell of old car, mold, and dust greeting me.

"So, why did Jean Watkins really come to see me?" I asked C.C., starting up the engine.

C.C. mewled. Maybe she felt like I did when my friend Barbara was at the wheel.

"Does she really think I'm going to investigate?" I asked as I pulled out of the driveway.

C.C. didn't even answer. She turned her furry rear to me and sulked.

"Do *I* really think I'm going to investigate?" I persisted, once I was on the main road.

I thought I heard a sigh from the cat carrier.

That was the end of our conversation until we got to the veterinarian's and pushed the glass door open.

There were two patients ahead of us in the big waiting room. A Maltese in the convenient cat jail that the vet had installed for those who brought their cats in without cat carriers, and another cat that I couldn't see but could definitely hear in what looked like an ice cooler. The cat in the cooler was howling, much to the embarrassment of its well-dressed daddy.

C.C. howled back as I approached the receptionist and the ululation wars were on.

"Name?" the receptionist shouted.

"C.C.," I shouted back.

"Last name?" she demanded over the escalating howls.

"Cat?" I offered loudly. C.C. didn't actually have a last name. But that was embarrassing to admit.

"No, yours," she corrected me impatiently.

"Oh, right," I yelled, "Jasper!" taking the woman in for the first time. This wasn't the usual receptionist. The former receptionist had been elderly with a memory like an elephant, an android elephant with a computer chip for a brain. This woman was young, steely eyed, and clearly unhappy. Maybe it was the howling. Maybe it was the smell of antiseptics and cat. Maybe it was her paycheck. I didn't ask. After an afternoon of unwanted confidences, I was afraid she might tell me.

After explaining C.C.'s need to see the doctor, I took a seat on the easy-wash, military-green vinyl couch against the back wall, cat carrier and opera cat in place in my lap.

The outer glass door swung open again. And Gilda Fitch walked in, a more modern plastic cat carrier on her arm, a tabby peeking out, green eyes wide.

My eyes must have been wide too when I first saw Gilda. It was true that Avis Eldora and Jean Watkins had tracked me down at home. But now, another suspect in Dr. Sandstrom's murder had found me at the vet's. How likely was that? Even C.C. had quieted down. Did she sense danger? Gilda saw me and her head jerked back. She frowned for a moment, then seemed to take a breath and winked my way. Was my presence as suspicious to her as hers was to me?

"Gilda Fitch," my suspect announced to the receptionist in a moment of relative silence. "I rang up earlier."

"Name?" the receptionist demanded.

"Mordecai," Gilda answered.

"Last name?"

I bent forward.

"Poor little bugger doesn't have a last name, now does he?" Gilda answered, with a great, shining smile. "And I've already given you mine, my good woman."

And then I was laughing. Suspect or not, the woman didn't put up with bureaucratic nonsense.

The receptionist ascertained that Mordecai seemed to be undergoing a disturbing attack of sniffles and then waved Gilda away from her desk.

Gilda joined me on the easy-wash couch, and Mordecai essayed a small, mewing sound. C.C. answered with vigor and the howling chorus went into second session, with the unknown cat from the ice cooler joining in.

"Well, m'dear," Gilda greeted me over the noise. "We seem to meet in the most squalid places." Then she appeared to lower her voice, though I could still hear her clearly. "Though

Mordecai does have the taint of bastardy in his blood. No last name, you know."

We laughed together. It was too easy to like this woman whose dark skin belied the characteristic long nose, round eyes, and shining, slightly buck teeth of the British aristocracy. She could have been a browned Windsor. Maybe she was.

"But Mordecai has to see the putty-tat quack, much as I abhor the breed."

"Ducks?" I asked, now thoroughly confused.

"No, doctors, m'dear. Doctors are not so affectionately, but commonly, referred to as quacks, across the big puddle."

"You don't like doctors?" I asked, the light finally dawning.

"Got it in one," she told me. "Visited a series at home. All misdiagnosed me. Positively terrifying. Ten years of rubbish before a piece of luck brought me to a woman who figured the whole lot out."

I was beginning to be able to understand her. And I understood something else too. This woman had a grudge against doctors. And of course the late Dr. Sandstrom had been, well, a doctor.

"Most of the quacks I've seen have been bloody pieces of work, but I wouldn't go postal, now would I?" she assured me. Or tried to.

"Huh?" I said. She'd lost me again.

"I toil for the post office," she reminded me.

"Oh, got it," I whispered. Her wit had almost struck me mute. But I was curious enough to risk a stupid question.

"Is that your real accent?" I asked. I couldn't help it.

Gilda threw back her head and laughed.

"Yes and no," she finally answered. "My mother is truly a British woman of a certain class." I must have still looked confused. "Upper," she explained. "Though my papa, his fatherhood unbeknownst to him, was an African exchange student. So I was raised 'black as coal' in the clutches of minor aristocracy. When I first came to the States, people were positively shocked by my accent. Teetered right off their chairs, some of them. So I decided to lay it on even thicker, even snootier. Put a twist in their tails, it did. Especially when I mixed in a bit of Cockney."

I smiled, imagining.

"Ever think of acting?" I asked her.

"And what would a nice young woman like me be doing that for?" she asked, suddenly Irish. "Actually, I'm keen on little theater. Done quite a bit of that. But it hasn't led to fame and fortune. The post office may be my true route in life."

"Did you know Avis was an actress?" I asked.

"Really?" Gilda stretched the word out in a way no American could have. "Should have guessed. She's got the fatal signs—"

"Ms. Jasper?" the receptionist shouted across the room.

And suddenly I remembered where I was and why.

There were usually two vets on call here. Dr. Murray was a graceful woman of grand proportions who always smiled, patted my shoulder, and made me feel better while stitching up kitty boo-boos with love and compassion. And then there was Dr. Peckinpaw, a stick of a man who tended felines tenderly, but generally treated humans with frowns and brusque recriminations.

I got Dr. Peckinpaw. The receptionist probably planned it that way, I decided as I stepped into the sterile examining room.

Once inside, I opened the cat carrier door and C.C. rocketed out onto the metal examination table, sliding to a stop exactly where Dr. Peckinpaw lay his arm across her path. He didn't say a word as he gently inspected her. She crinkled her eyes up at him adoringly and barely flinched as he sterilized her wound, and applied ointment.

"And a little something to keep her from worrying the bite," he finally said, adding yet another ointment. C.C. didn't look so adoring anymore.

Then Dr. Peckinpaw turned to me. His sour face was pinched into a glare.

"It appears that C.C. has been under some unusual stress

lately," he told me. "Cats will often self-mutilate if they feel stress or neglect—"

"*Self*-mutilate?" I yelped.

"Of course. Can't you see she did that herself?"

I looked down at C.C. She stared back up at me smugly.

"But why?"

"Probably because of something you have done to cause her stress," he answered quite seriously.

"Murder?" I asked just as seriously.

"This is no joking matter, Ms. Jasper. Have you neglected your cat, left her alone, left her out—"

"Well, my sweetie and I did get married," I told him, then added hastily, "It's really a secret, though."

"Did you tell C.C?" he asked.

I could feel my mouth drop open.

"Did you tell your cat, Ms. Jasper?" he persisted. He would have made a great prosecuting attorney.

"Well, no," I answered. Suddenly the room seemed un-bearably small. "But she's just a cat. I mean—"

"You should have told C.C.," he declared, shaking his head. He drew in his cheeks until he looked like a standing skeleton. All he was missing was the string from the top of his head to hold him up. He glared at me for an infinite amount of time, then turned and solicitously stuffed C.C. back into her carrier, yelling, "Next!"

I scurried out of his office, carrier in hand, passing Gilda just coming in. She rolled her eyes and whispered "Peckinpaw, the putty-tat quack," before entering the den of the beast. Her attempt at humor helped smooth out the guilt a little. But I still felt as if I should do hard time. Especially after the re-ceptionist gave me my bill and ointments and instructions.

I talked to C.C. on the way home.

First, I asked her if she'd like a formal adoption.

She mewled like a kitten. Had she really heard me?

I told her I didn't mean to hurt her feelings.

She lifted her head and blinked. If she was crying, all that was missing were the tears.

I apologized. And apologized again.

By the time I'd reached home and turned off the engine, I began to hope she'd forgiven me. A little of her favorite cat food didn't seem to hurt.

I sat down at my desk, C.C. now safely snoozing in the kitchen, and looked at my Jest Gifts paperwork. I wanted to know more about Dr. Sandstrom. I was beginning to know more about some of the suspects, but the doctor was the center of this case. And besides, I assured myself, visiting his office wouldn't be as dangerous as visiting suspects. But this time I asked C.C. if the trip would be all right with her. She seemed to shrug her shoulders. I took that as a yes and told her I'd be home soon.

Finding Dr. Sandstrom's office was easy. He was listed in the Yellow Pages, located in downtown Mill Valley, not far from where I'd visited Dr. Peckinpaw.

The office was in a well-kept, redwood-shingled building on one of the little streets off East Blithedale. The sign on the door read Dr. Sandstrom, Dr. Yamoda, General and Family Practice.

I was beginning to lose my nerve as I stepped through the doorway into the comfortably furnished waiting room. It was a room meant to be gentle on the eyes, salmon-blush walls with white accents. Salmon and teal furnishings. And a blond young woman behind the reception desk, her eyes and nose a painful red in her pale face. She sniffled and asked if she could help me. I could smell antiseptic, but no cat. And it was quiet. A vast improvement on the last office I'd visited.

"I came to ask some questions about Dr. Sandstrom," I told the young woman behind the desk. Somehow, I couldn't resort to subterfuge while she was crying.

Maybe I should have.

"He's not here!" she wailed. And wailed. She couldn't seem to stop. Maybe this office wasn't such an improvement, I decided, looking back longingly at the door I'd come in.

An older, Asian woman, her glossy black hair tied back in a severe knot came out wearing a white coat . . . and a frown.

"Melanie, what is it?" she asked.

"The lady wants to know about Dr. Sandstrom," she whimpered, pointing my way. "And he's dead!"

"You must have really liked him," I said to Melanie, not knowing what else to say."

"He was my friend," she whispered. "He never treated me bad. He was a nice man."

That was enough for me. Avis hadn't just been kind when she'd described Dr. Sandstrom as a gentleman. Here was another human who had found something in him I hadn't seen. And then I remembered the few moments when he'd seemed concerned about my vegetarian diet. Maybe I'd seen another man, too.

"I should go," I murmured. "I'm very sorry for your loss."

But the older woman wasn't having any of my inept apologies.

"Who are you?" she demanded. "What do you want to know about the doctor?"

"I . . . I was in the group the night he was killed," I admitted. "I just wanted to know who he was . . . I—"

"I'm Dr. Yamoda, Dr. Sandstrom's partner," the woman announced, putting out her hand. I shook it, and noticed her eyes were red-rimmed too. "Come with me," she ordered.

I went with her to a tastefully appointed office in the same color scheme as the reception area. There was a lone rose in a vase on her white desk. She must have noticed my glance.

"For the doctor," she said softly, then turned back to me.

"Are you from the police?" she asked.

"No," I answered. "I was in the group—"

"I know that's what you said," she cut me off. Her voice was harsh. "You're not a reporter?"

"No, I just have problems with deer," I shot back.

"So did the doctor," she breathed. She even smiled a little.

"Coffee-can Claymore mine," I pronounced to ensure my credentials.

This time she really did smile. And she sat down.

"Dr. Sandstrom was my partner. He made me a partner in

his practice, despite my race, despite my gender. He was a good man and a good doctor."

I sat down too, introduced myself, and we talked a little while longer, but she had already summed up all there seemed to be said about Dr. Sandstrom. And I believed her. In this office, the doctor had been everything he hadn't been the night of the Deerly Abused. I doubted that whatever had brought his death had come from here.

Twenty minutes later, I got up to leave.

"Ms. Jasper," Dr. Yamoda called to me as I opened the door. "If you find out anything, let us know."

I nodded.

"And if you need more help in your investigation, please come back," she added.

I wanted to tell her I wasn't investigating, but I didn't. I couldn't. I just nodded back. And said a quiet goodbye to Melanie in the reception area.

I was still thinking about the doctor when I pulled into my driveway. The good doctor, the bad doctor. Who was he really? It took me a moment to even notice the ring of protestors on my deck. And even when I saw them, I wasn't sure I'd really seen them. I got out of my car and approached warily.

Two men and three women, all wearing camouflage beige and deer antlers were holding picket signs. When they saw me they held their picket signs higher and walked in a circle.

Then they began to chant.

It was even louder than the vet's office. And stranger.

"Deer are human too!" they cried out together. "Deer are human too!"

Ten
✗

Theirs were not voices I wanted to hear without musical accompaniment. Or with musical accompaniment, for that matter. In fact, the only two of the voices on key just seemed to accentuate the three that weren't. The shrill notes were from the tallest of the group, a man dressed in beige jeans, T-shirt, obligatory antlers, and a necklace from which hung a round planet Earth, which bobbed on his chest as he marched and chanted. The angriest tones came from a small woman dressed similarly but without the planet Earth. Maybe she'd lost hers.

The closer I got, the louder they got, only now the words had changed.

"Deer count!" they chorused, marching even faster in the tight little circle the radius of my deck would allow. Their picket signs showed deer faces with melting brown eyes . . . and not a rosebush in sight. I checked out their shoes, hoping for the moral high ground of their leathered feet, but saw cloth sandals with wool socks instead.

When I finally reached the bottom of the stairs to my own house, I was working up the nerve to ask the picketers why they were on my deck. I opened my mouth.

"Deer killer!" the small angry woman accused.

The others immediately took up the chant.

"Deer killer! Deer killer!"

Whoa. That was scary. Perspiration drenched my shirt suddenly. I took a second to think.

"Sheep oppressors!" I yelled back. It felt good to yell. And justified.

After all, I'd seen their wool socks. And I was pretty sure they hadn't asked the sheep for shearing rights. All those vegetarian magazines I'd read over the years were finally coming in handy. I'd never been very good at the recipes. But I had a good store of ammunition for those cumbersome arguments about animal ethics.

A tall dark-haired woman looked down, her face reddening, recognizing the jab. The rest of them seemed struck dumb. They had that sheep-in-the-headlights look. That was all right by me.

I bolted up my stairs, hoping to get by them before their brains returned. Or at least before their mouths did. C.C. came out of her cat door to eye the contestants.

"You're Kate Jasper," the small woman declared as I was almost to the door. I could smell the anger on her. At least a week's worth of anger. It wasn't pleasant.

"And you are?" I shot back. That ought to keep them on their woolly toes.

"We're Deer Count, an organization to protect the rights of deer in Marin County," she declared and hefted her sign even higher.

I longed to ask, *Do deer count with their little hooves?* but I resisted. "Who gave you my address?" I asked instead.

"We have our sources," the shrill man answered smugly.

"Well, I haven't killed any deer," I informed him. "So your sources must be confused."

"You are in the Eldora Nurseries Deer-Abused Support Group, aren't you?"

"The nursery group is not a hunting group," I objected, trying to keep my voice even. Still, the realization that they knew that much about me slowed my pace just as I was ready to lunge at my front door.

"But you were there to find ways to get rid of deer, weren't you?" my inquisitor persisted.

I shouldn't have stopped to consider the question.

"Deer killer!" the small woman shouted again.

"Look, I don't know who you guys are, but I haven't done anything to hurt a deer—"

"Deer persecution clearly is happening at the change of the millennium for a reason," the other man in the group told me, his eyes intent under his antlers.

I took a breath, lunged, and stuck my key in my door.

"Those who think not of the sheep whose souls have been sheared for their own pleasure shouldn't cast the first stone at nonviolent gardeners," I announced in biblical tones. I turned the key. "And I'll bet none of you have gardens either," I added, shoving my front door open.

It worked. I swiveled my head to see their blank faces as I stepped inside and slammed the door behind me, locking it in place.

I put my hand on my heart to steady its thudding and then flopped into a swinging chair, my clothes as wet and sticky as if I'd spent the afternoon in the tropics. Only in Marin, I told myself, pushing off with my feet. Only in Marin would a group of picketers attack a gardener trying to protect her own roses. Actually, maybe they'd do it in Berkeley too.

Little bits of conversation drifted through my closed window.

"Souls?"

"No, soles."

". . . talking about our feet!"

"Socks . . ."

"Wool is from sheep?"

"Of course it is, you numbskull!"

And after a while their voices died away completely. I peeked through the slit between the living room curtains. Deer Count and all their antlers were gone. But they were not forgotten. I wanted to know how they had found me. Felix? The police? Avis Eldora?

I could check on the last guess at Eldora Nurseries. But I had to ask C.C. first. I found her in the laundry basket and picked her up to check out the hole in her side. It already looked healthier to me than it had pre-vet. I reached down and stroked my cat's sleek head, murmuring sweet nothings to her. I would have been embarrassed if anyone had heard me. But they couldn't. And C.C. couldn't talk. Though she sure knew how to communicate. Chew a hole in your side. Maybe I'd try it sometime. She purred contentedly, her paw extended in full control.

"Is it all right if I go to the nursery?" I asked.

She stopped purring.

"I'll only be a little while," I told her.

She slitted her eyes my way.

"Food?" I tried.

It was the magic word. C.C. went scooting and meyowling all the way into the kitchen for a special treat.

I snuck off to Eldora Nurseries while she was still slurping. I couldn't figure out if I felt guilty about C.C., or completely bamboozled.

Eldora Nurseries was doing a brisk business in spite of any bad publicity it might have received. Or perhaps because of that publicity. Avis was busily ringing up flats of plants and bags of fertilizer at the cash register, and a young woman was carrying the purchases out to the patrons' cars. The air was soggy with the smells of dirt and plants. It wasn't until the young woman came back into the store that I recognized her round face and curly hair. Avis's helper was none other than Darcie Watkins.

Avis whispered, "Jean asked if I'd pay her to help out one afternoon a week. I can use the help, and Jean . . ."

"Bullied you into it," I finished her sentence. Avis smiled from beneath her hat. But were thirteen-year-olds even allowed to work?

Darcie pulled her baseball cap down further over her curly hair and smiled at me, big teeth showing. "This is really cool, and I'm getting paid too," she assured me.

"That's great," I told her, deciding that child labor laws had no jurisdiction here.

Avis rang up a flat of foxgloves and Darcie cheerfully carried it out to yet another car.

"Avis," I whispered urgently in the lull, "there're these goofy picketers called Deer Count—"

"I know," she cut in, her voice low with some emotion I couldn't quite identify. Sadness, anger?

"They visited me today," I told her. "Did you tell them who I was?"

Avis shook her head wearily. She reached out both her gloved hands to hold mine and looked into my eyes.

"They came here this morning. I don't know how they knew about the group. But they charged the place, pushing their way into the store. And then they saw the roster . . ."

"And what, Avis?" I demanded. Her gaze was fading, her hands limp now. "Did they eat the roster?"

"No." She giggled and released my hands. "They stole the roster. Luckily, I have a copy. But I never imagined they'd harass you. I need to talk to them, to tell them we mean no harm to deer. I tried to look them up in the phone book, but they're unlisted. I want to tell them that we're peaceful here."

"Ask them about their policy on sheep," I suggested.

"Sheep?" she asked, confused. Then she blinked and whispered, "Maxwell is here if you want to talk to him."

"Really," I whispered back. "Where?"

"Out by the ground covers," she told me.

So I sauntered out to look at baby's tears, mosses, and succulents.

I recognized Maxwell's slim, well-dressed figure from the back, but moved past him, my face averted, waiting for him to discover me.

"Oh, Kate!" he exclaimed as his eyes came up from the thyme he was inspecting. "I'm so glad you're here. I need to discuss all of this with you—"

"All what?" I asked hesitantly, suddenly wondering what I

hoped to accomplish by sneaking up on him. He couldn't hit me with a statuette out here, could he?

"You'll know what to do," he assured me. He pulled back his shoulders, readying himself for speech. I just hoped it wouldn't be a long one. "I'm fairly successful in my life," he began modestly.

"Very successful," I corrected him. I may not have owned a TV, but even I had heard of *Everyone's Talking.*

He grinned, that well-groomed impish Asian grin. No wonder he was a success.

"If you insist." He bowed and kissed my hand. I could smell his cologne. It was good enough to eat. "Okay, I am *very* successful. By your decree." Then his face turned serious again.

"But I'm at a complete loss about this murder." He paused. "And I don't like being at a loss. Especially when I knew the victim."

I started. "You knew the victim?"

"I was Dr. Sandstrom's patient," he answered. "And I think we might have been friends."

My mind reviewed the night the doctor had been killed. Hadn't Dr. Sandstrom made some crack about Maxwell's sexual proclivities? That didn't sound friendly to me.

"I went to Dr. Sandstrom as a patient last year. I was feeling run-down. My 'friend' was afraid I might be HIV positive, though we've been tested again and again. My friend is frightened. Sometimes, I am too. So I went to the doctor."

Maxwell paused, looking out over the flats without seeing them. I could hear the buzz of insects in the brief silence.

"I tested negative . . . again. Sandstrom was great. Told me to stop worrying. He said I just worked too hard. In fact, he was the one who suggested I take up gardening. I started and haven't stopped since. And my garden is really—"

"Perfect?" I guessed. I had a feeling everything Maxwell did was perfect.

He laughed. "As perfect as it can be, except for the deer. I called Dr. Sandstrom and he suggested the deer group. I know he didn't act as if he knew me at the meeting. That was the way he was. Absolutely discreet. Even our relationship was confidential to him."

"Even his staff didn't know," I murmured. Dr. Yamoda hadn't mentioned him, or Felix for that matter, when I'd gone down my suspect list.

"Yeah," Maxwell agreed. "They're professionals. In my business, I require a certain level of professionality. And I liked the doctor—"

"But didn't he make homophobic remarks that night?" I asked, trying to remember exactly what the doctor had said.

Maxwell smiled. "No, not homophobic. Never from Dr. Sandstrom. Believe me, I have heard truly homophobic remarks. In fact, I hear them daily. No, the doctor was just to the point, professional as always. I can't say he was a career charmer, like myself. But he was honest. I enjoyed his company, his character."

I believed Maxwell. In fact "honest" seemed a good assessment of the doctor. And "professional." At least now I had a hint of why some people might have liked the man.

But I also began to wonder just how many members of the Deerly Abused had been Dr. Sandstroms's patients.

Maxwell's soothing voice cut into my thoughts. "My dilemma is whether I should go to the police and tell them about my relationship with the doctor or not," he said. "I don't want to throw myself in their way as a target, but I still want to do everything possible to help them solve this crime—"

"Kate, Maxwell!" came a raspy voice behind us. A voice filled with the joy of meeting friends unexpectedly.

We turned and saw Natalie Miner beaming at us, her heart-shaped face sparkling like an aging cherub's in the sunlight, haloed by her curly blond hair.

Natalie reached out with both arms and hugged me tight to her stale-cigarette-smelling bosom. But Natalie wasn't really a friend. My one and only shared experience with her had been at the Deerly Abused the night before, hardly an experience on which to build a friendship. But apparently Natalie thought differently.

"I am so glad to see y'all," she told us once she'd let go of me. "Lord knows I've been wanting to talk to someone about last night. But Avis seems so busy."

Avis was busy, but I wondered if she was making herself appear even busier to avoid Natalie.

"Shoot, I just don't know what to think," she went on, patting her pockets. She pulled out a pack of cigarettes, then put it back. "Dear God, what a thing to happen to the doctor—"

"Did you know Dr. Sandstrom?" Maxwell Yang cut in quickly.

Natalie blushed under the tan foundation that coated her face.

"Not as well as I would have liked to," she admitted. She reached for her cigarettes again but only got halfway this time before pulling her hand back. "Dr. Sandstrom was a very attractive man, you can appreciate that." I wondered if by "you" she meant Maxwell or me, but I didn't interrupt. "We met right here at the nursery. Talked up a storm. He was a very intelligent man. And a brave one. He served in Vietnam, proud as could be."

Her smile faded. Was she remembering his death?

"Were you ever his patient?" I tried.

"Oh, no, honey," she trilled, her smile appearing again. "Never let a man who might be courting you see you in your underwear. That's what my grandmother always said. She married a doctor. South Carolina—"

"But you were friends?" Maxwell shepherded Natalie back to the subject with a skill he must have learned as an interviewer.

"Yes, I should hope so," Natalie replied. "We talked just endlessly about roses. All the different kinds and such. He was going to come to my house to help me out with my garden design. I'd hoped . . ." Her mascaraed eyes teared, the droplets looking like diamonds on her dark lashes. "And now the poor man is dead. Dear God, it just isn't right."

"Well, it was good seeing you again," Maxwell murmured politely, and then he was gone. Vanished. Probably another skill he'd learned as an interviewer. One I obviously needed to work on. I was still there with Natalie.

"When my late husband died, it was different of course. He'd been sick a long, long time. Prostate cancer. Not that I could eat a bite for months afterwards, mind you. I was devastated."

"I'm . . . um . . . sorry," I put in inadequately.

"Never you mind," she told me, lifting a finger to wag in my face. "Life is for the living—"

"I'll bet your grandmother told you that too," I commented, smiling at her. I couldn't help it. She was such a friendly puppy.

"You're so right," she cooed. "When my Buddy died, I could almost hear Granny telling me to get on with it. I've been selling real estate, you know. And looking for the right man. Thought maybe Dr. Sandstrom might be the one. Surely was a shock, the way he was killed. I just can't seem to comprehend it, somehow."

I nodded. "You have any whodunit theories?" I whispered, woman to woman, gossip to gossip.

"A million and one," she whispered back, moving her face closer to mine. "That Reed Killian didn't like anyone stealing his show, the good Lord knows. And Lisa and Darcie were downright rude, if you want to know the truth. And something is truly strange about that Gilda woman." She swiveled her head back and forth in a quick, sweeping motion. "Not to mention Avis," she added.

I kept nodding, though I hated to hear Avis included in the list.

"But still," Natalie went on, hand reaching down toward her pocket again and returning empty. "I may not have an ounce of sense, but I can't make a murder motive out of any of it. Can you?"

"Nope," I answered honestly.

"I thought, now, what if one of our group had seen the

doctor as a patient," she went on. I hoped my face didn't show that I knew of at least two who had. "Maybe they had some terrible disease they were ashamed of. But then I said to myself, Natalie, you aren't making sense. Why would they come all the way to a deer-abused support group to kill him?"

"To cover their motive?"

"The police are bound to find out they're patients," she pointed out.

I was beginning to guess that Natalie had way more than an ounce of sense. She probably inherited it from her grandmother.

"Then," she continued, "I looked back on the evening and thought of everyone the doctor had insulted. Lord, he was in a mood, wasn't he? That Howie Damon with his manuscript, for instance. But, shoot, it still doesn't make sense to me."

I shook my head. So far, nothing she'd said added up to murder for me either.

"First, I thought it might be that strange little man who came in late—"

"Felix?" I asked.

"Felix, uh-huh," she confirmed. "My, my, he wasn't up to any good, now was he? But the doctor was hit twice with the same statue and Felix wasn't even here for the first time. It just doesn't make any sense."

"It doesn't," I agreed glumly.

"But you can't just let a few little old obstacles get in your way," she added. "It's a challenge—"

"Your grandmother again?"

"It surely was my grandmother who said that, hon," she admitted. "You're one smart girl. I know you'll figure out who did it, Lord willing."

"Me!" I squawked.

But someone tapped me on the shoulder before I was even squawked out. I jumped under the weight of the hand and whirled around to see Darcie smiling my way, oblivious to my moment of panic.

"Ms. Eldora told me to tell you wassup," she explained. Or tried to.

" 'Wassup'?" I asked.

"You've got a visitor," she translated and pointed over her shoulder.

I followed the direction of her finger.

Lieutenant Perez of the Abierto Police Department stood at the entrance of Eldora Nurseries with his arms crossed over his chest. His dark eyes were brooding. One of his heels was tapping. And he was looking straight at me.

ELEVEN

✗

Emily Bronte's Heathcliff came to mind as Lieutenant Perez's eyes burned into mine. But Heathcliff hadn't been a policeman. Though he had been a trifle miffed with Cathy as I remembered. Was the lieutenant miffed with me?

I stepped forward hesitantly on weak legs, then told myself to cut it out, and strode forth to meet Lieutenant Perez, centered, balanced, my spine straight. No one suspected me of this murder. Right? Then I started thinking of all the possible and impossible reasons that might lead the lieutenant to suspect me. By the time I'd reached him, I was wilting again and ready for the Typhoid Mary of Murder speech.

"Ms. Jasper," Perez muttered in greeting when I reached him.

"Lieutenant," I murmured back, hoping my voice was low enough that he couldn't hear the tremor.

"We have a little problem, Ms. Jasper," he went on.

"Problem?" I asked. Could he mean the murder? "Problem" sounded more like an illegally parked car or—

"I know you've been involved in these things before, ma'am," he told me.

My body stiffened, ready for the lecture.

"Thought maybe you could help us out on this one," he finished up.

It took a very long time for his words to make sense to me.

Maybe it was a minute, maybe a century. Long enough that the lieutenant peered into my face for a response.

"You want help?" I asked. "From me?"

"The Abierto Police Department doesn't get involved with many murders," he explained. "And the chief, well . . ." A look of pain crinkled the lieutenant's eyes, real pain. Did he really care that much about his chief? I reached out a comforting hand and then pulled it back before I touched him. This was a policeman after all, a very handsome and appealing policeman.

My cheeks flushed. Married less than a week, and already I was noticing other men.

"I don't really know the players here," the handsome lieutenant told me, his voice low. It was a sexy voice.

Damn. I shook my head. I didn't want to think about the quality of his voice.

"Ma'am," he asked, anxiety tingeing his sexy voice. "You okay?"

It was the "ma'am" that did it. The realization that Lieutenant Perez probably saw me as an older woman, and that I probably was, in fact, at least ten years older than he, was like a splash of cold water on any sexual fantasies I might have been ready to kindle.

"Fine," I answered him curtly.

"Anyway," he said, getting back to his point, whatever his point was. "I've talked to Sergeant Feiffer from the County Sheriff's Department. He says you're good, that you'll be nosing around anyway. All I ask is that you tell me what you learn."

I nodded, still trying his words on for size. He wasn't telling me to keep away from his case. He was inviting me in.

"Well, um—" he said.

"Lieutenant," I burst in, suddenly beginning to actually think. If he wanted to tell me things, maybe I could ask him things too. "Did Felix Byrne do an article about the murder for the *Marin Mind*?"

Perez shook his head, a small smile tugging at his lips. "I

had a little talk with the people at the *Marin Mind* about the appropriateness of a suspect covering the story. They did a brief crime report. Unfortunately, the names of all the members of your group were mentioned."

"Unfortunately," I repeated. Then I asked. "Do you guys have any idea—"

He cut me off with a curt shake of his head.

"Well, I'll be glad to help, Lieutenant," I told him belatedly. "I want this solved too."

"Thanks, ma'am," Perez said. I waited for him to tip an invisible Stetson my way. "We need to know who did it."

"Right," I agreed, shifting my gaze to his shoulder.

"Even if it's you or your husband," he added.

And then he walked away.

Me or my husband? The words wouldn't go away. Was he threatening to arrest me or my sweet Wayne if I didn't solve this? No, I told myself. He was a policeman, the good guy. The guy who'd probably illegally pressured the *Marin Mind* into putting a lid on the story to protect his chief. What else would he do?

"Kate," a voice murmured solicitously behind me. If I hadn't realized it was Avis, I probably would have whirled around and kicked. Instead, I just turned stiffly. "Did he scare you?" she asked.

"Yes, he did, Avis," I admitted.

"Oh," she whispered, pulling her smock tighter around her thin shoulders. "I'm so sorry, Kate."

It wasn't until later that evening in tai chi class while I was doing the sparring called single push hands, sinking to the rear and turning my body and arm in retreat, then circling forward to seek the center of my partner's resistance, that I realized the lieutenant had probably scripted his words about me and Wayne, counting on my being frightened enough to help him. My body stiffened as I retreated again. My partner took advantage and pushed me gently backwards. I thanked her sincerely. That's just what the lieutenant had been doing. Pushing me gently, finding my weaknesses. And that sexy voice and those burning eyes—were they just another form of manipulation? I consciously relaxed my body and circled more softly this time, catching my partner off guard. By the end of the round, I wondered if Perez really wanted my help at all. Or was he just testing me? And of course, I stiffened again.

I learned a lot from push hands that night. If I stiffened from fear or resistance, the lieutenant could topple me. If I relaxed, and remained true to my principles of balance and centering, I might just find a murderer. And then I left the tai chi hall for the real world and immediately forgot my lesson.

Saturday morning, I told Wayne we had to talk. His face took on that unmistakable look of dread that statement inspires in most males.

"It's about C.C.," I told him. "We have to adopt her."

He lifted his eyebrows and smiled tentatively, waiting for the joke.

But then I showed him her wound and told him what the veterinarian had told me.

Twenty minutes later, after a whispered consultation, Wayne and I sat on the denim-and-wood couch, C.C. enthroned between us.

She moved her head from side to side, eyeing each of us suspiciously.

"We want to tell you that we're married, C.C.," Wayne began.

C.C. licked a paw. *Tell me something new*, she seemed to be saying.

"And we want to adopt you," I put in quickly.

C.C. looked up at me, her eyes wide-open now. I could have sworn she was actually listening.

"We, hereby," Wayne and I chanted in unison, "take you, C.C., as our lawful, legitimate cat who we will love and take care of for as long as we are married." The three-by-five card I'd prepared before our speech helped the simultaneous nature of the broadcast.

"Merowr?" C.C. said hopefully. And then we each petted her.

Wayne and I were still ogling long after C.C. had left the room, her tail held high, her steps purposeful as she pushed her way out of the cat door to make some other local animal's life a misery.

"Did she really understand?"

"I think so."

"But she's just a cat."

"A legitimate cat."

And so it went until it was time for Wayne to go to work. Whether C.C. had understood us or not, Wayne and I felt better. We were a family now: woman, man, and cat.

And I was ready to protect my family. I was ready to find out who killed Dr. Sandstrom. I hadn't forgotten Lieutenant Perez. And it was Saturday, a good day to catch members of the Deer-Abused Support Group at their respective homes. But I needed backup.

Felix.

Ugh.

It was a horrible thought, but one that actually made some sense. And if there was any trouble, I could always use Felix as a human shield . . . or a semihuman shield anyway.

I punched out the numbers of Felix's phone guiltily, my stomach objecting with each jab.

He answered within a ring.

"All right, Felix," I told him, getting the words out of my mouth as quickly as I could. "You win. I want to investigate."

"Far friggin' out," Felix breathed after a second of silence. "Listen, I know I've been a potato-brain, man, talking about spreading the poop around about you and your Big Guy to your family. I was just being a wiseacre. Holy socks, I wouldn't really say anything."

"Fine, Felix," I answered through clenched teeth. I didn't stoop to reminding him that he had already told my brother, which was the equivalent of telling my whole family.

"I've been sweating over some cool-as-pool announcements for you," he went on.

It took me a moment to remember what he was talking about. Post-wedding announcements, the answer to all faux pas.

"See, I got this really hot-as-jalapeños idea, man. They could look like friggin' newspaper headlines, but on this classy paper. I did a quickie-wham-kazaam sketch. I can bring it."

In the short silence that followed, I realized that he was serious. Felix Byrne was trying to be my friend. I was still scanning my brain for the words to answer him by the time he'd told me he was on his way, "burning rubber" to my house, and hung up the phone.

Fifteen minutes later, the doorbell rang, and the man was there himself, mustache, soulful eyes, and all. He flashed a sketch my way. THEY DID THE DEED was printed in bold-face across the top. An impossibly rendered bride and groom were below, labeled Wayne the Swain and Kate the Mate.

"I'm . . . I'm . . . touched, Felix," I finally choked out. It was better than choking him.

Scratch the announcement idea, the still-functioning part of my brain told me.

"So, let's visit Howie," I suggested quickly.

Felix's grin disappeared for a moment, but then reappeared as quickly as cat hair on trousers.

"Wow, Kate, you're really ready to sleuth the truth!" he whooped.

We were rolling out of my driveway in his vintage '57 Chevy, complete with foam dice, before he had time to ask for feedback about his announcement. I wondered how long I could keep him away from the subject.

"So d'ya think Howie's the weirdo-in-the-works?" he asked eagerly once we were on the highway, heading toward Howie's address in Green Valley. Felix wasn't such a bad partner. He had everyone's address already in his little spiral notebook. And he knew how to get anywhere in Marin County.

"I don't have a clue, Felix," I told him. "But I want to talk to the members of the group I haven't seen since the . . . incident," I told him.

"Holy moly, you mean you've already seen some?" he breathed.

"Just Avis and Jean Watkins," I began. "And Darcie and Maxwell. Oh, and Gilda. And Natalie," I added defensively. How *had* that happened?

That's what Felix wanted to know. And I still hadn't answered him to his satisfaction by the time we reached Howie's. But at least he'd forgotten the announcement.

Howie seemed surprised, but not unhappy to see us at the door of his little cookie-cutter duplex. His round, undistinguished features reflected a mild curiosity if anything. I was even more curious as I surveyed his front yard. Gray stones, a few boxed plants. Was Howie really a gardener? Not even the remains of a rosebush were in sight. Maybe he had a magnificent backyard, I told myself.

"Terrible thing, Dr. Sandstrom's death," he commented, ushering us into his living room. Or maybe I should say "library." Books were scattered liberally across the room, spilling out of shelves onto the coffee table, chairs, and even the floor. This was his real garden. A garden of literary delights. The smell of old paper tickled my nose.

He cleared off a couple of chairs absently, his mouth moving as if he were talking to himself. Cataloging the books he was removing?

"It was a very painful experience," he amplified, once we were all seated.

"Pretty good friends with the old doc, eh?" Felix led the witness. Or tried to.

"No, I never met him before," Howie answered, his face a study in innocence. "But I'm sensitive. Every man's death is important."

I didn't ask him what he thought of women's deaths.

"Well, we thought we'd ask a few questions—" I began.

But Howie's small eyes filled with a sudden recognition of Felix that stopped my mouth in its tracks.

"You're the reporter, aren't you?" he asked.

"Yeah, that's me, I scoop all the poop," Felix assured him cheerfully.

"You know, you might like to do a feature article on my manuscript," Howie suggested eagerly. "Three generations of Californians. It will be important, really."

Felix barely had time to blink. Howie's eyes went out of focus as he launched blissfully into a dizzyingly long summary of his manuscript.

We left, twenty minutes later. And Felix was carrying a complete copy of Howie's work.

"Jeez, what a friggin' geek," he exploded when we made it back to his Chevy. "Everyone and their friggin' iguana thinks they're a writer."

"But is he a murderer?" I asked.

"Single-minded sucker, that's for sure," Felix replied thoughtfully.

"All right," I agreed. "If Dr. Sandstrom had some way to block publication of Howie's manuscript, I'm sure Howie could have overcome his sensitive nature to do the act—"

"But the doc didn't have diddly to do with Howie or his friggin' manuscript," Felix pointed out.

"Right," I said, and we rode the rest of the way down the highway to Lisa Orton's house without further conversation.

Lisa's house was not a cookie-cutter job like Howie's. Hers was produced by a cookie *couturier*, and protected in a gated community. The guard at the gate took a while for secret communications before we were allowed in to drive past minimansions, set back on full-acre lots, with identical fluted columns and double doors. But one look at Lisa's garden when we arrived told me the gates didn't keep the deer out. Her garden was filled with deer fodder, the remains of rosebushes, clematis, and Korean lilac, giving her garden a Bosnian sort of character. Why had she planted all the very flowers and shrubs that the deer loved so well? Lisa for one, appeared to need the information that the Deerly Abused had to offer.

She met us at the door, unsurprised, having been warned by the guard. I stared at her large, childlike eyes, her freckled cheekbones, and her sucked-in lower lip and wondered how she'd wound up in a mini-mansion. (What did she do for a living?)

"My father died," she explained before I asked, before we were even through the doorway. "My mother was already dead, died when I was a kid. I inherited a whole bunch of money." As we crossed her double-doored threshold, she pointed to a marble mantelpiece with an eight-by-ten picture of a severe-looking man whose face was neatly crossed out in Magic Marker.

"Oh, how—"

"I deserve wealth. I deserve to be happy after his abuse. And I'm tired of working as an accountant."

"I'm sure you—"

"And now I have the money for therapy. He would have a fit if he knew," she said proudly, then lowered her voice. "But he doesn't. And I am becoming a fully actualized woman, finding my goddess within—"

"Did you know Dr. Sandstrom before?" I inserted abruptly.

"No, but I know his type. My father was a doctor. If it weren't for my therapist and my survivors' group, I don't know what I'd do—"

"Did you put out the doc's lights?" Felix interjected, his voice raw with frustration.

"Huh?" Lisa replied.

"Did you kill him?" I translated.

"He killed himself," she declared, her eyes widening even further. "Karma," she whispered.

Felix and I let ouselves out as Lisa went back to being a goddess or whatever she'd been doing before we arrived.

"Whoa, not logged-on," Felix muttered as we drove back by the security guard.

"But a murderer?" I asked.

"Karma." He smirked.

"Be good, Felix," I warned him. "You're still in Marin County limits. Karma will get you."

He laughed, and so did I. But I wasn't absolutely sure I was joking. Anyway, we still had one more stop to make. I didn't want to offend the parking gods.

But there was plenty of parking at Reed Killian's house. His place wasn't a cheap, cookie-cutter house or an expensive one. It was . . . itself, a rambling brown adobe with little cutouts in the walls all along the outer edges. The cutouts were fun. Each one had a puppet or a rubber dinosaur or a piece of pottery or—

"Don't spend all day like a friggin' tourist," Felix hissed in my ear. "We gotta grill the poss-perp."

"The what?"

"Possible perpetrator, Kate," he explained impatiently. "Your friggin' hearing going or what, man?"

"What, man," I answered, but Felix was already ringing Reed's doorbell.

I was admiring the deer-proof lantana bordering the pathway to the front door when the door opened. The sound of Tibetan bells with a salsa beat greeted us.

Reed Killian was unshaved, dressed in short-shorts and a Hawaiian shirt, and playing. His living room was filled with toys. Light-activated sculptures barked and twinkled as we followed him into the room. Banks of black built-in stereo equipment stood at attention. Travel guides littered the room. But Reed only had eyes for something that looked like an oversized synthesizer linked to a computer screen.

"Wow, you guys have to see this," he told us, as if we'd been friends since childhood. "I just got it last week."

He pushed some buttons and a saxophone blared Bach to a rock beat.

"Is that a synthesizer?" I asked. I wanted to play too. But he didn't offer.

"No, no," he said, pushing another button. Harps played a happy tango. "This thing could be a whole recording station, it's so cool. You can pick style, rhythm, instruments—"

"We wanted to talk about the murder," I told him.

"Talk," he declared. "And music will answer you."

"Avis Eldora—" I began.

A pastoral symphony with the hint of a shimmy came wafting our way.

"Lisa Orton?" Felix tried.

Discordant jazz, with too many instruments, filled the room. An organ joined in sorrowfully.

"And you." Reed pointed at Felix.

Rapping drums pounded, obliterating all other sound. Felix? Yep.

"So who did it?"

Reed turned from his new toy with obvious sadness.

"I'm a doctor, a plastic surgeon, not a detective. I play at a lot of things, but Hercule Poirot isn't one of them."

He turned back to the synthesizer recording station, and a frantic harpsichord played.

"Howie Damon?" I guessed.

"Yeah," he agreed, grinning. Then his grin faded. "But I don't think he did it. Look, I just want to have fun. I was going hang gliding next weekend. But this whole thing is a downer, especially for Avis."

Classical music brought an auditory image of Avis into the crowded room, and once again some instrument played a mischievous shimmy in the background.

Reed turned the machine off. Only then could I hear my ears ring in the silence.

When he turned back to us, his eyes were serious, pupils dilated.

"I've thought and thought," he told us. "And I've come up empty. Solve it for Avis," he ordered.

"Friggin' easy for him to say, man," Felix complained not too long afterward as we sat in the Acorn Grows restaurant. Felix asked for three burritos and a side of refried beans. I asked for a soba noodle salad.

"No venison," Felix told the waitress when I ordered. She smiled.

How Felix could wrap waitresses around his finger was a mystery to me. Maybe it was the magic of first contact. Or maybe they just wanted good tips. But they always smiled at Felix. I told myself to forget the waitress and tried to get a word in edgewise. Felix was ranting. From what I could make of his words, he thought detecting should be easier. Because with these last three visits, I'd had a second shot at talking to each and every one of the suspects, and I wasn't a whisker's breadth closer to knowing who did it. And Felix was not a happy camper. Karma.

After Felix dropped me off in my driveway and sped away, his foam dice swaying, I grinned. He'd forgotten about our wedding announcements in his post-detection snit.

I walked up my driveway, listening to a burst of unexpected birdsong and smelling what was left of my garden. The scent of grass, rosemary, lavender, and a few remaining roses mingled with the smell of dirt and barbecue smoke from next door. I was too busy enjoying the feel of the sun on my neck to look up until I got to my front stairs. I should have kept my head down. Kevin and Xanthe sat on my front deck. Frantically, I looked over my shoulder for Felix. But Felix was long gone. And for the first time since I'd met the pit bull reporter, I missed him.

"Hey!" Kevin shouted. "Guess what?"

TWELVE

✗

"I don't want to guess what!" I shouted back, ascending the stairs cautiously for all my volume. "In fact, I don't even want to know. Maybe if you just left—"

"Katie, what's happened to you?" Kevin whined, his Wookie face showing hurt somewhere beneath the dark glasses. "It's like you're in a totally different emotional zone or something. You didn't used to be so mean."

"Did too," I told him. Family brings out the real Oscar Wildeian wit in me.

"It's that man she's *married* to," Xanthe intoned. She shook her blond poodle head and threw back her shoulders, exposing the full Mae West effect of her body under her tight T-shirt. "A man can do that to a woman, take away her power, her individuality, her woman-soul—"

"Wayne has not taken away my woman-soul!" I barked. "If anything, he's helped me grow into it. He's a kind, sweet—"

"Hey, Katie," Kevin interjected. "We're just here to help."

I stood for a moment, my mouth hanging open, panting like a dog.

"Help me what?" I finally asked, knowing an instant later that I shouldn't have.

"Help you with this murder situation, Katie. You need to take a more cosmic approach. Maybe it's some kinda reincarnation thing. Could be the murderer knew his victim in a past life—"

"Kevin," I murmured, controlling my voice, "I thank you for wanting to help. Truly, I appreciate your concern. But there's nothing you can do here."

"Oh, Katie," Kevin insisted, "why do you think we were born into the same family? We've probably had tons of past lives together. Helping each other, sharing . . ."

Not to mention arguing, hitting, kicking, fratricide, that kind of thing. I tried to tune him out.

"And you still haven't decided on the pyramid—"

That I heard. "The decision is *no*," I told him. Then I repeated myself, poofing out my lips like a megaphone. "*No.*"

"It'll take you a while. I understand," he answered. "Holistic financial planning is harder for some people. But we'll be here—"

"What do you mean 'here'?" I shouted. "Not 'here' as in this house—"

Xanthe began a slow, keening noise, her large, mascaraed eyes shrinking to black blobs.

"Stop it," I told her.

It was then that I felt someone walk up from behind me on the stairs. Or maybe I heard him, not only his footsteps but his breathing. There was something about his gooey inhaling and exhaling that told me he had allergies. Or a broken nose.

I turned slowly and saw a man with a scraggly beard and squinty eyes. His eyes held an expression that I remembered from my days working at a mental hospital.

"Who are you?" I asked, keeping my voice slow and calm.

The man didn't answer. He just smiled, revealing missing teeth. And he flexed his considerable muscles. Crazy or not, this guy worked out, I realized. And he sweated. And he didn't bathe a lot. I was a regular Sherlock Holmes of eyes, ears, and nose. But I still didn't know what it all added up to.

"Are you a solicitor?" I asked. "Because if you are—"

"No, Katie," Kevin objected. "This is our friend Slammer.

He's going to provide you with some logistical help in your murder situation."

"Your name's Slammer?" I asked the man, just to be sure.

He smiled again. Slammer was missing more than his teeth. Reality was not present in his face. At least, not my version of reality.

"Yeah, Slammer," Kevin answered for him. "You know, like the governor's hotel."

"Prison?" I yelped. I hadn't meant to yelp, but I was pretty sure no one heard me anyway.

"And he likes to hit people a lot," Kevin went on happily. "Slammer's his own name for himself. I think we all should be able to name ourselves for our unique—"

"Kevin—" I muttered menacingly, still not turning my back on Slammer. I was sure he *had* named himself for his unique qualities, and I didn't want to find out about them personally.

"We thought you could use some muscle," Xanthe added helpfully.

Muscle? Muscle head was more like it. But why would they think I needed muscle?

"Is this your idea of a bodyguard?" I asked, realization finally awakening.

"Yeah," Kevin and Xanthe answered together. They sounded pleased with themselves. Of course I couldn't see their faces, because I was afraid to turn back and take my eyes off Slammer. They were trying to help me. First Felix, now Kevin and Xanthe. How could I get so lucky? Or maybe they weren't trying to help me. Maybe this was a trick.

"Xanthe?" I asked softly. "Why are you trying to help me?"

"Because I like you," she insisted. "I told you that."

"If you like me, then why do you curse me?" It seemed like an appropriate question.

"Oh, I get mad," Xanthe answered lightly. "I know I shouldn't, but hey, better than keeping it all bottled up, right?"

I didn't have the heart to tell her I'd rather she kept it in the bottle.

"Well, I thank you all for coming," I assured them after a

few cleansing, calming breaths. At least, that's what they were supposed to be. "But I can handle everything just fine on my own from now on."

There was silence from behind me, silence in front of me. "No" was not going to work here. I was outnumbered. *Lie,* my body ordered me.

"Oh!" I cried out melodramatically, lifting my wrist to peer at my watch. "I'm late for my appointment!"

I slithered around Slammer as quickly as any tai chi student could. (Running away can be the best of all moves.) Then I flew down the stairs, ran to my car, started it in record time, and backed out of the driveway, popping gravel. Backing out, I momentarily faced the three figures who were left in front of my house. None of them moved. The Wax Museum of nightmares. I jerked the wheel and turned onto the road, still in reverse, then jammed the shift into Drive and sped away, my seat belt buzzer still screaming for my safety.

I was sweating when I finally landed in the parking lot of the health food store. Health was what I needed. Continued physical well-being. It was worth a trip. I locked up and entered the store through gliding glass doors, heading for the tofu section to see what was new. Tofu pepperoni was what was new, and it looked good. I was just grabbing for a log when a voice startled me out of my gourmand fantasy world.

"Just not cricket," the voice announced.

I jumped and turned. Yep, it was Gilda Fitch standing behind me.

"Tofu pepperoni," Gilda went on, a smile lighting up her maple-brown face. "A bit much, don't you think? I mean, is it ground from little tofu piglets or what, eh?"

"What are you doing here?" I blurted.

"A bit of shopping," Gilda replied. "And you?"

I regrouped. There was no reason Gilda couldn't be shopping at the same store as I was. And taking her cat to the same vet. Right?

"So how's . . . um"—I searched my memory for her cat's name—"Mordecai?"

"Oh, positively terrific," she assured me. "And how's your little puss?"

"My? Oh, you mean C.C. Well, we adopted her," I finished lamely.

Gilda laughed. "Jolly good," she congratulated me. "Adopted your puss, eh? Rather a piece of luck for her, hah-hah."

"The vet told me to," I answered defensively. I didn't know if Gilda thought I was kidding. Actually, I didn't know if Gilda was the one kidding. I didn't even know if Gilda was a murderer. In fact, I didn't know if Gilda was stalking me.

"The puss had her tail in a twist?" Gilda asked.

"No, she bit a piece out of her side," I explained.

"Ow," Gilda commented, stepping back from me. "Ornery little blighter, eh?"

I opened my mouth to defend my cat, then closed it again. C.C. was an ornery little blighter, adopted or not.

"So, any progress with the grand deduction?" Gilda asked, her face coming a little closer to mine than it had been before.

I shook my head. I was getting cold. I figured it was the refrigeration in the soy section. I lay the tofu pepperoni back down alongside the other logs.

"Positively terrifying thing, this murder," Gilda declared, twiddling a curl in her topknot. "And your chum Avis called to set up another confab for Sunday. Think it's safe to go, what?"

"Oh, sure," I answered Gilda, remembering that the meeting had been my idea. But what if it wasn't safe? What if it would just give the murderer another chance to do harm? Damn. I hadn't even thought of that possibility. "As safe as driving," I amended.

Gilda laughed merrily.

"Got me there, old bean!" she whooped. "Driving, indeed. Got your statistics handy? Deadly machines, those horseless carriages. Hah-hah. Well, must run. Cheerio."

And Gilda strode away with the posture of a dancer and the

leg muscles too. Maybe that's what carrying letters did for you.

What Gilda did for me was to give me the willies. I was sweatier now than I had been when I'd entered the store, and cold on top of it. What if she'd brained me with a tofu pepperoni?

I had a feeling Gilda and I would be instant friends if it weren't for a little murder and her constant vaudevillian appearances. But there was that murder. I shook my head. I'd figure out who she really was later. There was tofu to peruse.

Maybe you can't buy over forty versions of tofu anywhere else. But you can in Marin County. I left with teriaki tofu balls, Mexican tofu patties, and yes, the tofu pepperoni. Soy paradise.

And even better, when I arrived home, no one was on my front deck. This time I checked before I got out of my car.

I walked in the front door, calling out for C.C., who serenaded me as she came sliding around the hall corner like an ice skater.

I told her I loved her. She smirked. I asked her if she'd like some tofu. The smirk disappeared, and she left in a huff. And there are those who don't believe cats are psychic.

The phone rang before I'd made room in the refrigerator for my soy groceries, or chased down C.C. to apologize.

I slammed the refrigerator door shut and ran to pick up when I heard the voice on my answering machine. "This is your mother," it informed me.

"Mom?" I whispered into the receiver.

"Do you have another mother?" she asked, sadness marking each word.

"No," I answered dutifully.

And then I heard a sniffle. Uh-oh.

"Mom?" I asked again, my pulse gyrating in my ears.

"Oh, honey," she breathed. "It's all my fault."

"Um, what's all your fault?"

"You're afraid of weddings!" she sobbed.

C.C. heard my mother and sobbed along with her. I would

have sobbed too, but I had to be calm. Someone did.

"Mom, I'm not afraid—"

"It's all because of me. Remember Aunt Rita's wedding? Oh, of course you don't. I was still pregnant with you. But they say that babies in the womb are ultrasensitive. And you know how that wedding was."

"Actually, I wasn't there," I reminded her.

"Oh, but you were!" she cried. "There in my belly. The whole thing was a fiasco. The cake fell. The mother and step-mother were arguing. Everyone hated each other." She lowered her voice. "Rita divorced him within a year."

"But that wasn't your fault," I assured her.

"But I should have never gone while I was pregnant. You picked it all up. All the negativity. All the arguing. No wonder you and Craig didn't last. Womb trauma. And now you're afraid—"

"Oh, Mom. It's not your fault. Really."

"Then what is it, baby?"

She had me there. But I attempted an explanation. A reasonable, nonhurtful explanation.

"Mom, I had one fancy wedding with Craig," I tried. "I wanted it to be different with Wayne."

"Because of me!" she wailed.

It was a long time before I got off the phone. I think my mother felt better for the conversation. I hoped so. Because I certainly didn't.

And then I ran the messages off my answering machine. My mother wasn't the only one upset about my wedding. I counted nine friends and six relatives, three I hadn't spoken to since I was a child. They all wanted to know why they hadn't been invited. But how had they all found out?

Whatever the reason, it was time to start making phone calls. I prepared a script.

"Hi," I greeted every indignant/hurt/inconsolable nonatten-dee. "I just called to tell you that Wayne and I were married last week. I wanted you to be the first to know." Lying was becoming more and more easy for me. A career in law was clearly next. Or maybe acting.

I was just staring to call number eleven when the doorbell rang.

I told myself that as long as Kevin and Xanthe weren't at my door, I could use a break from phone calls and groveling. A break? I must have been completely rattled to have even thought it.

Because when I opened my front door, I looked into the dark, brooding eyes of Lieutenant Perez of the Abierto Police Department.

"Ms. Jasper," he murmured, his tone deep, and . . . was it suggestive? Only to me, I decided. This guy was too good-looking to be a policeman.

"Lieutenant," I returned his greeting briskly.

Then we stood for a few moments.

"I guess you'd like to come in?" I finally said.

He nodded.

I sighed and pointed the way to the living room, where he took a seat on the wood-and-denim couch and I flopped into one of the hanging chairs.

"Well?" I said finally.

"Have you learned anything?" he replied.

I took a long breath. Conversing with this guy was like swimming in a small hot tub. Nearly impossible and uncomfortable to boot.

"Look, Lieutenant," I began, determined to crash the verbal logjam. "I just got a call from my mother telling me I had womb trauma at a wedding before I was born. I also had fifteen other calls from people who are having hissy fits because they weren't informed that I'd married Wayne. My cat bit a hole in herself. We had to adopt her. And my brother and his crazy girlfriend are visiting and want me to buy into their pyramid pyramid scheme. If I have learned anything, I don't know what it is, except that I need a vacation."

"I meant, have you learned anything about the murder, Ms. Jasper," the lieutenant corrected me mildly.

I wondered if he ever really smiled. Then I got real.

"I've talked to all the people who were there the night Dr. Sandstrom was killed," I told Perez. "And nobody said anything about themselves or anyone else that made me think that anyone was a murderer."

"Have you really thought it through?" Perez asked.

"Of course—" I began. But then I answered truthfully. "No, I guess I haven't really thought it through."

"Ms. Jasper, you may have noticed that Captain Thorton is slightly disturbed . . ." Perez said.

I nodded and tried to stop my mind from going through the list of euphemisms: *light's on, nobody's home*; *elevator doesn't go to the top floor*; *one sandwich short a picnic . . .* But they just kept spinning out while I remained silent.

"The captain's been through a lot," Perez finally went on. "He needs a break. And he doesn't need a lot of outside attention."

I nodded again.

"I have to solve this thing, and I don't know how," Perez admitted. "Please help me."

Help him? I'd marry him. Wait, I was already married. Okay, I'd help him.

"Will you try, Ms. Jasper?" he asked.

"Of course," I murmured.

"Thank you," he said simply and rose from the couch, leaving my house without a backward glance.

I sat in my hanging chair. Had I been manipulated? If I had, I was still pretty sure that Lieutenant Perez was telling the truth. And I'd promised to try to find a killer. How was I going to do that?

The phone rang before I had a chance to torture myself with any more unanswerable questions.

This time I didn't even wait for the message. I just picked it up.

Jean Watkins was on the other end of the line. She wanted me to come to her house to talk to Darcie. She said Darcie was afraid.

I never quite understood what it was that Darcie was afraid of, but I did hear a real urgency in Jean's voice. Would visiting grandmother and grandchild help me help Lieutenant Perez? Or would it get me killed? I left a long note for Wayne, detailing my time of departure and my destination. Hopefully, I'd be back before he got home and could rip it up then. Otherwise, it was my insurance policy. I thought of calling Felix and inviting him along. But there are, after all, some things worse than possible death.

I was walking down my front stairs, heading for Jean Watkins's house, when I noticed that my "deer-proof" daffodils were not where they were supposed to be. They were supposed to be rooted in the ground, their bright yellow blossoms facing the sun. Instead, they'd been ripped out, bulbs and all, and lay limply expiring on top of the earth.

I ran to them, remembering how long it had taken me to plant those bulbs, my face heating up with the memory of the exertion. And with new rage. Deer!

But then I bent to look closer. A deer would have at least nibbled at the daffodils, not just uprooted them and flung them aside. Was this destruction caused by a human hand? A deer or Deer Count?

And then, suddenly, the heat left my face. Left it cold. What if the murderer had torn up the bulbs to scare me off?

Thirteen

✗

Deer, human, murderer. I told myself it didn't really matter. What mattered was breathing life into my expiring daffodils. I felt like a paramedic as I got down on my knees to inspect them. Their roots were torn, but their lives still might be saved. I ran to the toolshed for a spade. Then I knelt down once more to dig even deeper holes for the ailing bulbs as the sun warmed my shoulders and the hard ground bit into my knees. It wasn't easy. It'd been hard enough to dig the six-inch holes in the first place. But in less than half an hour I had all the daffodils lined up again. I sprinkled them with water, took a moment to inhale the twin scents of dirt and vegetation, and to listen to the buzzing of the neighborhood, and then mouthed a request to the goddess of bulbs that my daffodils live and prosper. Finally, I looked at my watch and remembered that I'd been on my way to Jean Watkins's house.

I walked to my car with one look back at the daffodils, wondering if telling them they were adopted might help. Or promising vengeance when I found their despoiler. *A little too attached to the garden*, my inner Zen master chided. I laughed. Which was crazier, listening to an inner Zen master or talking to bulbs? Of course, neither would be cause for alarm in Marin County. C.C. came outdoors just as I reached my car. I told her goodbye and asked her to guard the daffodils. Why not?

Still, I refrained from communicating with my Toyota when

I put the key in its ignition. Usually I gave the two-decades-old car a pep talk, but as far as nonhumans were concerned, I was all talked out. So I just drove, first to Highway One and then north in the direction of Stinson Beach, feeling the imprint of the spade in my palm each time I turned the wheel to negotiate the curves in the road.

Jean Watkins and her granddaughter, Darcie, lived in a house off Highway One about halfway to the beach. It was a big house set on at least a half acre of prime Marin property, surrounded by a high redwood fence. I almost drove past, but turned just in time when I glimpsed the tasteful numbers on the mailbox at the side of the road leading to the front gate. I skidded off the winding highway, drove up the dirt road, and parked next to a Volvo that seemed to shriek newness next to my ancient Toyota. Somehow, Jean Watkins hadn't struck me as the moneyed type, but I was obviously wrong.

Maybe there was no such thing as "the moneyed type," I decided as I pushed open the gate to the front yard. I stood, shocked for a moment once I was through the gate. I closed it firmly behind me. Money or not, Jean's fences weren't high enough to deter deer. Decimated rosebushes stood side by side with all the proper "deer-proof" plants: yarrow, salvia, and lavender. But the healthy plants just seemed to emphasize the sad state of the roses.

I shook my head and made my way to the front door on a pathway of slate paving stones. The house was a marvel of design, even from the outside. The front windows were expansive and in some spots I could see all the way through the house to the back windows. Something about people living in glass houses came to mind, but Darcie popped out the front door before I could complete my thought.

"Hey, wassup?" she greeted me.

She wore her usual baseball cap, jeans, and a black T-shirt. Her curly hair sprang out from under the cap, and she smiled, her prominent teeth dominating her face.

"Hi, Darcie—" I began

"Gramma!" she hollered before I finished.

And then Jean Watkins appeared next to her granddaughter, her own square face red with what might have been exertion. Or maybe embarrassment. She smiled, exhibiting the same big teeth as Darcie's. The look was engaging in her homey face.

"Yo," Darcie said, pointing at my knees. "You're all muddy."

I looked down. I'd never changed clothes after saving my daffodils. My knees looked like a garden before planting. Little patches of unblemished soil. I was afraid to look at my behind.

"I was gardening," I murmured.

"Of course you were," Jean replied assuringly. "If you weren't a gardener, you wouldn't be part of the deer group."

I could have hugged her. But I was too muddy.

"A whiskbroom?" I asked. "So I don't mess up your chairs?"

But Darcie became a human whiskbroom, enthusiastically using her hands to brush off my knees and my rear end for good measure. I felt like a prisoner who's been frisked by the time I crossed the Watkins's threshold.

And it was some threshold. Slate-tiled floors were covered with Moroccan rugs. The roof slanted up at an impossible angle from walls rough with bits of stone and glittering hints of metal. The whole place was filled with light—and cooking aromas, and a floral scent that must have been room freshener.

"My late husband was an architect," Jean explained as I stopped in my tracks, taking it all in. "I was a social worker. I still volunteer. And it was a good marriage. Please, come on in, Kate." She held out her hand. I took it and let her lead me into the amazing room.

Jean seated me on a couch covered with nubby taupe linen next to a carved stone coffee table; then she and Darcie took seats across from me in matching chairs covered in the same nubby cloth. Darcie crossed her legs yoga-style and snuggled up in her chair. Jean sat with her back straight and her legs bent at a ladylike angle, knees together.

"Nice house," I managed weakly.

Jean laughed.

"It is incredible, isn't it?" she agreed. "But then so was my late husband."

"Gramma really loved the old dude," Darcie muttered wistfully. I wondered if the "old dude" was Frank Lloyd Wright. Wright, Watkins? I decided against it.

"And I really love you, young dudette," Jean told Darcie. Then her softened face turned businesslike. "Now, tell Kate what's going on."

"Well, I'm . . . um . . . like . . . scared, maybe," Darcie told me, looking at her feet.

"Of what?" I asked gently. It was an effort to be gentle. I wondered if there was a fast forward button anywhere on the young woman.

"I don't trust those dumb cops," she answered angrily. She brought her head up. "They're nasty-asses, all of them, messed up, you know?"

"And?" I prompted.

"And just 'cause I thought that old doctor dude was a wickety-wack old man, they think I killed him."

"Wait a minute," I ordered, holding up my hand. "What makes you think—"

"If I was going to kill anyone, it'd be my dad," she went on, ignoring my order. "He's nastier than that old dude was. But they think a teenager is full of it, you know? Like we'd do evil crap like kill people."

"Darcie is actually quite responsible, especially for her age," Jean put in mildly. "And her fears aren't entirely unreasonable."

"But why tell me?" I asked.

"Well," Jean said, her face reddening with something that looked like embarrassment again. "We understand that you're investigating Dr. Sandstrom's case unofficially."

"Me?"

"That's what the reporter said."

Reporter?

It took a few breaths of cooking smells and air freshener before I remembered Felix.

"You mean Felix Byrne told you I was investigating?" I demanded, leaning forward on the sofa. *And never told me he talked to them, that little weasel.*

Darcie and Jean nodded, looking very much alike, despite the difference in their ages, both of their square faces holding wide-eyed expressions of anxiety.

"It's all right," I told them. Reassurance seemed important here. "Felix does stuff like that."

"Is he really a reporter?" Darcie whispered.

"Oh, yeah," I answered. "He's really a reporter, but I wouldn't believe much else that he told you." I looked across at Darcie and her grandmother. "Was he here?"

"Oh, yes," Jean responded. "Sitting right where you are now. He wanted to know how we felt about doctors for some sort of report he was doing.

I opened my mouth to expose Felix's fraudulence, but then realized that *I'd* like to have the answer to his question myself. My mouth took a left turn.

"What did you tell him?" I asked innocently.

"Yuck," Darcie put in succinctly.

Jean laughed, though not very comfortably. She shifted in her chair.

"I don't particularly care for doctors after my last eye surgery," Jean told me. "It was, well, botched."

"And there was that messed-up dude you took me to after dad threw me out," Darcie added.

"Dr. Peterson," Jean agreed, nodding. "Dr. Peterson is a therapist of the new school. He sees incest everywhere. He can't seem to understand that not all wounds are sexual."

"And the wackhead tried to hypnotize me, tried to make me believe my dad did all that yucky kinda stuff with me."

"Now, that man was irresponsible, as irresponsible as my eye doctor," Jean Watkins declared, her voice rising. "What if he had made Darcie believe such a thing? I've read that hypnotists can implant false memories."

"And he wanted me to take this stupid doll that was supposed to be my dad and hack it up," Darcie went on. "Yuck."

"And," Jean added to their catalog of complaints, "there was the doctor who missed a whole set of symptoms because he thought I was having some kind of 'female problems.' He thought I was hysterical. I almost was, four years later when it turned out my symptoms were real."

"Poor Gramma," Darcie muttered, reaching out to her grandmother from her chair. "What a wack-off."

"I don't know about the language, but I'll agree with Darcie's diagnosis," Jean commented dryly, linking hands with her granddaughter. "I guess if we were to be accused of disliking doctors, we'd be found guilty."

"How about Aunt Louise?" Darcie put in. Somehow, I had the feeling that they'd covered this ground before, and often.

"Oh, poor Louise," Jean answered. "Fine-looking woman. But that wasn't enough for her. She thought she was getting old. Wanted a face-lift. Ended up with one side of her face higher than the other. Not to mention the neurological damage."

"Yuck."

Yuck, indeed. But how did all of this relate to Dr. Sandstrom? I didn't need to ask. Darcie was way ahead of me.

"That ole doctor at the deer thingy, he was a mean-ass," she pointed out. "Wanted to blow up deer. All for his roses. Gramma had roses too before the deer ate them, but she doesn't want to blow them up."

"Some actions are irresponsible," Jean agreed.

"Right," Darcie said, and the two of them leaned back in their chairs with their arms crossed, identical twins separated by some forty or fifty years. No wonder they got along.

"So, Darcie," I began, bringing the conversation back on track. "You're afraid the police suspect you."

"Yeah! Those wackheads—"

"Darcie," I interrupted. "I've talked to at least three people now who think the police suspect them. I'll bet that's how

Lieutenant Perez wants it. Everyone afraid. Everyone off guard."

"Really?" Darcie breathed, obvious relief in her face. What had Perez said to her that frightened her so much? No more romantic thoughts about that lieutenant, I decided. He really was a manipulative . . . wackhead.

"But a man was killed," Jean pointed out. "That's not right."

"No," I agreed. "And maybe between the group members, we can find out who did it."

"Yes," she pronounced seriously. "Kate, we must find out."

I left the Watkins home not long after that. I liked the grandmother and the granddaughter. But I'd liked murderers before, I reminded myself. They weren't off my suspect list, yet. Not quite, anyway.

The first thing I did when I got home was rip up my note to Wayne. No need for him to know I'd visited the Watkins. Then I walked outside to check my daffodils. For the most part they stood up vertically if limply. I thanked the goddess of bulbs. And finally, I went back inside and looked at my answering machine, remembering that I still had four calls to make to apologize for my wedding. I punched in numbers and got four answering machines back. Yes! So what if their owners would just return my calls later. For the time being, I was off the hook, so to speak.

And then the phone rang.

It was my aunt Shirley from South Carolina.

"Honey," she said, affront flavoring her tone. Affront and nobility. "I jest can't believe you married without inviting the family . . ."

I speechified. I lied. I left Shirley feeling better, though she gave me the impression that she would never be entirely whole again. I sighed. Who knew one little marriage could crater the lives of so many.

The phone rang again. Probably one of those callbacks. I acted quickly, shutting off the machine so that the phone would just ring and ring. And ring. No human would answer.

No android would answer. I told myself this was the way Alexander Graham Bell intended it.

I only hoped the caller wasn't Wayne or someone who wanted to give me a new contract for Jest Gifts. I counted as the phone rang fourteen times.

I wanted to leave the house. Immediately. But I didn't have any more excuses. I'd already bought tofu. Still, I could do more investigating. But if I did, I'd make sure it was safe investigating. I had promised Wayne . . . What was it I'd promised Wayne? Whatever it was, I'd be careful.

I'd call Avis. Avis was my friend. I refused to think she was a murderer. And Avis knew everyone. She was the key.

I punched out the number for Eldora Nurseries . . . and got an answering machine. It was only then that I looked at my watch. It was after six o'clock. No wonder I was so hungry. But that didn't stop me. I called Avis's home number.

A voice I'd never heard before answered, and that voice was not happy. In fact, it was downright peevish.

"Kate who?" it asked, then yelled, "Mother!"

Avis came to the phone next. "My daughter, Olive," she explained. I thought I could hear strain in her voice.

"Would this be a good time to come over?"

"Oh, yes! It would be lovely if you visited," she answered. There was a note of pleading in her voice. Was Olive that bad?

I had a bite of tofu pepperoni and was ready to drive to Avis's. But first I checked the landscape through my window. No one was ripping up my bulbs. Kevin and Xanthe were not on my deck. And there was no sign of Deer Count or Felix. Or Lieutenant Perez. Safe. I was exhaling relief when C.C. snuck up behind me and whacked my ankle with her paw. I jumped and came down on that ankle in a way that would not have made my tai chi teacher proud.

But I fixed C.C. a supper of Fancy Feast anyway, and told her once again that I loved her before I took off for Avis's. On the way out, I took an instant to wish that Wayne was with me, but Saturday was his big night at the restaurant. I was on my own for investigation, and worse, I was on my own for dinner.

Luckily, I'd visited Avis in her San Ricardo country cottage before. I was prepared for the perfect garden, filled with un-nibbled plants: succulents, jasmine, wisteria, forget-me-nots, and lamb's ears, to name a few. Her old two-story Victorian, white with blue shutters, greeted me like a friend.

However, the woman at the door didn't.

"I'm Olive," she told me, hands on hips, as if daring me to argue. Olive was probably fifty-five or sixty, but she looked older than her mother, her skin leathery from the sun, her hair colored badly, and her face pinched into an angry shape that almost obscured the delicacy of the features she'd inherited from Avis.

"Kate!" Avis cried out and came running to hug me.

"Grrrumph," Olive snorted.

"You've met my daughter?" Avis asked, hopefully, diffidently.

"Oh, yes," I answered cheerfully. "A real pleasure." It's always such a joy to confuse an unpleasant person. Olive squinted uncertainly.

"Olive has moved back in with me . . . temporarily," Avis said softly.

"After that s.o.b. left me and my lease ran out, I didn't know what else to do," Olive added helpfully.

"She's had a few jobs, she even worked for me at the nursery for a while, but she . . ."

"Scared off the customers," Olive finished for her mother. "So screw 'em. How am I supposed to be cheerful after a divorce? I was married for over thirty years, thirty goddamn years . . ."

"She's been divorced for almost nine months," Avis murmured as her daughter's complaints went on.

"What am I supposed to do now? Live on the pittance he's giving me for alimony?"

"It's more than a pittance," Avis whispered.

Olive heard that. She put her hands back on her hips.

"It's easy for you, Mom," she accused. "You were an actress."

"Neat, huh?" I put in positively.

"Oh real neat," Olive snarled. "My mom, the star of soft-porn."

I could see Avis's color change from ivory to shell pink under her hat. Suddenly I wondered if she wore the head-to-foot clothing so that no one would recognize her from her earlier, less savory movies.

"Well, how about something to eat?" Avis suggested with forced cheer.

"Right," I agreed, still trying to imagine the fastidious Avis as a porn star, soft or otherwise.

Olive and I sat and glared at each other from worn, comfortable chairs with crocheted throws as Avis made herself busy in the kitchen.

"Your mother's done a great job at the nursery," I tried.

"Grrrumph," she replied.

Luckily, it wasn't long before Avis returned with a loaf of orange-date bread, rye bread, sliced raw vegetables, dill and tahini dips, and a plate of cold marinated leeks. Maybe dinner without Wayne wouldn't be so bad. If I could stand the company. The dill dip was garnished with a jaunty sprig of rosemary.

I was stuffing myself when Avis suddenly went still. The marinated leeks were perfection.

"There shouldn't have been any rosemary in the area where the doctor was killed," Avis said softly. "He was in the bedding section."

"Rosemary for remembrance?" I mumbled, mouth full.

Avis shrugged, her eyes lost in thought. "I wonder. But who? What could they remember of him?"

"Who was this doctor?" Olive asked.

"He was a very supportive individual—"

"Oh, supportive, huh?" Olive leered.

"Olive, please stop that. If we must live together, let's do it in harmony."

I gave Avis an inner cheer.

"You'd love to throw me out, wouldn't you?" Olive challenged. "But it wouldn't do for the all-so-kind-and-giving Avis Eldora, now would it?"

"Olive, please," Avis begged.

Olive sighed and bit down into a slice of orange-date bread.

"Anyway, Dr. Sandstrom was a very kind man usually—"

"Mom likes everyone," Olive interrupted.

And I realized that Olive was right. Avis rarely had a bad word to say about anyone. Even about her loathsome daughter. A wonderful trait, really. But not in a murder investigation.

"Well, there'll be another meeting tomorrow," I said, trying to cheer Avis. "Another chance to guess who—"

The doorbell rang. This time Avis answered it. The caller was Reed Killian. And when he put his arm around Avis, I no longer had any doubt that they were a pair.

Nor did Olive apparently.

"Mom's pushing eighty, and she's got a man nearly half her age," she whispered, loud enough for anyone in the room to hear. "She gets all the luck."

Reed sat down next to Avis, ignoring Olive. He reached out for Avis's gloved hand.

"Oh, Reed," Avis murmured, then turned her hat-brim-shadowed face to him. "Why did that man have to die?"

Reed frowned.

"Sometimes, surgery is inevitable," he answered.

Fourteen

✴

"Surgery?" I muttered, startled by Reed's pronouncement. Then I remembered that Reed was a doctor himself, a plastic surgeon. But still . . . "Did you see Dr. Sandstrom as a disease?" I asked.

"No, no," he answered impatiently, tapping the fingers of his left hand on his thigh. His right hand was still grasping Avis's. He was probably going through synthesizer withdrawal. He didn't even seem to notice the food on the coffee table. "Jeez, I just meant that someone that moody and abrasive was pretty much asking to make enemies. And he probably made a really bad one."

"What was he like?" Olive asked, her face oddly softened by her curiosity.

"He was okay, I guess," Reed murmured. He wriggled around in his chair as if he couldn't quite get comfortable. "But he didn't know how to have fun. He'd rather argue and make people mad—"

"And someone killed him for that?" Olive interrupted, shaking her head. "It's lucky *I'm* still alive."

Three mouths restrained themselves as one. Reed, Avis, and I all just sat and looked into the air.

"Maybe it wasn't just the doctor's unpleasantness," Avis suggested after enough time had gone by to change the subject. "Maybe it was a secret he knew."

"A doctor," Olive mused. "Abortions, transmittable diseases, insanity—"

"Or maybe someone inherited," Reed put in. "Do we know who his heirs are?"

Now that was a point. Had Lieutenant Perez looked into the question of Sandstrom's heirs? He must have, right?

"His wife was dead," Avis reported, frowning. "But I think he had grown children."

"Look," Olive put in. "Maybe someone was jealous of him."

"For what?" I asked, taking one last bite of orange-date bread while waiting for her answer.

"I don't know," she shot back, throwing up her hands. "Could be anything. Success—lots of people are jealous of success. Or maybe he had affairs with more than one woman." Olive wrinkled her nose. "Men!" she finished up.

"He was a doctor." I offered my own theory. "Maybe he was guilty of malpractice." I thought of the Watkinses. But neither of them had mentioned Dr. Sandstrom in their screed. And he wasn't an eye doctor or a plastic surgeon. Though Reed was—

"Maybe he made a pass at someone," Olive cooed, her eyes on her mother.

But Avis didn't even catch the look.

"How can anyone kill another person?" Avis asked, rubbing her arms and dislodging Reed's hand in the process. "It's too hard to even imagine."

"Oh sure, Mom," Olive sneered.

Avis looked at her daughter then, concern in her eyes.

"Hey, Avis," Reed suggested, his voice high with enthusiasm. "Let's go on a little trip. I know some friends who are taking a sailboat down the coast. It'll be fun—"

Avis laughed. One look at her clothing should have given Reed a clue that sailboats wouldn't be her idea of fun.

"I love it when you say those things," she told him.

Reed smiled, looking as innocent as a puppy dog. Olive was right. Avis had luck when it came to men. Reed was smitten, no doubt about it.

"Well, then, let's just do it. We can both make arrangements to take the time off, then I can call my friends, and—"

"Betcha the police won't let you go sailing off into the sunset," Olive piped up. "You're suspects."

That was a real conversation killer.

In the silence that followed, I saw Olive smile for the first time. Then she stood up and left the room.

Reed and Avis looked at each other. I couldn't see Avis's face under her hat just then, but I could see Reed's. And Reed was not a happy plastic surgeon.

"Cripes," he muttered under his breath.

"I think she's probably right," Avis whispered, turning to me now. "Kate, we have to figure this out."

Why "Kate"? How many people had included me in the "we" of whodunit since Dr. Sandstrom was murdered? Did I look like a detective or what? It had to be the "what." But I didn't know what the "what" was. Unless I had a sign that read "sucker" on my forehead. I actually raised my hand to feel my forehead, then jerked it back.

"Tomorrow, Avis," I told her. "We'll get a better idea what's going on tomorrow."

I left not long after that, suggesting that Avis and Reed take a motel room until Olive left. They both giggled at my suggestion, suddenly seeming very suitable for each other despite their age difference.

I thought about the pair on my drive home. Something about Reed bothered me. Was it just his relationship with a much older woman? Or his nervousness? Then it hit me. He was a doctor. After talking to the Watkinses, maybe that was enough to indict him. But not for murder, I decided as I backed into my driveway, carefully positioning my car for the possibility of a quick getaway. I don't know what I thought I'd need to get away from, but the possibilities of relatives, reporters, police, and suspects seemed statistically significant enough to justify a different way of parking.

I was just in the door when the phone started ringing. I

waited for the answering machine to pick it up. Some time around the seventh ring, I remembered I'd turned the machine off. I picked up the receiver cautiously.

"Kate, it's me," the voice on the other end of the line announced.

"Me" was Jade, my warehousewoman at Jest Gifts. I was expected to know this. And expected to know that when she announced herself this way, something was really wrong. I waited. It didn't take long.

"You know the guy who's supposed to make the new computer mouses," she began.

I nodded. Apparently, she heard me.

"Well I found out what his little problem is. I tried to call you yesterday, but your line was always busy. And today no one answered at all."

"What's his problem?" I asked, not really wanting to know.

"He's in jail."

"Jail!"

"Yeah DUI, driving under the influence," she filled me in. "He thinks he can make a deal to go into rehab, but he's not going to make our computer mouses."

I grabbed my manufacturers file, thumbing through frantically for a new mouse-maker.

"Kate?" Jade asked in a tiny voice, way too tiny for her.

"What?" I asked impatiently. Was she in jail too?

"Did you get married?"

My heart contracted. Damn.

"Um . . . yeah," I confessed.

Then I heard her crying.

"Jade," I began. "No one was supposed to know. You would have been one of the first—"

"Really?" she asked nasally.

"Of course. You know Wayne and I care about you . . ."

Half an hour later I hung up. And while comforting my warehousewoman, I'd also searched my manufacturers file and found at least three leads to follow on Monday for replacing our imprisoned, and hopefully sobered, mouse man.

The phone continued to interrupt me for the rest of the evening as I worked on badly neglected Jest Gifts paperwork and worried about mouse manufacture. The whole Northern Hemisphere now appeared to know that Wayne and I were shamefully married. The rest of the world was waking up to the news too. And a few entities on other planets were probably gossiping about it as I worked and apologized over the phone. At least Kevin and Xanthe seemed to be gone.

Wayne came home late that night. My eyes opened from a light sleep to see him gliding around the room quietly, trying not to wake me. A ghost with a body. A nice body. A nice body that smelled of Wayne. He was almost in his p.j.s when I ambushed him.

Sunday morning, Wayne and I lay in bed, staring out the skylights into the morning sun . . . and discussing murder suspects.

It felt like a morning to snuggle under the covers and sniff the sweaty roses. But Wayne had other ideas.

"Who have you talked to?" he asked, rolling my way, his eyebrows lowered to half mast.

"Um . . . everyone, I guess," I told him. Better to get it over with now.

He rolled on his back, glared, and crossed his arms over his bare chest. C.C. came ambling in, took her place beside him and glared at me too. I shifted into striking position and kissed Wayne on the forehead. C.C. was on her own. Wayne sighed. I kissed his mouth, gently. He sighed again, but this time the sigh had an underlying note of contentment.

"It's our honeymoon," I reminded him coyly.

"Can't have a honeymoon without the traditional dead body, now, can we?" he retorted.

Now it was my turn to roll on my back and cross my arms.

"Okay," he mumbled. "Who do you think did it?"

"I don't know," I answered impatiently.

"You probably know more than you know," he said.

That was a thought, though I wasn't sure what it meant.

"How about a word-association test?" he suggested. "I'll say a name and you say the first thing that pops into your mind."

"All right," I agreed, uncrossing my arms and closing my eyes.

"Avis Eldora?" he shot off.

"Nursery," I responded. That was easy.

"Howie Damon?"

"Manuscript." That was even easier.

"Lisa Orton?"

"Therapist."

"Reed Killian?"

"Synthesizer."

"Synthesizer?" Wayne asked.

"You know, like for music," I explained.

He paused to digest that. I felt, rather than saw him shake his head. And then he went on.

"Darcie Watkins?"

"Baseball cap."

"Jean Watkins?"

"Social worker."

"Gilda Fitch."

"Cheerio."

"Maxwell Yang?"

"Smooth."

"Natalie Miner?"

"Southern belle."

There was a long pause.

"I can't think of anyone else," he finally admitted.

"How about you?" I suggested.

"Wayne Caruso?" he murmured, confused.

"Sexy," I purred.

I didn't see him coming with my eyes closed, but I felt his warm, gentle hands and his soft lips.

After a few minutes, I pulled away and asked, "Are you sure it's dead bodies that are traditional on honeymoons?"

He pulled me back.

"Live ones," he mumbled through our joined lips.

It sounded right to me. Actually, it felt right to me. Deliciously right.

But all honeymoons must end. Or at least endure intermissions between acts. An hour later, we were up and showered and breakfasted, ready for the meeting of the Deer-Abused Support Group, minus one, at Eldora Nurseries.

On the way out, I checked the daffodils. They were weak, but alive. Condition critical.

When I told Wayne about the bulbs, he frowned a gargoyle frown that might have killed those bulbs if it had been directed their way.

"Don't like this," he announced. "You're right, Kate. Can't just run away. It's come to us."

He was seriously silent as he drove his Jaguar to the nursery. I didn't even try for light conversation.

When he parked the car, we saw a flurry of people near the entrance. Was that our group? Then I saw the picket signs and deer antlers. Deer Count had joined the Deerly Abused.

As Wayne and I got out of the car, we heard the raised voices.

"Deer count, deer count!"

And saw the picket signs bobbing in a circle.

"We are attempting a harmonious solution," came Avis's voice floating over their chants. Those years as an actress must have taught her how to project her voice.

"Deer killers!"

"How can you accuse us of killing deer?" Jean Watkins challenged the picketers, standing her ground on sturdy legs. "We're here to find natural solutions to their eating our gardens, not to kill them."

"Yeah, tell those wackheads, Gramma!" Darcie added loudly, yanking the bill of her baseball cap.

"Deer are human too!"

"People are more important than deer!" Lisa Orton shouted, hands on her hips.

None of our group had the slightest impact on the chanting picketers.

"Deer count, deer count!" they began again.

Maxwell Yang and Gilda Fitch stood off to the side, whispering back and forth and laughing, as if the whole performance had been staged for their enjoyment. It did have its comic aspect, the bobbing signs and antlers.

But Reed Killian wasn't laughing. He emerged from the main building and stood in front of Avis, addressing the pickets.

"I've called the police," he announced firmly. "This is private property. You picketers will have to leave. So please go take care of the planet somewhere else."

Deer Count skedaddled as fast as C.C. did when she was caught shredding curtains.

"Oh, Reed, that was so smart," Avis told him. "I didn't even think of the police."

Reed grinned. "I didn't really call them," he admitted.

"And a bully, bully for you," Gilda said. Reed's grin turned into a diffident smile. Was she really complimenting him? I wouldn't have bet on it.

But Deer Count was gone, and I, for one, was grateful. However, all things wonderful are not always possible in the same moment. Felix Byrne showed up just as the last antler had bobbed out of the nursery. And it seemed that Felix had assumed a Clint Eastwood persona for the moment.

"So, which one of you put the doc under the lilies?" he asked by way of a greeting. He smelled of garlic and frustration.

Maybe someone would have answered Felix, but Howie Damon was the next to arrive. And Howie had news.

"I've got a publisher!" he whooped.

"For your California manuscript?" I asked, hoping the incredulity wasn't evident in my voice.

"A small press," he answered me. "They do all California history."

"Well, congratulations," I told him, holding out my hand.

He shook it, his own hand moist with excitement.

And then everyone was congratulating him. I just wished

we could've had a party to celebrate his success, instead of rehashing Dr. Sandstrom's murder.

Natalie was the last of our group to arrive, her eyes reddened, her baby face a sad baby's. I wondered what was wrong, but was afraid to ask. There were enough things wrong for the time being. She smiled briefly upon hearing Howie's news, though, and then asked where we were going to meet.

We all filed into the main building, seating ourselves on metal folding chairs arranged in the same semicircle as on the night that Dr. Sandstrom was killed. Only Reed didn't stand at the podium today. He had clearly abdicated his duties as class teacher.

I began to shiver as we sat down. Was it just the memory of the doctor's death? I locked my hand with Wayne's. *His* usually warm fingers were cool too. Maybe the room was just cold. The smell of earth, plants, and fertilizer floated on the air. I even thought I smelled roses.

"Okay, you guys," Felix demanded. "You got any friggin' idea how the doc bought it?"

Silence was his answer.

"Anything?" he asked more softly.

Reed looked thoughtful. "There was the pill," he said.

And suddenly, I was even colder.

"What?" Avis asked sharply.

"I remember a green pill," Reed went on, his eyes almost dreamy. "Dr. Sandstrom pocketed it after the first time he was hit with the deer statuette."

"So what kind of gonzo clue is that supposed to be?" Felix asked. "Probably was his own friggin' pill."

But Reed didn't answer him. "Maybe the statuette had a Freudian significance," he theorized instead. "I used to read Freud."

"Freud was a lousy therapist," Lisa declared. "He was the worst kind of testosterone-based life form. I heard he took a bunch of women who were actually abused by their fathers and labeled them hysterics. He made a whole career out of it—"

"As opposed to those who are making careers out of women who *weren't* abused and are convincing them they were," Jean Watkins interrupted.

"Was on the couch once, myself, eh what," Gilda put in. "Always wondered what the guy sitting behind me was doing. A bit much, I say. And for a tidy sum, to boot."

"Did you know psychoanalysis came to California quite early?" Howie put in. "Even in the earliest part of this century, California always had room for new ideas."

"All therapists are wack-offs," Darcie told us. "Bunch of jerks."

"Well, most of them are," Lisa conceded. "But not mine. You oughta try her. She's wonderful."

"Huh!" Darcie snorted.

"Excuse me, but we don't want to talk in terms of generalization," Jean Watkins piped up. I had a feeling we were in for a lecture. "Generalization leads to stereotyping. Just because one therapist is bad doesn't mean they all are. And the same goes for doctors. I've had my troubles with doctors, but Reed seems like a fine man."

Avis smiled in agreement.

Maxwell winked. "All I can say is that Freud would make a fantastic subject to interview if he were alive. Did he consciously accuse women of hysteria who'd actually been abused? Did he realize it? Did his views just reveal his own hang-ups?" Maxwell paused. "A fantastic interview, but not a fantastic friend, would be my guess. The man was probably homophobic, to begin with."

"And Dr. Sandstrom?" Avis put in, bringing the group back where they'd started. Where they should have stayed.

"He was a jerk," Darcie put in.

"He was a doctor," Jean reminded us.

"He was a gardener." Avis commended him. "A man who had his loves and his hates."

"He was a deer killer," Lisa snarled.

"An officer and a gentleman," Maxwell offered, without irony, as far as I could tell.

"So, who whacked the old fart?" Felix bawled in frustration. The conversation went downhill from there.

And then, suddenly, Natalie Miner spoke up. I realized she'd been silent the whole time.

"The doctor was seeing another woman," she said quietly.

"What?"

"I just found out. From my hairdresser," she explained. "Hairdressers know everything."

"Dr. Yamoda?" I guessed.

"No," Natalie said, shaking her curly head. "Though it was another doctor. Just not his partner. A woman named Dr. Larkin. She has a practice on Tepper Street.

"Good for him," Avis murmured wistfully.

"Listen, you potato-brains," Felix started up. "At least one of you knows something, and I'm—"

"Have we said all we need to?" Reed asked, suddenly impatient. He stood up and brushed invisible dirt from his knees.

"Yes," the rest of us answered nearly in unison and rose with him, splitting into smaller clusters to talk and wander around the nursery. Somehow, we of the Deer-Abused Support Group had bonded. At least, I thought so. Though there was the murderer to consider. Had the murderer bonded?

Natalie came to me. I looked into her reddened eyes and saw real sadness there.

"You didn't know?" I asked.

"Not till he was dead," she answered. "Good Lord knows there's nothing sillier than an old woman looking for a man."

"Now, now," I told her. "You're not old. And you're young at heart." I don't know how those words jumped to my lips, but they did.

And they seemed to help. Natalie smiled tentatively. And then she talked. Too bad Freud wasn't there to listen. And as she talked, I wondered. What if Natalie had found out about Dr. Sandstrom's affair with Dr. Larkin before his death? How much hope had she invested in him?

Other members of the Deerly Abused wandered out the doors of the main building as I listened to Natalie, a woman

whose age felt hurtful and vulnerable to her, for all of her
bright makeup and bouncy, curly hair. My heart went out to
the woman, even as I suspected her of murder.

Once Natalie was all talked out, Avis beckoned me over to
a corner.

"Did you learn anything?" she asked.

"Not that I know of," I told her. "But then I probably know
more than I know."

That confused her long enough for me to find Wayne where
he stood listening to Howie Damon next to some flats of pan-
sies and sweet alyssum.

Let's go, I mouthed.

"That's wonderful," Wayne interrupted Howie, and then we
moved quickly, making our way out of the building to the
main gate.

We were almost there when I tripped over something.
You'd think I'd learn not to look down.

But my gaze moved to the ground of its own accord.

Reed Killian lay dead there in the dirt, with a hoe to his
bloodied head. I didn't even have to check. He couldn't have
been alive with his skull split open like that.

Maybe Avis didn't have such good luck with men, after all,
I thought, and then felt the earth sway beneath me.

FIFTEEN

✗

I felt Wayne's big hand grab my shoulder, and the earth stopped swaying.

"The police," he growled, his rough skin pale, too pale, and beaded with sweat. I looked at the man I loved, and my body lurched again as if shoved.

"Avis," I whispered, my eyes burning with the effort not to cry.

Wayne's eyebrows shot up in understanding.

Avis. How much had she cared for Reed? What would this do to her?

"See if you can take her aside," Wayne suggested quietly. "And I'll make the call to the police."

"But what about—" I took a big breath and pointed down, my eyes closed. The breath was a mistake. I could smell the blood. At least, I thought I could.

"Nothing we can do for him. Let the police worry about evidence."

The police, I thought. The police that Reed had threatened to call to scare away Deer Count, but didn't. Had that decision cost him his life? And then I remembered Lieutenant Perez. Now I started shaking instead of swaying. Perez would never forgive me for this.

Forget Perez, I told myself. Avis was the first priority. The only priority for the time being. Wayne and I strode toward the main building, passing Maxwell, Gilda, and Howie on our way. Jean and Darcie Watkins, Lisa, and Natalie were inside next to the gardening books. And Avis and Felix were huddled near the sales counter.

"Avis," I called out, my voice sounding tinny in my ears. "I have to talk to you." I saw Felix's mouth begin to open. "And Felix, you go talk to Maxwell. He has something he wants to tell you," I lied. It seemed a small sin. And I was sure Maxwell could handle him.

As soon as Felix's mouth closed, I pointed outside. Our pit bull of a reporter was gone in an instant.

But Avis was still in front of me, a woman so fragile that she was swathed head to toe to protect her from something that I couldn't see or understand. Could I tell her about Reed? My mouth went dry as dirt.

I could see Wayne in the periphery of my vision, hovering near the phone, waiting till Avis was taken care of to make the call to the police. The room shimmered with light, but somehow it was blinding, not illuminating.

Then I heard a shout from outside. Someone else had found Reed's body. Now, I had to tell Avis, and quickly. I shook away my doubts and looked her in the face.

"Avis," I began gently, "Reed's been in an accident."

Another shout sounded from outside.

I moved my mouth faster.

"Avis, he's dead."

Avis just stared at me, her head tilted, as if trying to translate my words. Slowly, her mouth opened.

"Oh, but that can't be, Kate," she stated clearly. "He was just here and—"

I had to get through to her. I swallowed, then spoke again.

"He was killed," I told her. "I'm sorry."

I opened my arms just in time for Avis to fall into them. For a minute, she was heavy, most likely unconscious, but then she lightened again, writhing like a troublesome two-year-old.

"No," she muttered obstinately, her head down and shaking.

"No. I'm the old one. I'm supposed to die first."

"Avis, the police will come," I told her, holding her tightly. Wayne must have heard me. I saw him reach for the phone.

Avis's head came up, knocking my chin with the brim of her hat. Her green eyes widened.

"Kate, he, he . . ." she tried. She took a deep breath and straightened her spine. Carefully, I released her from my arms. When she spoke again, her voice was emotionless.

"He actually cared for me, in spite of my age. I never thought I'd have another romance, and then there was Reed. I . . . he . . ."

"You were lovers?" I prompted. Was that what was so hard for her to say?

But she shook her head.

"We were . . . we were courting," she told me, her voice lilting into a different range. Suddenly, she sounded like a schoolgirl. Was she acting? Or regressing? "It might sound strange, but Reed wanted to go slowly. At first, I thought he just couldn't bear to make love to an ancient woman like me, but that wasn't it." Her eyes lost focus. "Reed liked to play. He was Peter Pan, forever a boy. He wanted a long courtship, to talk about everything, to do new things. A few kisses. Then a longer kiss. Like it was when I was a girl. Reed loved anything romantic. He rowed a boat around Sontaris Lake and I let my left hand trail in the water, while I held my parasol with my right. I even took off my gloves. We could have stepped out of an old picture book."

Once again, I wondered why Reed had chosen her, a woman so much older than himself. But when I looked into her lovely face, I imagined what Reed must have seen. A true beauty from a more romantic age.

"No," she declared again, her gentle voice firm, no longer lilting. "Reed can't be dead. Reed is the most alive man I know. He—"

"Avis," I whispered. "It'll be all right. Reed's just passed on." I didn't really know what it meant, but it sounded good.

"Passed on?" A hint of a smile played on her lips. "Sailing

into heaven, playing his synthesizer?" Then even that hint of a smile was gone, and she shook her head violently.

I grabbed her arm and led her to a chair. Her body was trembling as I helped her down onto the metal seat.

"Oh, Kate!" she cried, as if I had just told her. Maybe she had only now heard me. "Reed's dead?"

I could only nod and hold her gloved hand.

"What's happened?" a voice asked from the rear.

I whirled around. I had forgotten everyone but Avis. And Reed.

Jean Watkins stood behind me. Once my heart dropped back down where it was supposed to be, I took in a deep breath of hope. Jean Watkins, social worker, grandmother, woman of reason. Who better to deal with Avis? And best of all, Jean wasn't me. Because I'd run out of ways to soften the impossible reality for Avis. Maybe there were no more ways.

"Reed Killian is dead," I told Jean, as quietly as I could. "And Avis had a special relationship with Reed."

Jean stepped back for a moment, but only a moment. Then she was there, by my side, ready to minister to Avis.

"Avis?" Jean asked slowly, clearly. "Do you believe in God, in Spirit?"

Avis nodded slowly. Jean knelt down and took Avis's two small gloved hands in her larger ones.

"Reed is in loving arms now," Jean told her then. "You must know that in your heart."

And finally, Avis began to cry. Jean held her hands and let her. And I began to cry too.

"Thank you, Jean," I whispered through my tears.

Avis was grieving now, loudly and wetly. I just hoped the early breakthrough would help her in the long run. And the short run. Because the Abierto police would focus on her relationship to Reed. I was sure of it. *Cry*, I beamed mentally to Avis. *Cry till the police get here.*

I turned around to make sure the police weren't already on the scene. They weren't. But I wasn't the only one who was witnessing Avis's reaction.

Darcie Watkins stared at us from a few aisles over. Slowly, she made her way to us, fear evident on her young face.

"Gramma?" she whispered.

Jean Watkins turned, never letting go of Avis's hands as Avis wept on.

"Darcie," Jean said, her voice low. "There's been another death. I need to take care of Avis. Can you stand with Kate?"

Darcie looked at me, her eyes still afraid. But the fear cleared when she saw my own tears. She put a tentative arm around my shoulders. And it felt good. Darcie might have been a thirteen-year-old, but she had the Watkins genes. I was comforted.

"All messed up?" she asked.

I nodded, and let her hold me. I felt almost peaceful, in the midst of Reed's death and Avis's grief.

"The other doc's been whacked!" a voice bellowed, barreling down on us. Felix, I'd know his voice anywhere. So much for peace.

"Felix!" I turned and put my finger across my lips, gesturing in Avis's direction, though I don't think Avis even registered his voice.

"But, Kate," he whined. "Another friggin' stiff—"

"Hey, wassup with you, you effing jerk?" Darcie demanded. "Can't you see people are sad here?"

Felix just stared at Darcie, at me, at Avis, and at Jean. I don't think he'd really seen us before. And maybe he still didn't.

"Whoa!" he objected. "Don't get your high-tops in a twist."

"What's that supposed to mean?" Darcie shot back. I could almost feel the heat of her anger.

"Hey, man," Felix muttered, backstepping out of her range. "I'm outa here, okay?"

And he left, picking Wayne as his next victim. Wayne, who was still on the phone. I had a feeling communications with the Abierto Police Department weren't going so well. Wayne glared and waved Felix into silence.

"Guy's a real wickety-wack," Darcie commented. "Talks weird too."

I swallowed my laugh and thanked her. I even hugged her. Her grandmother was right. Darcie was a good girl. I just hoped neither of the Watkinses was a murderer. Because now that Avis was being taken care of, I was realizing the odds. There weren't that many of us left, and one of us had killed Reed Killian.

I took Darcie's arm and walked toward Wayne, raising my hand in question.

"They're calling in Perez," he told me, his hand over the mouthpiece.

"Cop shop won't do a thing," Felix announced. "They're a bunch of potato-brains. We gotta do this, Kate. We gotta get the poop on this one."

"Shhhh!" I hushed him. And with Darcie for backup, he hushed.

But the four of us weren't alone for long. I saw Natalie and Lisa approaching.

"Dear God," Natalie Miner breathed. "Is it true? Was the other doctor killed too?"

Wayne, Felix, and I nodded.

"But why?" she wailed. "What's happening here? I just can't understand. It doesn't make an ounce of sense—"

"Maybe it's not supposed to," Lisa Orton put in.

"What's that supposed to mean?" Darcie asked before I could.

But she never got an answer. Maxwell Yang was next to join our circle, trailed by Howie Damon and Gilda Fitch.

"Are you okay now?" Maxwell asked Felix, raising one sardonic eyebrow.

Felix blushed as he nodded.

"Why, what'd he do this time?" I asked.

"Well I found Dr. Killian," Maxwell explained. He gave his head a slight shake. "Pretty much tripped over him. I must have cried out. And then your friend came running up. And he passed out."

"I didn't friggin' pass out," Felix objected.

Maxwell merely pursed his lips and opened his eyes wide in Felix's direction.

"I just had to lie down for a minute," Felix insisted. Then he turned and stomped off in the direction of soil enhancers.

"I'm afraid I didn't do much better, myself," Maxwell murmured. "It was a real shock. I always thought I was competent enough in a crisis, but the sight—" He stopped himself.

"It must have been awful," Lisa offered softly.

"It was," Maxwell agreed.

"Bloody awful," Gilda added in support from behind him. "A bit thick, two dead bodies in how many days?"

Maxwell looked up and counted in the air. "Four," he answered brusquely.

"Everyone's traumatized," Lisa put in. "Maybe we all need to go to a grief group."

I turned to look back at Avis. She was still crying, but more softly than before. Jean stood at her side now. Maybe grief counseling would work for Avis. The rest of us needed post-traumatic stress pay.

And then I looked at Howie. I'd forgotten Howie. He stood at the back of the pack, his round face dazed.

"Are you all right, Howie?" I asked.

"What?" he muttered.

I repeated my question.

"No, I guess not," he answered, his voice flat.

I had a feeling Howie Damon was in *serious* shock.

I turned back to Wayne, who had finally hung up the phone.

"Police will be here soon," he growled.

I nodded toward Howie. Wayne walked over to him and put a hand on his shoulder. Howie looked up into Wayne's face as if he'd never seen him before.

"Howie, you've had a traumatic experience," Wayne told him. "But it'll pass."

"It was my day to celebrate," Howie whispered.

The manuscript. Poor Howie. Today, of all days.

I looked around and realized that we were all in shock,

varying only by degree. And we were bonding like survivors of a shipwreck. Only this was no shipwreck. One of us had killed Reed.

Jean joined us. "I think Avis will pull through," she told me. "She's a strong woman, a survivor. She wants to be alone for a bit."

I looked over to where Avis sat, her back straight and her eyes red but dry. Avis *was* a strong woman, not frail. I only hoped her strength could see her through.

"I have an announcement," Jean declared. "I know the police have been called. But it may be up to us to settle this. I've talked to Avis. We can meet here again on Tuesday night, if the murderer hasn't been apprehended by then. We will stay together, only move around in twos. And we *will* figure out who did this."

I believed her. Some people are born leaders. And some are born followers. "I'll be here," I piped up.

"I don't know," Lisa whimpered.

"It might be dangerous," Natalie agreed.

"Whoever doesn't come is a friggin' suspect," Felix put in. He stopped short of saying "nyah-nyah," but just barely.

Actually all of us were suspects, I thought, whether we showed up or not. But Felix's not-so-original approach was bringing the backsliders into line.

Lisa grumbled but agreed to come. Natalie looked around and saw universal nods of assent.

"Oh shoot, I suppose I'd better," she sighed.

"So, we'll all be here, seven o'clock," Jean said firmly. She spoke, and things happened. Truly, a born leader.

Then we heard the police sirens.

My skin tightened all over my body. The police. Lieutenant Perez. Guilt.

Officers Ulric and Zenas were first on the scene, but Lieutenant Perez and Captain Thorton weren't far behind.

The lieutenant took Avis for questioning before the rest of us. And then he sent her home with gentle words. Darcie promised she would close up the nursery for her new boss. I felt a few muscles relax. Perez had some kindness in his heart.

Then he asked to talk to me.

I couldn't look into his dark eyes.

"Another man was killed, Ms. Jasper," he said, his voice a sad accusation.

"I didn't do it," I told him.

He ignored my words.

"Why the two of them?" he asked softly instead.

"I don't know," I told him pitifully.

He just gazed at me.

"Maybe because they were both doctors," I guessed frantically. "Or maybe Reed saw something the night Dr. Sandstrom was killed. Maybe he confronted the murderer."

Captain Thorton wandered by, humming "The Lusty Month of May," and playing with his hands. He was only a couple of months early.

"Another accident, eh?" Thorton asked. "Lot of that going around."

The lieutenant sighed deeply and returned his accusing eyes to mine.

I shrank into my metal folding chair.

At least Perez let me go after a few dozen more questions. He tried to establish the movements of the suspects, their relationships, anything. And he tried to draw out the details of Avis's relationship with Reed. But I didn't have a clue to any area of his investigation. And interrogation by guilt can only go so far.

His interrogation of Wayne was even shorter. And then we were free.

Carefully, Wayne and I walked out to his car, arms around each other's waists, leaning on one another as if we were suddenly elderly.

Thankfully, there was a crime scene team surrounding Reed's body. Its members blocked our view. We were almost to the car. I felt like a long-distance runner at the finish line.

But two yards away from Wayne's Jaguar, there were more

hurdles. The media had arrived. And, worse, Deer Count had returned.

At least Deer Count had new picket signs. They read, "Murder a deer, then a human!"

"Go away," I told the first picketer.

And then a video camera was shoved into my face.

"Kate Jasper is speaking to us today," a disembodied female voice told the viewers. "The woman who has become the . . .

I sang the phrase with her.

". . . Typhoid Mary of Murder."

And then I got mad.

Sixteen
✶

"I am not the Typhoid Mary of Murder!" I exploded.

I'd been trying to keep my face and voice calm. But my ears were ringing from my own explosion. Somehow, I figured I'd lost the battle in the voice arena. I just hoped the TV cameras weren't catching my raging pulse on tape as well. I could feel the veins at my temples bulging. *Boink, boink, boink.* I made a conscious attempt to soften my facial expression.

"Calling Ms. Jasper such a name is legally actionable," Wayne warned from my side, his voice deep and wise. He could have been on the bench, ready to pronounce judgment. "I wouldn't use that segment on the air unless you want to spend a lot of time in court."

The camera moved back like a dog slapped with a newspaper.

"Maybe the guy's right," someone stage-whispered. "He some kinda attorney?"

"But you kill deer!" a picketer screamed, not dissuaded by law or reason from the species at issue.

"I do not kill deer," I tried again. This time my voice just sounded strangled.

The picketer waved his sign in my face.

Another TV camera began rolling. The Typhoid Mary of Murder versus Deer Count had to make great footage. Better than mud wrestling. Then I remembered a little factoid I'd pushed to the unused section of my brain some time ago.

"Do you guys eat honey?" I asked the picketer.

"Honey?" another picketer responded. I recognized this one from our previous encounter, a tall, dark-haired woman. "What's honey got to do with it?" A little music and a new Tina Turner song might have been born. But I nipped it in the blossom.

"Eating honey oppresses the bees." I lobbed my factoid their way, trying to remember where I'd heard it. "Bees go to all that work to produce the stuff, and then people, people like you, steal it right out from under their little antennae."

Deer Count picketers' faces were coming into focus, horrified under their antlers.

"Do you really believe that?" a reporter asked.

I'd forgotten about the reporters. Damn. Now I'd be on the evening news spouting bee propaganda.

"What do you think?" I shot back. Very clever. And my angry face was probably looking great on camera.

"Well, you said—" the reporter started, shoving in closer. Way too close. Her microphone touched my nose just as her body touched the hand I'd held up to protect myself. Without even thinking, I centered myself, let her push me even further to the rear, and then moved forward, using her own momentum to shove her back.

The shot of her and her microphone flying through the air would probably look even better on camera than the bee debate with Deer Count. I looked down at my perfectly placed feet in shame. True, she'd shoved me first, but tai chi should be used judiciously on the uninitiated. I just hoped my tai chi teacher still didn't own a TV.

"Cute," Wayne whispered affectionately in my ear. "But I think we'd better leave now."

And we did. The media parted like my hair on a good day as we made our way to the Jaguar. And the Deer Count people were still too busy arguing over honey to get in our way.

"But isn't sugar worse?" someone asked as Wayne unlocked

the passenger side. "Don't they, like, filter it through horse's bones or something?"

I climbed in the car quickly, snuggling up in the leather seat and hoping no one would notice it was leather.

"Well, I'm not using aspartame—" was the last thing I heard before I slammed my door shut.

Wayne had taken the driver's seat before I had a chance to breathe, and then we were rolling out the gates.

We were at a stoplight when I heard a smothered snort from Wayne. Startled, I looked his way. His face was red and he was squinting. Was he choking?

A sudden guffaw changed my concern to anger. He was laughing!

"Are you laughing at me?" I demanded.

"No," he muttered breathlessly, waving a hand. "At *them*, Kate. At *them*. Just glad you're on my side."

And pretty soon the confrontations with the media and Deer Count seemed funny to me too. We were both chuckling by the time we sat down for lunch at the Green Forest, Reed's death necessarily forgotten for a while.

The Green Forest sported an Amazon motif. Except that the waitresses weren't bare-breasted; they wore sarongs. Did Amazon women wear sarongs? And the men wore loose white linen shirts, opened to the navel. Yummy. The food was very green. Chili-spiced green bean salad, cilantro pesto and spinach noodles, broccoli habanero, green chili enchiladas, spicy lentil patties.

At least the tofu on my artichoke tostada wasn't green, although almost everything else was. The green salsa was perfect, though. That's why we went to the Green Forest. Though the white linen shirts didn't hurt. I took a lingering bite of tostada.

"Dr. Killian and Dr. Sandstrom," Wayne muttered through his pesto, laughter forgotten. "Both doctors. What else?"

I swallowed and thought.

"Men," I offered. That cut out half the population. "Um . . . gardeners."

I took another bite of artichoke, savored its spicy flavor, and thought some more. Reed and Dr. Sandstrom? Humans, lived in Marin County, dead.

Luckily, Wayne didn't ask for those thoughts. He was probably having them himself. Reed was Dr. Fun Guy and Dr. Sandstrom had been a grouch. There was no home team for the two men. They might have been different species. But someone had thought they had something in common, something worth killing over.

"Kate?" Wayne asked softly, once I'd finished my tostada. "Investigate with me from now on? Don't do it alone?"

I nodded, not wanting to verbally commit.

"Please," he added, obviously hearing the hesitation in my silence.

"I'll try," I promised, meaning it.

"Love you," he explained, looking down at his empty plate.

That look was enough. I'd really try.

We talked on the way home. But neither of us had any idea why the two men had been killed. Dr. Sandstrom had at least made people angry. But Reed?

We were still talking as we climbed our front stairs and saw Kevin and Xanthe waiting for us.

"Hey, there," Kevin greeted us, smiling beneath his dark glasses. Xanthe just stared our way, and then turned her gaze to the far end of the deck.

I followed her gaze, and saw Slammer. Slammer was checking out my roses, safely planted in giant terra-cotta tubs, guarded by the deck railing. So far, the deer hadn't climbed the stairs to visit them. But Slammer had. He sniffed a rose, then petted it, jabbing himself on a thorn, midstroke.

"Wow," he muttered, looking at the red dot of blood on his palm. Then he laughed. Maybe he hadn't seen a rose in a while.

I looked at Wayne, but Wayne just raised a brow.

"Who?" he whispered.

Right, I remembered. Wayne hadn't had the pleasure of meeting Slammer yet.

"So, Wayne," Kevin said, bringing our attention back to the front door. "Kate said you had a few questions about the pyramid investment. You know, so did I at first, but that's always true when you're on the leading edge. You don't see things quite like everyone else . . ."

Kevin was right. He didn't see things like everyone else. There didn't seem to be much advantage to his viewpoint, though.

Wayne's eyes were drifting toward Slammer again.

". . . zoned in on the cosmic potential," Kevin went on.

"He's their friend," I whispered into Wayne's ear. "Some guy from the loony bin—"

"Not the loony bin," Xanthe interjected helpfully. "Prison. Slammer's from prison."

"Right," Kevin cut back in, changing tracks as easily as a locomotive. And about as subtly. "Hey, Slammer's just the guy to help you now, for the right amount of money—"

"Kevin, no," I said firmly.

Xanthe glared. "I'm glad I tore up your bulbs," she told me.

"You!" I cried out. I hadn't even considered Xanthe.

"I try to help you, but do you give me credit?" she demanded before I even had a chance for *my* tirade. "Huh, huh? I like you, Kate. But do you give an inch?" She squinted her raccoon eyes. "I call upon the gods and goddesses—"

"Xanthe," Kevin put in gently.

"But—"

"Remember, you decided the cursing might not be holistically sound—"

"Fine," Xanthe spat out. "We're outa here. Come on, Kevin. Come on, Slammer."

And they were outa there.

I opened the door and pulled Wayne in after me as fast as I could. You never know when a Koffenburger will return.

"Who—" Wayne began again.

But the ring of the phone cut him off.

"Slammer is some kind of nut Kevin and Xanthe picked up. Just out of prison, I think—"

The phone rang again.

"He wants to be a bod—"

I stopped myself as the phone rang for the third time, and my own voice began its recorded answering spiel. I was going to say "bodyguard," but that's what Wayne had been when I'd met him. And he hadn't been a successful bodyguard. It was still a sensitive point.

"He wants to be paid to protect me—"

"Kate, are you there?" someone asked through the speaker.

I stopped again, trying to place the voice.

"This is Olive," it said. "Avis is all upset—"

I picked up the phone. Olive told me that her mother was really "knocked for a loop." Olive sounded genuinely worried. And that was enough to worry me. I promised her we'd be right over, and hung up.

"Avis is having a hard time," I told Wayne. "Um . . . I said we'd—"

"Let's go," he agreed, then added more softly, "both of us."

On the way to San Ricardo in my Toyota, I explained Slammer to Wayne as much as Slammer could be explained.

By the time I'd parked in front of Avis's, Wayne had summed up Slammer, Kevin, and Xanthe.

"Family," he said, and we walked through Avis's perfect deer-proof garden to the front door of her Victorian cottage.

Olive greeted us before I even knocked.

"Mom's acting really weird," she announced at full volume, her overtanned face pinched with what might have been concern. Or maybe just aggravation.

If Avis was within fifty yards, I'm sure she'd heard her daughter.

"I'm not actually acting weird, Olive," came Avis's voice from across the living room. Her gentle tone held a weariness, though, rather than anger. "Come on in, you two."

We tiptoed into the living room, followed by the clomping of Olive's footsteps, unsure what we would see. Avis was ensconced in one of her comfortable chairs with a crocheted throw tucked around her legs. And she wore neither a hat nor gloves. No wonder Olive was worried. Minus the hat, I could see her beauty clearly. Her skin was wrinkled, but otherwise flawless. Her hands were the same. Maybe there was a logic to the hat and gloves beyond the fear of skin cancer. Avis's green eyes were tinged with red, though, and her elegant cheekbones seemed to droop.

"Reed was a wonderful man," she murmured dreamily.

Wayne and I looked at each other, unsure what to say.

"Oh, don't worry," she assured us. "I know he's dead. I'm mourning his passing by remembering the good times. That's what he would have wanted. Sit down and we can talk."

So we sat. I could smell the mixed scents of lemon and cinnamon from my seat. Air freshener or cooking? I wondered. Or incense. Incense for Reed? My eyes returned to Avis.

"Reed showed me his synthesizer," I threw in.

"That's what I mean, Kate," Avis said eagerly. "Did you ever see anyone who enjoyed life as much as Reed did? Reed lived life to the fullest—"

"Playboy," Olive muttered.

"He loved to play, if that's what you mean," Avis conceded, her eyes moistening.

"Mom, don't cry!" Olive ordered, panic in her voice.

"Olive, I'm all right," Avis told her daughter. "I know I never cried much when you were growing up, but there's nothing wrong with crying. Nothing wrong with remembering."

"But—"

"Listen," Avis insisted. "I'm strong, I'll survive. Reed went out like Peter Pan, young and healthy. I think that would have been his wish." Her eyes went out of focus. "Certainly it's better than a lingering death."

"Mom, you can't know that, not yet."

Avis's eyes came back to focus. She shook her head.

" 'Not yet'?" she repeated, laughing. "Olive, you *are* good for me."

Olive's eyes narrowed.

"Avis," Wayne threw in. "Kate and I are trying to imagine why anyone would want to kill Reed."

All the humor left Avis's face.

"So am I," she murmured, shaking her head. "So am I. And I just can't think of a reason."

So instead we talked about Reed hiking, and Reed skateboarding, and Reed singing. And about all the other things he'd done. Avis seemed sad but steady by the time we got up to leave. And Olive was angry again, angry that Reed had managed to have such a good time while he was alive. Mother and daughter were fine. Situation normal.

When Wayne and I got home, no one was standing on our front deck. The phone wasn't ringing. It was a pleasant Sunday afternoon. We sat down together in the swinging chair and pushed off with our legs. The movement of the chair was hypnotic. I had almost dozed off when Wayne spoke.

"Kate," he whispered. "Think I understand now."

"What?" I asked, snuggling closer to him, to his warmth.

"A public wedding means a family wedding," he went on. "It's your family, isn't it?"

I sat bolt upright as the tumblers fell into place. Click, click, click. He was right!

Hours later, we were still talking. Not only did Wayne understand why I didn't want a formal wedding, he forgave me. I watched him cook me dinner and wondered how I'd gotten so lucky. And then I thought of Avis, and how easily it could all be lost.

Love was sweet that night. And I really believed that I would never investigate without Wayne again.

Monday morning, I worked to solve Jest Gifts' problems like a good little entrepreneur, calling mouse manufacturers and actually lining one up to replace our jailbird supplier. Then surreptitiously, I got out my suspect list and stared at it. What could I really do to get information? There had to be something. I was failing Lieutenant Perez. I was failing Avis. I was failing Jean Watkins. And I was failing the two dead men. Did the motive for *both* deaths lie with Dr. Sandstrom? His girlfriend, I thought. Maybe she knew what had motivated the killings. It was time to check out the woman. What was her name? Natalie Miner's words did an instant replay in my mind. Dr. Larkin, a woman named Dr. Larkin with a practice on Tepper Street.

I turned in my swivel chair, away from my desk, ready to hop in my car. And faced Wayne's belt buckle. I jumped in my chair, bouncing as I came back down. Wayne—I'd forgotten Wayne. Already.

"What?" he demanded.

"Dr. Larkin," I replied.

His brows lowered, trying to place the name. Then he had it. "The other woman."

Bingo. Wayne insisted on calling before we drove over to see Dr. Larkin. She told us she had a cancellation right before lunch. We were on for eleven o'clock.

Dr. Larkin was a gynecologist. It was right on the glass door to her office: Obstetrics and Gynecology. Wayne looked around nervously as we entered the reception area. A glimpse into a room equipped with a stirruped examination table didn't do him much good. Nor did the smell of antiseptic clogging our sinuses.

"Don't worry," I whispered in his ear. "You're a boy."

He flinched, neither amused nor comforted.

I was just apologizing when the receptionist showed up. She was a small woman, small and wizened. She couldn't have been a day under eighty. She eyed Wayne suspiciously.

"Husband," I told her.

"Huh!" she snorted.

Could this be Dr. Larkin's mother?

"Eleanor?" a voice called from the rear. "Are there people out there for me?"

"Guess so," Eleanor conceded.

"Then send them back."

Dr. Larkin was a large woman with maybe ten years on me. Her curves were voluptuous, her hair gray and clipped short, her actions neat and controlled. And her voice was brusque, but maybe only for us.

"You wanted to ask some questions about Searle?" she began once we were seated in the thinly padded chairs in front of her desk.

My brain searched for a match. Searle?

"Yes," Wayne answered. "Dr. Sandstrom."

Of course, Searle Sandstrom. The man had to have a first name. I'd just had yet to hear anyone actually use it.

"And why should I answer your questions?" Dr. Larkin asked.

"We want to find out who killed the doctor," I said. "No one in the support group—"

"You were there?" she interrupted. "You're members of this Deer-Abused group?"

"Uh, yeah," I answered, squirming to find a more comfortable spot on the chair. There wasn't one.

"Heard another man was killed," she commented.

I had a feeling she was going to interview us, not the other way around.

"That's exactly why we want to know as much as possible," Wayne put in.

"How do I know you didn't kill them?" she demanded.

"You don't," I told her. "But we didn't."

"Saw you kung-fu that reporter on the news last night," she said, smiling at last.

"Tai chi—" I began, correcting her.

But Wayne was way ahead of me.

"Kate gets things done," he cut in. "She's already talked with everyone from the group, but we still don't have a feeling for Dr. Sandstrom. What was it that caused his death?"

"A blow to the skull, I heard," she answered.

Ow. That was cold. But at least she wasn't sniffling and crying. Maybe she heard my thought.

"Okay," she said finally. "I'll tell you about Searle. He was a man who couldn't abide bullshit. He was strong, straightforward, and occasionally obnoxious." A gentle smile flitted across her face. "We made a good pair. I could care less if he wanted to kill deer. And he didn't need a bunch of feminine folderol."

Yeah, I could see them together.

"Do you know of any reason—" Wayne began.

"No. The police asked me all that," she interrupted, slashing her hand in the air.

"Do you know who his heirs were?" I pushed on.

"His kids, I think. Both grown now."

"Do they live around here?"

"No, back East somewhere. I've never met them, but neither of them needs money. Both doctors themselves, the son and the daughter."

There wasn't a whole lot to say after that. I didn't even know what questions to ask.

"Listen," Dr. Larkin said, rising from her desk, "I'll call you if I think of anything, but I can't imagine that I will."

We got up and turned to go.

"Oh, and Mr. Caruso," she added, looking at the card he'd handed her. "If you're ever pregnant, you know where to come. Don't be a stranger."

We could still hear her laughing after we closed the office door behind us.

We drove home in silence and found Barbara Chu on our doorstep. I didn't mention Dr. Larkin's little joke to my friend.

"I'm here for lunch," Barbara told us.

And Wayne cooked. Fresh gazpacho, herbed biscuits, and a fruit and biscotti platter. He was a lot calmer once he'd finished cooking.

And I was a lot calmer once I'd eaten.

While we were tucking away the last of the biscotti, Barbara congratulated us on our insight.

"Into the murder?" I asked eagerly.

"Sheesh, no." She laughed. "Into the reason you don't want a formal weddng."

Seventeen

✗

"Barbara!" I howled.

"What?" she asked, her lovely Buddha-face as innocent as . . . well, the Buddha's. But her mind wasn't. She knew why I was howling.

"The issue under discussion is why Dr. Sandstrom and Dr. Killian were murdered, not what kind of formal wedding Wayne and I are or aren't going to have."

"But I don't *know* why the two doctors were killed," she replied reasonably.

"You don't?" I whimpered, my eagerness sinking into a lump of undigested biscotti.

She shook her head. "Not a clue."

"But you're psychic!"

"You know murder fritzes my psychic circuits," she reminded me cheerfully.

"Then just think like a normal person," I ordered.

"Kiddo, you also know I'm not a normal person," she fired back.

Wayne nodded judiciously. I reminded myself I loved him. I'd strangle Barbara instead.

"Great meal," she told Wayne, smiling his way.

Wayne blushed becomingly. Barbara rushed around the table, a hug-missile, grabbing Wayne first and me second. She kissed my cheek, and then she was gone. By the time we got up from the table, we could already hear her Volkswagen bug screeching out of the driveway onto the road.

I sat back down with a sigh.

"All right, I will not find Barbara and kill her," I assured Wayne. "I will move on. We must have other sources of information that we haven't thought of. What? Who?"

"Use our little psychiatric gray cells?" Wayne tried.

"How about Ann Rivera?" I shot back, remembering my friend, my friend *and* psychiatric-hospital administrator. Now, that woman knew how to use her gray cells.

I caught Ann at the hospital. She'd planned a quiet evening alone after work, but I was determined to convince her to visit. I tempted her with dinner. She wanted to know if Wayne would be cooking, and, if so, what was on the menu.

Negotiations satisfactorily begun, I handed the telephone to Wayne and wandered off as he murmured about tempeh samosas on greens with gado gado dipping sauce, sweet potato salad, and berry sorbet. My body had barely absorbed the last feast, and I was salivating again. When Wayne hung up the phone, he told me Ann had agreed to dinner. She probably would have agreed to marriage if he'd asked, but he was already taken.

Wayne made a list and went out for groceries. I went back to my desk to scale the mountains of Jest Gifts paperwork.

Some three hours later, Ann was sitting with us at our kitchen table, oohing and aahing over an early dinner that had taken Wayne most of those hours to prepare. And a meal that had taken me most of those hours to smell and savor before eating. The shades were drawn, and three candles provided a romantic light for our gourmandizing. My best, and only, china was on the table. Then, after all those hours of cooking, the three of us just dived in and devoured the samosas, greens, and sweet-potato salad like so much granola. I was surreptitiously loosening my waistband to make room for the dessert course when the inevitable question came from Ann's lips.

"So why didn't you tell me about the wedding?"

"A secret," Wayne answered brusquely. "Like a good rec-
ipe."

Ann laughed, a toothy grin appearing in her brown face.
She twiddled a curl.

"I'll forgive you," she announced. "I'll even congratulate
you. Congratulations."

I reached out and squeezed her hand, gado gado sauce and
all. Because she meant it. She wasn't hurt by our negligence.
She wasn't crying foul.

"Thank you," I murmured sincerely. "You're a true friend."

Her skin flushed, a rich terra-cotta shade in the soft light.
A true friend who was embarrassed by compliments.

"So, tell me about your murders," she ordered.

Telling her about the murders took us through the berry
sorbet and crunchy carob topping.

"Both men were doctors," Ann recapped, wiping her lips
with the steaming lemon-scented napkins Wayne had provided. Not only did Wayne cook when he was nervous, he
embellished.

Wayne and I bobbed our heads in enthusiastic unison at
Ann's recap, causing the candle flames to flicker.

"A doctor's a classic father figure for some," Ann told us.
"For others, the bearer of bad news. And maybe even the
violator, armed with the tools of surgery."

"All possible motives for murder," Wayne growled.

"I can't see Reed as a father figure," I pointed out. In my
mind, Reed would always be a child who never grew up.

"But he certainly had the tools of violation as a plastic surgeon," Wayne shot back.

We all nodded then, united in a labyrinth of confusion.

"And either could have borne bad news," Wayne plodded
on, his tone softening as his mind took over.

"What if the motives were different for the two men?" Ann
put in.

"Like Dr. Sandstrom, because of his unlikable nature—" I
began.

"—and Reed because he knew something," Wayne finished for me.

"But who?"

"Who hates enough?" Ann asked. The candlelight was suddenly eerie, no longer romantic.

I ran the suspects through my mind, each face lit by murky candlelight, each filled with hate. I shivered.

The phone rang, and all three of us started in our chairs.

I picked it up before the announcement, wanting a break from the brooding. A break from the not-knowing.

"Keep out of it," a muffled voice warned, and then the handset on the other end of the line was slammed down.

I wasn't brooding anymore. I was shaking now.

To tell or not to tell? I asked myself as I took a few deep breaths before returning to the kitchen.

Ann and Wayne stared at me as I sat back down. Somehow, I felt the words I'd just heard must have been written on my forehead.

"Who was on the phone?" Wayne asked.

I flinched.

"I don't know," I answered honestly. Male, female? Young, old? No imprint had been left but the words themselves. "Some breather," I lied.

"Spooky," Ann commented. This from a woman who spent her days in a psychiatric hospital. But she was right. It was spooky.

I took another breath and tried to forget the call. Tried to forget that it had probably been the murderer. No, I wouldn't tell Wayne. I wouldn't even tell Lieutenant Perez. I knew from experience that the police wouldn't be able to trace what had to be a local call. Then I wished I had one of those new doohickeys on my phone that might have come up with the caller's number.

"Any more ideas?" I asked Ann.

"Be careful," she suggested, and rose from the table. "And thanks for dinner," she finished up.

And then she left for her quiet evening at home. Lucky Ann.

I was glad when Wayne turned on the lights and snuffed the candles to do the dishes. Good, clean, artificial light made the phone call seem unreal.

I was drying cutlery when it came to me.

"Wayne!" I whooped. "I do have a source."

"Who?"

"My hairdresser."

Wayne smiled. He'd met Carol, my hairdresser, once. The woman who knew everything. Snip. Talk. Snip. Talk. That was Carol. And what local gossip she didn't know, didn't exist. *And* she worked Monday evenings.

I called the Golden Rose, and let Wayne finish drying. Could Carol fit me in that night? Yes, if I came in right away. I told them I would, and gave Wayne a quick kiss goodbye.

Backing my car out of the driveway, I remembered just why I loved the Golden Rose, a beauty parlor of the old school: inexpensive, pink, and patronized by a few people who still preferred iceberg lettuce to radicchio. The Golden Rose was a time warp in Marin County. And the time warp included prices. I could get my hair cut there at half the price of any other place in Mill Valley.

I ran my hand through the few curls on the top of my head as I drove to the Golden Rose. I didn't really need a haircut. And I knew Carol was apt to snip at the same rate that she talked. My new attempt to grow out a little braid from the rear of my head might suffer a setback if I really got her going.

"Hiya, honey," Carol greeted me, her voice rasping a welcome at the Golden Rose's pink portals. She eyed my mini-braid hungrily and snapped the ever-present scissors in her hand. "Early for this month, huh?"

I nodded apprehensively. Maybe this would be too much of a sacrifice. My hair for the murderer's identity?

"Probably wanna look good for TV," she opined, without waiting for confirmation. She shook her cascade of blond hair as if to give me a few pointers. "Saw you on the news last night."

I groaned and closed the door behind me. And inhaled the

scent of hair spray and peroxide. My dinner felt heavy on my stomach.

"Hey, at least they didn't call you the Typhoid Mary of Murder this time," she said consolingly, and led me to her station at the rear of the shop.

I climbed up into the pink vinyl barber chair, and Carol wrapped a rubbery golden sheet around my neck.

Snip. A short brown curl dropped to my lap.

"I suppose you wanna know about the folks who were at that goofy deer group," she whispered intimately.

The few late-night hairdressers and their clients all turned our way. Carol's whisper could go on stage. By itself. It was hard to believe that volume came out of her skinny body. But years of Coca-Cola and cigarettes had probably helped.

"Yeah," was all I had to say.

"Well of course, you know I do Avis's hair," she began. Snip. "Very classy haircut for a very classy dame. You know all about her *movie* days," she breathed. Her tone made it clear which movies she was talking about.

"Uh-huh," I muttered.

"And then, that old movie producer died and left her all that money. She is one helluva rich woman. Doesn't have to work for a living, that's for sure."

"She inherited her money?"

"Yep." Snip.

"I didn't know that," I murmured. A man dies and Avis inherits. Was that a motive? I wrinkled my forehead, trying to think. It was the wrong murder, even if it was a motive.

"Lots you don't know," she commented, then added, "Too bad about Reed. Avis was stuck on that boy for sure."

"Did you know Reed?" I asked, and was glad to see her raise her scissors away from my head to think for a minute.

"Didn't know him, but I knew quite a few of his ladies. He never stayed too long, but he was real good to his ladies, real romantic, I guess you'd say. Like Willie Nelson maybe, you know?"

I nodded to keep her going. But I wasn't quite sure about

the Willie Nelson part. Much as I liked his singing, I couldn't see a resemblance to Reed.

"Did he get his . . . ladies from his plastic surgery practice?"

Carol shook her head emphatically, blond cascades shimmering under the fluorescent lights.

"No, he was real serious about his business stuff, they said. Especially after that suit." Carol shook her head. "Poor lady wasn't real good lookin' before the surgery, but at least her nose matched her face. Guess she didn't like her new nose, so she sued. Anyway, that man could meet a woman anywhere," she confided. "From the way the ladies talked, I wouldn't have minded a fling with him myself. He was a real gentleman. I'd bet on it."

Carol bent over my head again. I covered the end of my two-inch braid with my hand.

"Any split ends?" she probed.

"Nope," I told her, hoping she'd take my word for it. It had taken months for me to grow a braid of any length at all, split ends being the excuse for inches of trimming.

"Jean Watkins was in that group too," she informed me. Snip.

"You know Jean?" I asked. Silly question.

"Oh yeah, her and her no-good son. She used to get her hair cut here. Michelle did her. That son put her through hell, and with that sweet granddaughter too."

Sweet? I wondered if she'd ever met Darcie Watkins in person. Snip.

"Used to be a nun."

"Darcie?" I asked.

"No, Jean."

"A nun, like in an order and everything?"

"Sheesh, Kate," she protested. "What other kinds of nuns are there?"

"Right," I conceded meekly. "But what happened?"

"Jean lost her vocation. Left the order. Became a social worker. Married this architect."

"Oh," was all I could muster. Jean? I tried to picture her sturdy body in a habit.

"And Lisa Orton," Carol went on. "Camille did her until her father died and she got all that money. A real nut case. One group after another. Wanted us all to join a group to share our experiences about customer abuse. As if her guff wasn't enough. Hah! And then that group for deer." Snip. Snip. "No offense."

"No, that's fine," I told her, my mind working overtime. "Do you think Dr. Sandstrom could have been Lisa's father's doctor?" Now we were talking possible motive.

Carol tilted her head. "Nah," she finally concluded. "His doctor was an old codger named Drucker."

"You sure?" I asked, motive slipping away.

"Of course I am," she told me. Snip. Snip. Snip. "Now Natalie Miner, she was a sad one."

"She get her hair cut here too?"

"No, but my brother-in-law knew her late husband. She makes all this money in real estate, but she just messes up with men. Too eager. Men don't like that in a woman."

Her scissors hovered near my braid menacingly. I held it by its tail again.

"Thought I saw some split ends," she challenged.

"Nope, no split ends," I reiterated, putting up a warning hand. "You know Gilda Fitch?"

"Oh, the gal that delivers the mail, sure. She's a kick in the pants. And her mother's some kind of Lady or Dame or something. For real."

"Who else?" I asked.

"Didn't really know Howie Damon or Maxwell Yang, but I heard that the Damon guy had some kind of book he was trying to sell. It's got all kinds of juicy bits about old California families. Oughta raise a stir."

Now there was a motive . . . to kill Howie.

"And Maxwell Yang?"

"Everyone says he's real nice for a celebrity. But he wants

a real job. Wants to be a serious reporter. No more second-rate Oprah." Snip.

"How about Dr. Sandstrom?"

"Depends who you ask. Had a lady who told me he was a mean s.o.b., but Dr. Yamoda swore by him."

"She get her hair cut here?"

"Nah, I know a friend of her sister's."

"You know who murdered Dr. Sandstrom?" I asked. It was worth a try.

"Not Avis," she told me. "Don't know about the rest of them." Snip. That time, she got the end of my braid.

"Murder's an interesting thing," she reflected, happy to have won over my split ends. "They say there's something missing from a murderer, some kind of chemical or something. They oughta check everyone's chemicals." Snip. "But they probably can't with all these laws and such." Snip. "Probably be real easy if they could." Snip.

"How do you know all this stuff, anyway?" I demanded.

"Whaddaya think I do for a living?" she retorted.

I thought about the CIA for a moment. It was possible. What a cover. Mrs. Pollifax, move over.

"So, are you going to tell me about your wedding?" Carol asked. Snip, snip, snip.

I sat up so quickly that Carol's scissors stopped for a moment. That was good. I might have been entirely bald otherwise. I told her about my wedding, in detail. I had my hair to consider. Of course, now *everyone* would know about Wayne and me. Carol's knowledge was a two-way street. It went in, and it went out. Once I was done telling, I jumped from the barber's chair with my braid primarily intact, paid my bill, tipped Carol double, and ran out of the Golden Rose, my mind swirling with new facts.

"Well?" Wayne prompted when I got home.

"Avis didn't do it," I told him. "Carol says so."

He ran his hand through what was left of the hair on the top of my head. I closed my eyes, knowing for a moment the bliss of the well-petted cat. Carol just didn't have the hands

Wayne did. Then I reached up to return the favor.

The doorbell rang.

I opened the door slowly. It didn't stop Felix from rocketing past me, mouth in gear.

"So?" he prodded. "How goes the friggin' sleuth for the truth? Got any good poop for my scoop?"

I looked at Wayne. He sighed, but closed his eyes, a good sign he wasn't going to kill Felix on the spot.

Felix caught the sigh and the look, and was comfy on our denim couch before you could say "pit bull."

"Man," he grumbled as Wayne and I dropped into the swinging chair. "Those cop-shop guys are totally gonzo. All they wanna do is take information, not give it. Don't the potato-heads know we're trying to friggin' help them?"

Obviously, Lieutenant Perez hadn't taken Felix into his confidence. I suddenly felt better about the lieutenant.

"So who've you been grilling?" Felix asked before I could fully experience forgiving the lieutenant.

"My hairdresser," I told him.

"Come on!" he exploded. "What does your friggin' hairdresser know about these deer nuts?"

"Jean Watkins was a nun," I told him.

That stopped him cold.

"Holy socks, how'd she find that out?"

I smiled serenely, as if I knew.

"Betcha she didn't know Dr. Sandstrom's heirs," Felix smirked.

"His two kids, right?" I didn't tell him Carol wasn't my source on that one.

Felix jumped off the couch, scowling.

"How come you didn't take me if this woman is the friggin' KGB? Huh?"

I opened my mouth to answer, but I wasn't fast enough.

"Reed only had one heir, his sister," Felix announced, his hands on his hips. "No wives. No ex-wives."

"A will?" I asked.

"Nope, friggin' moron died intestate."

Felix was puffing up again, glad he had some information I didn't. He smiled and played with his luxurious mustache.

"Hey, I saw that Gilda Fitch clown," he added. "Went to get my morning caffeine injection and there she was. Weird-ass woman. Doesn't know how to speak English—"

"I think that's what they say about us," Wayne put in.

But I was thinking that Felix was right. Gilda was weird, the way she kept showing up. Or maybe she'd always been around, and I'd just never noticed her before.

"Did she talk to you, Felix—" I began.

But the doorbell cut me off.

At least I knew it wouldn't be Felix at the door. I jumped out of the swinging chair to answer. This time, Jean and Darcie Watkins were on my doorstep. I stared at Jean Watkins's round, guileless face. A nun?

Meanwhile, Jean peered past me and spotted Felix. She flinched visibly, as if she'd seen a bug. A big, hairy one.

"Please, come in," I said.

But Jean seemed to have changed her mind.

"We were just passing by and thought we'd drop in," she told me. "But I see you have company, so—"

"Hey, wait a friggin' minute!" Felix ordered, racing to the door to stand by my side.

"Young man," Jean reprimanded him. "Mind your tongue."

And Felix should have minded his tongue because his mouth fell open and the tongue in question was all too visible.

"I just wanna do a little talking, man," he finally shot back. "Why you put up with a space cadet like Kate, and won't talk to a real reporter like me—"

"Well, we'd best be going," Jean murmured and turned.

"Hey, you can't—"

"Young man, we can, and we will," Jean countered.

"Yeah," Darcie added. "You big jerk-head."

"Darcie," Jean warned, but I could hear the laugh in her voice.

Jean and Darcie could, and they did, leave.

Felix sat back down on the couch.

"What have I got, friggin' leprosy?" he asked, waving his hands. "I wasn't even there when the nasty-ass doc got bashed the first time. Holy socks, they can't think it was me that—"

I didn't hear the rest of Felix's sentence, because my front steps were clattering. Or someone or something was clattering on the steps.

I jumped out of the swinging chair once more and ran to the door. But there weren't any guests on my doorstep.

My guests were at the far end of the deck nibbling the roses in my terra-cotta pots. Three deer.

"No!" I screamed and ran at them.

EIGHTEEN
✤

The deer looked at me as I charged them, their eyes round and surprised in the dim light. Then they ran . . . in my direction. The deck didn't allow them any other exit. I'd forgotten that when I'd charged. I stopped too late, closed my eyes, and waited for the impact. Deer dented cars . . . by mistake. And then I imagined being gored. An instant later, I heard the deer veer to clatter past me and back down the stairs. My heart was beating as loud as their hooves. I wondered who was more frightened.

I opened my eyes slowly. A few roses were left in the rear-most terra-cotta pots. The rest were chewed to the stem. I clenched my fists. I probably would have charged the deer again if they'd stayed on the deck.

"Whoa, are you friggin' looney tunes?" a voice demanded from behind me.

Felix. Somehow, I'd imagined that he'd left with the deer, that all pests would stick together.

"I scared them away," I pointed out, my voice rising defensively.

Wayne was up to bat next.

"Kate," he growled. "You know a deer in rut can gore you. Even if they're not in rut, they're dangerous." His voice softened. "Please, don't do that again. My heart can't stand it."

"Oh, sweetie," I murmured guiltily, looking up at his

strained, pale face. I didn't think he was kidding. He certainly looked like a man in shock. "I'm sorry."

"How do you know if a deer is in rut?" Felix asked as I reached out to hug Wayne.

He didn't get an answer. This hug was a serious undertaking. My arms were around Wayne's waist. I heard his heart beating, too fast, and felt the cool cotton of his shirt against my face. And Wayne was holding me tight enough to break the ribs that the deer hadn't.

"The buggers look horny or something?" Felix pressed on.

Wayne loosened his grip. I let go too and reached my hands up behind Wayne's head to make finger horns, transforming Wayne into a five point buck. I grinned at Felix. The effort was childish, but strangely effective.

"Jeez-Louise," Felix objected. "I know when I'm not friggin' wanted. Gonzo, friggin' gonzo!"

And then he banged down the stairs, as noisily as the deer, gunning his engine before his Chevy flew out of our driveway, spraying gravel in its wake.

Wayne and I watched him go, our arms circling each other's waists; then Wayne turned to me.

"What did you do?" he demanded.

I showed him my finger horns, using my own head as a model. He smiled, his brows lifting, all anger gone.

"Think it'll work again?" he asked hopefully.

I couldn't promise him anything, but at least he let up on me for chasing the deer. In fact, an hour later in bed, he called me a "brave warrior," not to mention "fearless leader." I had a feeling he was relying on old cartoons for his lines, but that didn't make cuddling in his arms any less a pleasure.

Tuesday, I spent the day hard at work on Jest Gifts. Invoices, ledgers, and accounts payable spilled from my hands as Kris Kristofferson blasted from my tape deck. The "Deer Doctor Murders," as the papers had dubbed them, had taken too much time out of my business schedule. I wondered, and worried, about how Lieutenant Perez was doing, but kept on working until Wayne came home early from La Fête à L'Oeil. The murders had taken a chunk out of his time too. On the other hand, because of our meeting set for this evening Wayne had come home early enough to feed me a leftover dinner of vegetable paté, fresh baked bread, and sherried black mushrooms with shallots before we rushed off in my Toyota to Eldora Nurseries.

The taste of shallots was still on my tongue at seven o'clock when I pulled into the familiar parking lot. I climbed out of the car, looking both ways. I wasn't looking for traffic. I was looking for blunt instruments. Then I saw Lieutenant Perez against the beginning of a Maxfield Parrish twilight sky. The effect should have been magical. Instead, it was menacing.

"Ms. Jasper," he greeted me, nodding his head formally, his dark eyes conveying emotional injury.

"Lieutenant Perez," I answered, just as formally.

"Ms. Eldora told me about your meeting tonight," he continued. The implication was clear. I *hadn't* told him about the meeting. Uh-oh.

"How's your captain?" I asked, unable to meet his injured eyes.

"Singing. It's *The Music Man* this week." Perez told me. "We signed him out on health leave. Terrible flu."

"Ah," I murmured, nodding.

"Gives us a little more time," he bulldozed on.

I opened my mouth to wriggle out of my responsibilities, but Wayne was much quicker than I was.

"Us?" Wayne repeated. A breeze rustled the leaves and blossoms of thousands of neatly organized plants. And the breeze brought me Wayne's familiar scent. Only there was a uncharacteristic acidity to it now. "In view of the second death, shouldn't Kate be left out of any role in your investigation?"

Perez looked at Wayne with all the enthusiasm of a man observing the three-hundredth alien to land on his planet. And a particularly loathsome species of alien at that.

"No, sir," he finally answered Wayne. "The second death

makes Ms. Jasper's participation all the more important."

"Important, but not safe," Wayne tried.

"Safer once the murderer is found," Perez argued.

"My only concern is Kate's—" Wayne began.

I don't know how long the two men would have argued if Lisa Orton hadn't shown up just then. I wasn't about to get between them, no matter who the subject of their discussion was. No running at deer, and no standing between snarling dogs. No doubt about it, I was a new woman after the previous night's excitement.

"We need a grief group here," Lisa announced, standing alongside the lieutenant. The freckles stood out on her cheekbones. Her dark hair was pulled back in a ponytail. "Not Gestapo interrogation."

Perez turned toward her slowly.

"Do you feel particularly grieved, Ms. Orton?" he asked quietly.

Lisa sucked in her lower lip, and her round eyes widened.

"What kind of question is that?" she demanded, then added, "I want to talk to a woman officer."

Perez didn't physically roll his eyes, but somehow I could feel him doing it mentally.

"Ms. Orton, you began this conversation," Perez reminded her.

"Huh," she shot back. "Estrogen-deprived life forms are all the same. I make an intelligent suggestion and—"

"Officer Perez," a new voice interrupted. Natalie Miner's voice. Perez winced. He'd probably worked hard to go from Officer to Lieutenant. "I just don't know if I can bear it. The good Lord knows it's hard enough to see one man die, but two? Surely, there is something that can be done, isn't there, Officer?" She put her hand on the lieutenant's arm and looked up at him, her baby face quivering like a puppy's.

"Yes, ma'am," he replied neutrally.

"The shock is just too much—" she started up again.

"See, I told you we needed a grief group," Lisa declared, crossing her arms. "Look at this poor woman."

"A grief group?" Maxwell Yang echoed, striding our way. "I'm not sure grief is really what most people are feeling right now. Personally, I'll admit I'm frightened. And I am truly glad to see you, Lieutenant Perez."

Perez straightened his shoulders. Maxwell sure knew how to make people feel good. I wished I could learn that little trick myself.

"That's why I'm here," the lieutenant assured Maxwell. "No more incidents."

"Incidents?" Lisa parroted. "Now you're talking like your goofy captain."

Lieutenant Perez closed his eyes. I didn't blame him. If I could close my eyes and make it all go away, I would too.

"Hey, wassup?" someone yelled from the main building. Darcie popped out, her hands on her hips. "Yo, folks, the meeting's supposed to be in here, not in the parking lot."

Perez opened his eyes and sighed.

"The young lady is right," he conceded. "Time to go on in."

Inside, everything looked much as it had the night Dr. Sandstrom had died. A semicircle of metal folding chairs were set up near the cash register. Avis, Jean, Howie, Gilda, and even Felix were already seated. Actually, everything looked a lot like the night Reed Killian had died, too. The soil and plant smells made my nose tingle. The tingle extended to the hairs on my arms and the back of my neck. Who would die tonight? I told myself to cut it out and marched into the circle to take my own seat. Wayne hunkered down beside me.

When everyone was finally seated, Lieutenant Perez spoke loudly and firmly.

"Here are the ground rules," he began. "During this meeting, we will all stay together. If anyone leaves for any reason, they take a buddy. Is that clear?"

Everyone nodded, even Lisa. Though she sucked on her lower lip as she did.

The lieutenant turned toward Avis. "Ms. Eldora?" he inquired gently. "What would you like us to do now?"

I turned toward Avis, too. Under her hat and scarves she looked, if possible, even more delicate then usual, her cat eyes unfocused. I wondered if she was on some kind of medication.

"Well . . ." she answered hesitantly. Then her eyes came into clearer focus. "I would like to ask if anyone can tell me who killed Reed."

That was a simple request. A heartbreakingly simple request. But no one seemed able to give Avis what she wanted.

"Please," she whispered after a few moments of silence went by. "I have to know."

"Him," Darcie accused, pointing at Felix.

"Me!" Felix objected. His soulful eyes seemed to be pushing out of their sockets for an instant. "I wasn't even here when Doc Sandstrom got bashed the first time. Holy socks, everyone else in this friggin' circle is a better bet than me. Look at you, little Ms. Pronto, whiz-bang, accuse-the-reporter. All hopped up on adolescent angst, bustin' to trash anything in pants that walks in the door. And Granny, there, a friggin' nun. What do ex-nuns do for fun, knock off doctors?"

"You jerk-hole!" Darcie shouted, standing suddenly, her round face red under her Girls Rule baseball cap.

"Darcie, Darcie," her grandmother murmured.

"He *is* a jerk-hole," Lisa agreed. "Accusing a poor little girl like Darcie."

Darcie glared Lisa's way now.

"I'm no little girl, you, you—"

"Darcie." Jean Watkins's voice was firmer now. "Sit down." Darcie sat.

"Man, there're are a lot better suspects than me around," Felix began again. "Look at Natalie, jilted like a homeless hamster before she even friggin' started. And Avis, how do we know what hooey-wooey was really going on between her and Reed. And Lisa and Darcie would kill anything with the wrong equipment below the waist. And Maxwell—"

"Anyway," Lisa went on, as if Felix hadn't spoken. "Everyone knows men are more prone to violence. So that makes figuring this out a lot easier." She stared at each man in the group in turn.

"Lisa," Howie put in gently, "generalizations are just that: generalizations. They can be very hurtful to a specific victim of the generalization." His eyes strayed to Gilda. "For example, um . . ."

"For example," Gilda finished for him, "all wogs are stupid and lazy. There's one for you."

"Wogs?" Darcie asked.

"A racist term," Maxwell Yang explained, raising an eyebrow. "Originally meant 'wily Oriental gentleman,' I think."

"Right you are," Gilda confirmed cheerfully, "Though these days, anyone of color can manage a wog designation, don'cha know?"

"Wow," Darcie murmured. "Cool." I just hoped she wasn't incorporating the exotic slur into her vocabulary.

"Lisa, honey," Natalie broke in. "Not all men are cruel. Lord knows some are, but there's many a good man around if you just look in the right place." And Natalie was currently looking at Lieutenant Perez. The lieutenant had obviously noticed. He wriggled his shoulders and turned his head from her gaze.

"Yes, indeed," Maxwell agreed with a smile. "Lots of winners in this circle."

The lieutenant whipped his head around to stare into Maxwell's suddenly neutral, Asian features.

I resisted the urge to giggle. Whatever Maxwell had meant was lost beneath his Mona Lisa smile.

"Reed was certainly a beautiful man," Avis offered dreamily.

The urge to giggle stopped at my heart. Poor Avis. Hadn't she asked us to identify the murderer? Reed's murderer? What had happened to the original question?

"Yes, he was," Jean assured Avis. She reached for the older woman's hand and held it. "And for the life of me, I can't imagine any reason to kill him."

"As opposed to Dr. Sandstrom?" the lieutenant put in.

"Yes," Jean answered, without hesitation. "Dr. Sandstrom was opinionated, angry, and authoritarian. But Reed was none of those things."

"They were both doctors," Felix muttered, his face still flushed from his encounter with Darcie.

"They both loved gardening," Avis added.

"And they were both men," Natalie reminded us. As if the rest of us might not have noticed.

"What else?" Perez asked.

"They were both . . . um . . . involved in relationships," I offered feebly. "Though neither was married."

"They were both intelligent," Wayne tried. "Both attempting in their own, different way to discourage deer."

"Oh yeah!" Lisa sneered. "Dr. Sandstrom wanted to blow them up. Coffee-can Claymore mines. Real intelligent."

"And that upset you?" Lieutenant Perez prodded.

"Lots of things upset me," Lisa answered carelessly.

"Both had pots of money," Gilda threw in. She smiled for no apparent reason.

Now, there was something I hadn't considered. And I wondered how Gilda knew about the pots. But then, I had a feeling Gilda knew as much as my hairdresser about the postal patrons of Marin County.

"But no one here inherited," Felix countered.

The lieutenant looked at Felix with narrowed eyes. More information that shouldn't have been public.

"Both were attractive in their own way," Maxwell pointed out before the lieutenant could comment on Felix's information.

"Dr. Sandstrom was attractive?" Darcie objected incredulously. "That wickety-wack old man?"

"To some of us, honey," Natalie said, backing Maxwell. "Age is relative. To me, he was a handsome man. And Lord, that vitality." She sighed and shook her head.

Did any of this spell motive?

I glanced out the glass door as I tried to remember something, anything, that might solve these murders. And saw two large brown eyes staring back at me.

"Deer!" I shouted.

Avis was the first on her feet. "Did anyone shut the gates?" she asked.

We all shook our heads guiltily. Had that been Reed's job?

Everyone stood then as a group, moving toward the glass door. The lone deer turned as we got closer, taking to its hooves. But that wasn't enough for the Deerly Abused. Whooping and hollering, we poured out the door, running toward the deer, who was now panicked and charging through the ground cover at high speed.

"Turn!" I screamed. The deer looked up as if he'd heard me, and came back around through the bedding herbs, galloping toward the freedom of the still-open gate. We all turned with the grace of a lynch mob and chased him until he was through the gate to the street. So much for not running after deer.

"Hella tight!" Darcie yelled triumphantly as his tail disappeared into the evening.

"Well done, indeed," Gilda agreed.

Then we were all congratulating each other, and shaking hands, and hugging. All but Lieutenant Perez.

He glared at us, collectively and individually.

"We went as a group," I said, forestalling him.

"Do you have a garden, Officer?" Natalie asked.

"No," Perez answered curtly.

We all exchanged glances. Poor Lieutenant Perez would never understand the deer group. He was right about that. Wayne and I shut the iron gates, and I thought of Reed.

"If you did have a garden, you see, you'd understand," Avis admonished Perez gently.

And then he seemed to soften.

"Okay," he sighed. "Back inside."

"Shoot, the doctor would have liked that," Natalie said once we were sitting down. I guessed she meant Dr. Sandstrom, not Reed Killian.

Lisa Orton sat next to me now. She turned to whisper in my ear. I smelled mint on her breath.

"Would you come to tea, Kate?" she asked. "All my friends are from therapy. I could use an outside friend."

I looked at Wayne on my other side, congratulating Howie on the publication of his manuscript once more. And I nodded quickly. I knew Wayne wasn't invited. He was, after all, a man.

"Motive," Lieutenant Perez commanded.

Groans greeted his commandment, but we all tried.

Misdiagnosis, spurned love, jealousy, money, pure hatred, even deer channeling were discussed.

But no one came to any conclusion. The routing of the deer seemed to be the main event of the evening.

Perez told us he'd stand guard as we all went back to our cars. Avis and Darcie opened the iron gates.

Wayne and I began our careful walk back to my car. I didn't want to step on a body. I didn't want to even see one. We were almost to the Toyota, with Felix gabbling in my ear at each step, when I thought I heard something beyond the sound of cars starting up, something running somewhere in the nursery.

"Darcie must have a reason for accusing me," Felix insisted. "What if she's the murderer?"

"I don't think so, Felix." The sound seemed closer. Was I imagining it?

"Well, how about Granny, Ma Barker, nun-serial murderer?"

I shrugged my shoulders.

"And Maxwell Yang, he's too friggin' smooth for my taste. He's so big he thinks he's in a different time zone, but that still doesn't mean he didn't do it."

I didn't have an answer for him. And I could hear the running sound again. Wayne stiffened by my side.

"Kate," Felix whined. "Why is it that these gonzo potato-brains don't like me?

That question was from the heart. But could I possibly explain civilized behavior to Felix in a few minutes . . . or even a few days?

"Felix—" I began.

And then, in the darkness, the running sound became hoofbeats. A mass of beige came hurtling toward us, resolving itself into a deer as it closed in. A big deer.

Felix never heard it, never saw it. But he must have felt it when the deer's massive body knocked into his side, throwing him to the ground with a thud.

And then all was silent but for the hoofbeats, still running.

"Felix?" I implored as the beige mass continued out the gates. "Speak to me!"

Nineteen

✛

As I bent over Felix's small, slender body, I couldn't believe I was begging him to speak, the man I'd wanted to shut up from the moment I'd met him. But there was Barbara to consider. Barbara, my best friend, who loved Felix.

I squatted closer to his sprawled form, cursing under my breath in the cool night air.

"Felix, get up. There's a friggin' story in it for you," I whispered finally, remembering the magic words.

One of his eyes opened.

"Story?" he mumbled blearily.

"Okay, folks!" a voice boomed out from above me. I went from a squatting position to a sitting one the hard way, onto my tailbone. Lieutenant Perez looked down at Felix and then at me as Wayne reached out to take my hand. "Just what happened here?" the lieutenant demanded.

"Felix got run over by a deer," I explained, as Wayne pulled me up off the hard ground, my tailbone still protesting.

"A deer!" Felix objected, and his other eye opened.

"Wow, way cool," Darcie commented, and then I saw the rest of the audience surrounding us.

Had they been afraid Felix had been murdered? Jean Watkins's face was very serious in the moonlight. I couldn't even see Avis's expression as she moved in back of Jean. The nursery owner was a wraith, or maybe a garden fairy. Gilda was smiling, though. And Lisa's freckled face looked confused. At least that was appropriate.

I didn't see Maxwell, Howie, or Natalie, though. They must have been in the cars I'd heard starting up. At least, I hoped so. Now my mind buzzed more loudly than my tailbone. I swallowed. Could someone have been killed while Felix was dominating everyone else's attention?

"Lieutenant Perez?" I asked urgently. "Did the other three leave?"

I saw instant panic in the lieutenant's eyes. He jerked his head around, searching the shadows.

"Who's missing?" he barked.

"A friggin' deer," Felix answered fuzzily. "It was a big mother, brown, a nut case—"

"Not the deer!" Perez bawled. We all turned to him. It isn't good when the investigating officer gets hysterical.

Perez lowered his voice, grimacing. "Can anyone tell me who has already left?" he asked.

"Natalie Miner drove away," Avis provided quietly. "And so did Maxwell Yang." Avis turned for a moment. "Darcie, did you see Mr. Damon leave?"

"Yeah, the school dude who drives that crummy old Honda, right?"

Avis nodded.

Perez closed his eyes. I figured he was thinking. I hoped he wasn't fainting.

I searched my brain, and ticked off names on my fingers frantically. Natalie, Maxwell, and Howie had left. Gilda, Wayne, Felix, Lisa, Avis, Darcie, and Jean were still here. We were all accounted for. I felt my mind ease back into my body.

"I think that's everyone," I whispered to the lieutenant.

He opened his eyes, big brown eyes finally grateful for my help.

"Hey, are you guys logged off or what?" Felix demanded, sitting up suddenly. His shirt was torn, the side of his arm was scraped, and he was rubbing his head. But he was talking.

"I'm the one who got run over by Super-Deer. Man, that beast must eat iron ingots for breakfast—"

"No, roses," I corrected him.

Felix rubbed his side. "Ha-friggin'-ha," he snarled. "Just you wait till some gonzo deer takes you out, and—"

"Do you need a doctor?" Jean Watkins asked Felix.

Felix looked up at her suspiciously.

"Do you really friggin' care?" he shot back.

"Of course, I do, young man," she replied. "You might have internal injuries."

Felix paled visibly.

"D'ya really think so?" he asked, sounding pitifully un-Felix for a moment.

"Don't worry, you're probably fine," she assured him, bending over for a better look. "But you'd best have a doctor check you out."

"Hey, thanks," Felix murmured, turning his head away shyly. "You really do care."

Jean paused for a moment, and then spoke slowly. "Of course we care," she told Felix. "Isn't that right, Darcie?"

"Aw, Gramma," Darcie replied, squirming in place. I was just glad Jean hadn't asked *me* how I felt about Felix.

"You just need to trust people more," Jean instructed Felix. "If you treat people with respect, they'll return the favor."

Felix looked up at Jean Watkins like a cat who's just discovered the person with the can opener.

"I'll call the paramedics," Avis offered. She began walking to the main building. Then she turned back to Felix. "Now that you've tangled with a deer, you're one of us," she said.

Felix smiled, a real smile. Could Felix be domesticated?

"I'd have joined a lot sooner if I knew deer were such potato-brains," he tried.

"Maybe the deer was in rut," I offered.

"Piece of luck you're not a female, old bean," Gilda threw in. "Never know about the poor blighters' night vision."

Darcie and Lisa joined in a guffaw that could have risen from one mouth.

Felix frowned. The question was emblazoned on his wrinkled forehead. Was he being made fun of?

"Just lie back and enjoy it, Felix," I advised him. "These people are being nice. They like you."

Felix lay back on the ground, his eyes closing. "Thanks, Kate," he whispered.

I couldn't believe I'd heard those words from his mouth.

The paramedics arrived a little while later and declared Felix scraped, banged, and bruised, but probably unbroken and unconcussed. They snickered for a little while about deer muggings and then took Felix off to the hospital to make sure he was really okay.

I told Wayne I'd call Barbara, and then I drove out of the Eldora Nurseries parking lot, glancing at Felix's isolated Chevy in my rearview mirror. It looked lonely.

Wednesday morning, Barbara called me back to tell me that Felix had returned home and was feeling fine. And then she whispered, "Thanks, Kate," herself.

Everything should have been great. Felix wasn't permanently harmed, and he might even be learning social skills. I had a feeling that's what Barbara's thank you was about. But everything wasn't great. Two men were dead, and we still didn't have a clue why.

I resorted to chart-making, my drug of choice for stress. I shoved my stacks of Jest Gifts paperwork off my desk onto a chair. They immediately fell onto the floor. C.C. arrived just in time to roll in them. Groaning, I moved the stacks onto my bookshelves and then returned to the important stuff. I got out my biggest pad of paper and a ruler. Columns and rows, I told myself. Anything can be solved with columns and rows. At the end of each of my neatly aligned rows, I wrote a suspect's name. I even put myself in, but I left Wayne out. There had to be some limits. The column headings were sparse, though. Name, of course. Motive for Dr. Sandstrom's death. Motive for Dr. Killian's death. Then two more columns, for everyone's whereabouts at the time of each death. And then? "Other," I finally wrote.

I was staring at my chart, waiting for inspiration to fill in the rest of the columns, when Wayne walked up behind me. I didn't hear him until he put his big paw on my shoulder. Damn. After I landed in my chair again, I wondered if it had been a mistake to leave him off the suspect list. But then, I was still nervous after the telephone warning.

"Good," he growled.

"Good, what?" I sputtered. "It doesn't tell me anything. I can't fill it in!"

"You will," he assured me.

My mind translated his assurances. He was hoping I'd stick to charts and stay away from live, breathing people. Or dead ones, for that matter. I didn't really blame him.

I was staring at the chart again when he kissed me goodbye, and set off for La Fête à L'Oeil. After the kiss, I decided it *had* been a good decision to exclude him from the suspect list. No one who could kiss like that could kill.

I had just written "spurned woman" in Natalie Miner's row under motive for Dr. Sandstrom's murder, when the phone rang.

I dove for it thankfully. Even if it was someone upset about my wedding, even if it was my mother, it meant I could stop staring at my chart.

"Kate?" The voice on the other end of the line was high and anxious. It wasn't my mother. I tried to match it to a face. "This is Lisa, Lisa Orton. I thought maybe you could come to tea this afternoon. I get Wednesday afternoons off."

"Well . . ." I temporized. I looked around me. Wayne wasn't here to escort me, but was that necessary for Lisa Orton? I tried, but I couldn't begin to feel threatened by Lisa. What could she do to me, share her feelings? "Sure," I said finally.

We set a time and I hung up the phone. I thought about Lisa, aggressive one minute and shy the next. A member of more support groups than most states of the union could probably host. Why the sudden need for tea and sympathy? Did she know something? My fingers tingled. Maybe, just maybe.

I put my chart away and went back to the task of Jest Gifts paperwork until my appointment with Lisa. Who needed charts when you had live, breathing suspects to interrogate?

A few hours and a leftover paté sandwich later, I was ready for tea.

I gave the guard at the gate of Lisa's "community" my name and was allowed in. I just hoped his graciousness would continue if I ever really *needed* to get in. Or out. I parked my old Toyota in Lisa's two-car driveway, and made my way up her walk. At least her front garden had improved since my last visit. The rosebushes had disappeared from the landscape, and blooming fuchsias had magically appeared in their place. There were new ferns too, and blooming irises and daffodils, bordered by sweet alyssum. Either Lisa had a lot of time on her hands for gardening, or she had hired someone to do a lot of work. I suspected the latter. The transformation from flower Bosnia to paradise was too complete to have been accomplished by an amateur. A hummingbird shyly landed on a fuchsia. It was clearly a first date.

Lisa opened one of her double doors and peeked out.

"Kate!" she chirped as if I were an old friend who had surprised her with an unexpected visit.

And then I was in her living room. I'd forgotten how large that room was. And I'd forgotten the marble floors. Great for something, I was sure—maybe roller skating. Cozied up in the corner of the room was a round cherry wood table I hadn't remembered, surrounded by four wing chairs upholstered in maroon velvet. And a flowered china tea service on the table. I sighed, trying to imagine that cozy arrangement in my messy house.

"I made herbal tea," Lisa announced breathlessly. "I figured you'd like it. You do, don't you, Kate?"

I turned to Lisa, thinking it really depended on whether the herbal tea was intrinsically tasty or merely medicinal. There are herbal teas and herbal teas. The medicinal often featured a resemblance to brewed horse sweat. But Lisa's large round eyes were hopeful. I knew she was in her thirties, but her childlike face made it hard to answer honestly.

"I love it," I told her without equivocation.

"Oh, good," she sighed and led me to the table. "And I have cookies and everything. My therapist says I should have more fun, see more friends."

"Well, this looks fun," I tried.

The wing chair was worth the trip, as soft as well . . . velvet, and perfectly proportioned to my body. I sighed as I settled in.

"Perfect," I murmured.

Lisa's face brightened.

"I did this little corner myself," she declared proudly. "I think I could be an interior designer maybe. And I'm tired of being an accountant, but I want to be a psychotherapist too. People suffer—"

The doorbell rang.

Lisa jumped, nearly knocking over her new chair. Then she made the long trek across the marble floor to the double doors.

"Maxwell!" she chirped an instant later.

Was Maxwell Yang another guest for tea? An impromptu one, it appeared.

"Okay for an estrogen-deprived being to drop by?" he asked.

Lisa actually giggled.

"I was visiting an interviewee down the street, and I thought, why not?" he continued. Well, that explained how he got past the guard.

"Kate's here too," Lisa announced as she led Maxwell in.

It seemed as if a flicker marred Maxwell's impish grin for a moment, but then it was back in full-wattage.

"I admire your choice of residence, Lisa," he remarked, surveying the expanse of living room. "The whole deer group could meet here."

"And the deer," I added.

Maxwell laughed, and Lisa followed up a beat later. But something uncomfortable lingered in the air.

Why was Maxwell Yang here? I doubted that the talk show host lacked for friends. And I doubted that he would choose Lisa for one, even if he did. Was he here to investigate? Or—I couldn't stop my mind from wondering as Lisa brought out another flowered teacup—was he here to murder? Maxwell sat across the table from me and winked, almost imperceptibly. Did this mean we were both here in the pursuit of clues?

A cup of herbal tea of the tasty kind and a few oatmeal cookies later, the ambience was comfortable again. Maxwell Yang could tell a story. And he had already told us a few about the guests that came on his show. Suspicion dissolved into laughter as he spoke.

"The cat psychologist was one of the worst nightmares in my entire career," he went on. "The woman proposed to emotionally heal anyone's cat from the audience. So we had a studio full of cat carriers and screaming cats. She chose one young man from the audience at random. He brought up a precious-looking Persian in a basket and handed it to her. The cat jumped out and clawed our guest's face."

"No!" Lisa protested, her child's face lit up in wonder.

"Yes, but that woman was a trouper. She said, 'I sense some hostility here,' and the audience was laughing so hard, they forgot what had just happened."

"Did you ever interview anyone really famous?" Lisa asked.

"Jamie Lee Curtis," he shot back.

"Wow." Lisa's eyes went out of focus. She was probably considering a career in acting now.

"And the mayor," he added, rolling his eyes. "I hate interviewing politicians."

"Because you are one, yourself?" my mouth said before I gave it permission. Maxwell Yang certainly acted like a politician.

"How very perceptive, Ms. Jasper," he replied, doffing an invisible hat my way. "You have it in one. I give speeches, satisfy warring parties, and can be voted out of office on the whim of ratings."

"I'd hate that," Lisa muttered. "People are so stupid."

"There are parts of this job I'm not so fond of," Maxwell admitted, his automatic smile dimming momentarily. "But there's nothing like show business."

And with that, Maxwell Yang rose from our tea table. I rose with him. I wanted to catch him outside to ask him why he had come to Lisa Orton's in the first place. Then I saw the sad look on Lisa's face.

"Thank you, Lisa," I murmured and felt immediately guilty about leaving. This young woman wasn't really someone I wanted as a friend. If Maxwell had used her, so had I. I added hastily, "Your tea and your cookies and your furniture are all just wonderful. I had a really nice time." Lisa smiled.

Maxwell did me one better. He kissed her hand. Then she really smiled. I wondered if he felt as guilty as I did. But I never got a chance to ask him. My goodbyes lasted longer than his and I could only watch as his Mercedes pulled out of Lisa's driveway while I stood in her open doorway.

"Take care," I told Lisa.

"I will," she promised me.

All the way home, I fretted about Maxwell. What did he hide under his frivolous demeanor? In our whole "conversation," nothing personal had been said except when I'd challenged him about being a politician. Ambition motivated him, I was sure. But what did that mean? Was Maxwell Yang a murderer?

The phone rang the instant I walked in my door.

I stared at it as the answering machine picked up.

"This is Avis," she said after the beep.

I scooped up the phone before Avis began another sentence.

"Avis?" I asked. "Are you all right?" It was too easy to forget what Reed's death might have done to her.

"Um . . . I'm fine, Kate," she answered.

I waited. She had called me, after all.

"I wondered if you might be able to do me a favor. I think it's a positive thing. I hope so, but I know I shouldn't really ask. Still, I don't know who else—"

"What favor?" I stopped her. She had to be on some kind of medication.

"Oh," she murmured. "Sorry for rambling. Um, my daughter, Olive, has got a line on a job for a clothing wholesaler, but she needs recommendations."

"Will she go live somewhere else if she gets the job?" I asked.

"Yes," Avis whispered. I thought I heard her giggle. "Now, Kate, you don't have to do this. But I did wonder . . . I mean you're a wholesaler. A recommendation from you might carry some weight—"

"I'll do it," I told her. Years of business had taught me the skills to recommend anyone. Already I was reworking Avis's daughter's personality in my mind. Olive wasn't aggressive, she was enterprising. She wasn't nosy, she was interested in people. She wasn't nasty, she was good with words. And then, there was her boundless energy. Any good wholesaler ought to be able to translate my words well enough.

"Thank you, Kate," Avis murmured.

"And here's to your empty nest," I told her, wishing I hadn't used those words the minute they were out. "Avis, are you all right, really?" I asked.

"I am really," she declared in a much stronger voice. "Amazingly better. I know it will take a while, but Reed is fine wherever he is, I just know it. And I'm an old war horse. I can take it."

"You're a lot stronger than you look," I told her.

"Thank you, Kate. Not very many people notice."

We talked a little while longer, about gardening and food and life, and then we hung up. Avis really would be all right, I realized. I took in a deep breath. I finally believed it. Avis had enjoyed her short time with Reed. I was glad for her.

I looked out at the sunshine of the day. There was a lesson here. Before I did any more Jest Gifts paperwork, I would enjoy the sunshine.

I grabbed a glass of apple juice and walked out onto the deck, settling into a comfortable old deck chair and surveying my property. Sunshine lit the branches of the trees and warmed my shoulders. Birds argued. Traffic sounded from the main road. Life in all its glorious forms surrounded me.

I looked at the far end of my deck. The few roses that had been left in the rearmost terra-cotta pots had now been snipped as neatly as the hair of an insurance salesman.

TWENTY

꙳

The sunshine seemed to cool as my own temperature flared. They hadn't left me one bloom, not one! All right, so maybe I should have put netting or wire over the roses. But a rose is a rose is a rose. And a rose in prison just isn't.

Enough, I told myself, and clumped back inside.

No more Jest Gifts for me today. No more charts. No more apple juice on the deck. The afternoon wasn't over yet. I was going investigating. If I couldn't find the guilty deer who had murdered my roses, maybe I could find a guilty human who had murdered two doctors.

But who needed investigating?

I thought of my chart. There was one motive, one woman. Natalie Miner.

Twenty minutes later I drove up to Natalie's real estate office, which was housed in an old Victorian in downtown Abierto. I walked up a short path of cobblestones after parking on the street. The landscaping was sparse, a few rosemary bushes and vinca vines. There was no evidence of the kind of garden that would be plagued by deer. But maybe Natalie saved her more extensive gardening efforts for her home.

Inside the office, it was a different story. No computer cubicles marred the coziness of Natalie Miner's Pennsylvania Dutch motif. Rocking chairs, quilts, even stenciled rafters, gave her workplace the feeling of home. A calico cat lounged in a window seat. And the smell, was it apple-cinnamon? Either Natalie was a truly cozy woman or a fiendishly intelligent real estate agent. Or both. Who wouldn't want to buy a fairy-tale house after a visit to her office?

"Kate!" Natalie cried out. "Lord, it's good to see you."

"You too," I replied, and I meant it.

Natalie was looking better today. Her heart-shaped face was expertly made up, her blond, spiral curls were tousled perfectly, and her rosebud mouth was in full bloom.

She stepped my way on high heels and planted a kiss on my cheek. I caught a whiff of cigarette smoke underlying the apple-cinnamon scent.

"Richard, Zachary," she lilted, introducing a couple of young men sitting behind rough-hewn desks. "This is Kate Jasper from my deer group."

Both young men smiled my way, gorgeously. Could Natalie have been as desperate for Dr. Sandstrom's love as my chart theorized? Not with Richard and Zachary around. I tried to banish the lewd thought from my mind. Just because Natalie employed two much younger, handsome men didn't mean she had romantic designs on them.

"Hello, Ms. Jasper," both men greeted me simultaneously. They sounded like schoolboys.

No, Natalie would prefer a more mature man. I was sure of it after hearing the boyish voices. Almost sure.

"Natalie . . ." I began, hesitantly. I had considered feigning interest in new housing, but decided against it. "Could we talk about the . . . the deaths? I just can't help feeling—"

"Oh hon, of course we can," she agreed. "I can't stop thinking about them either. Both such attractive men. Dear God, what a waste."

Her eyes flicked back to Richard and Zachary. Maybe Natalie appreciated the male species of any age. There was nothing wrong with that, I reminded myself sternly.

"So you found Dr. Sandstrom attractive?" I prompted. I was remembering the grouchy doctor's narrow features and cold eyes under his aviator glasses.

"Oh, Lord, yes," Natalie whispered. "You see, he was such a *good* man."

"Good?" I was finding "good" an even more difficult adjective to apply to the doctor than "attractive."

"Oh my, yes. He set up vaccination programs in South America, you know, and AIDS awareness programs here. Shoot, he took patients for free who were without insurance. All kinds of things—"

"How did you know so much about him?" I asked.

Natalie blushed beneath her makeup.

"I had a friend who went out with him after his wife passed on," she admitted. "It didn't work out for her, poor thing, so she told me I might as well give it a try, you know, romantically. Lord, it sounds like hand-me-downs, doesn't it?" Natalie smiled nostalgically.

I smiled back. It was hard not to like this woman. Just as hard as it was not to like her office.

"Oh shoot, I haven't even offered you a seat," she apologized and pointed. I sat down in an old cane-backed rocking chair. A cannonball landed in my lap instantly. The calico cat.

"Jezebel," Natalie scolded. She looked up at me. "The poor little thing does love a warm lap. Do you mind, Kate?"

I shook my head. Jezebel was already starting to purr. I stroked her silky fur and wondered who had named her.

"Yes," Natalie went on, "Dr. Sandstrom was a good man, too good to have been murdered." Her eyes misted up.

I panicked. It was all over for her mascara if she actually cried. "What did you know about Reed Killian?" I cut in quickly.

Natalie shrugged her shoulders, taking a seat across from me. "Not a thing anyone else doesn't know," she shot back, tilting her head as she looked my way. "I truly just can't imagine what could have driven anyone to such ungodly acts." She sighed, and a sable-brown Burmese cat appeared from nowhere and leapt into *her* lap. Was there a cat for every client in this place? Probably.

"Was Reed a good man?" I tried again.

"Hon, he was a doctor," Natalie answered after some thoughtful stroking of the Burmese. "Where I come from, doctors usually are good men."

We petted our respective cats in silence a little longer. I wondered what Natalie was thinking now. And I wondered what place she came from where doctors were held in such high regard. Her brow was furrowed, no smile on her face now.

"Do you know why they died, Kate?" she finally asked.

"Not yet," I whispered.

I left Natalie's office once I'd lifted the calico from my lap.

Back in my Toyota again, I sat for a while, the gears in my mind turning but not meshing. Was Natalie Miner the woman she appeared to be? If so, I didn't think she was a murderer. But who was? I wondered if it would help to know more about Dr. Sandstrom. And Dr. Killian. It couldn't hurt, I decided, and aimed my car in the direction of Searle Sandstrom's office first.

Dr. Sandstrom's office didn't smell of apple-cinnamon when I stepped into the waiting room; it smelled of antiseptic. But then, it didn't reek of cigarette smoke either. And the salmon-and-teal decor was easy on the eyes. I wondered if Dr. Sandstrom had chosen the decor. He'd had a garden, maybe he'd had an aesthetic nature too. I shook my head. Coffee-can Claymore land mines didn't bring art to mind. Or goodness to mind for that matter. Or attractiveness.

"May I help you?" the young woman behind the desk asked me. At least she wasn't crying today.

"I'd like to see Dr. Yamoda about Dr. Sandstrom," I told her.

"Why?" she wanted to know.

"You may not remember me, but I was a member of Dr. Sandstrom's deer group," I said. And then her face pinched. Damn. Maybe she was going to cry.

But all she said was, "I'll ask the doctor."

After twenty minutes, a young, painfully thin woman left, looking unhappy. I hoped her illness wasn't serious. But before I could indulge in morbid fantasies, Dr. Yamoda strode into the waiting room.

"Ms. Jasper," she greeted me, her face lost in a frown.

"Dr. Yamoda," I returned her greeting, standing so as not to be intimidated. It almost worked.

"What do you want now?" she demanded.

"I want to know how a man who made land mines to kill deer could be a good man," I challenged her. "I want to know why he was murdered."

Dr. Yamoda's shoulders slumped, ever so slightly. She jerked her hand back and fingered her glossy black knot of hair for a moment.

Then she ordered, "Come with me."

I followed her to her office and was once again seated in the patient's chair. The rose that had been on her desk in memory of Dr. Sandstrom was gone now. Only the tastefully appointed room remained.

"Did Dr. Sandstrom pick the color scheme for your office?" I asked.

Dr. Yamoda smiled. And she might have been a different person.

"He did," she murmured, and I heard the tender sadness in her voice. "I wouldn't know white from ivory, but he had an eye for color, an eye for beauty."

I waited for more. It wasn't long in coming.

"You asked how the man could kill deer," she reminded me, strength returning to her voice. "Dr. Sandstrom's wife had a rose garden. She was in ad design when she was healthy, but you wouldn't believe the time she spent on that garden." Dr. Yamoda shook her head. "It was perfect in color, in design, in fragrance. And then she died. Ovarian cancer. Can you imagine how it was for a doctor to watch his wife die of cancer? Dr. Sandstrom changed. He was angry. And he took over his wife's garden, his shrine to her, I think. And the deer desecrated it. He couldn't kill the cancer cells that drained the life from his wife, but he could kill the deer." Dr. Yamoda bent toward me, pinning my eyes with hers. "Do you understand now?"

"Yes," was all I could say.

After a long moment, the doctor asked me, "Do you have any more questions?"

I almost said no, but I did have more questions. And knowing the goodness that had resided somewhere in Dr. Sandstrom gave me all the more motivation to ask them.

"Do you know who his heirs were?" I tried. I wanted confirmation from more than one source.

"His son and daughter," Dr. Yamoda shot back. "And don't look for a motive there. They're both physicians. No money problems. And they're both in shock over their father's death."

I couldn't leave it alone. This woman knew things.

"Were they acquainted with any of the members of the deer group?" I prodded.

Dr. Yamoda just shook her head.

"I can't tell you no for certain, but I can tell you this. The doctor's children loved him. They needed him more than his money. First, their mother, then their father."

I just nodded. I couldn't ask her any more questions. It was too painful. But that didn't stop her from asking *me* questions.

"I want to know who killed him," she told me. "Are you any further along in your investigation?"

"No, I'm sorry," was all I could answer. The answer was as painful as my questions had been.

"Is there any way I can help?" she pressed.

I shook my head, apologizing again.

"Damn it!" she barked and hit her desk with her fist. "There must be something I can do."

"There may be, later," I told her quickly.

She stared at me for what seemed a long time.

"Let me know," she ordered, and then turned her face away from mine.

It was all I could do to keep from running out the door of her office. So many people to see; so many people to disappoint.

After a few minutes of deep breathing, I looked up the address of Reed's office in the phone book I carried in my car. I wished I done it earlier, because Reed's office was back in Abierto. And I *was* going to visit his office. I made fists of my hands. Yes. I could do it. I just hoped there was no one like Dr. Yamoda there to upset.

I had learned something, I told myself as I drove back to Abierto. Dr. Sandstrom had been a complicated man, with his share of aesthetics, anger, and goodness. Now I had to figure if it was one of those attributes that had gotten him killed.

Dr. Reed Killian's workplace was not salmon and teal. It was glass and metal. OSTROW, KILLIAN AND FELDMAN, the plaque on the front door read. I opened it to a reception area filled with more glass and metal. There was no fragrance of apple-cinnamon here. Even the antiseptic smell was missing. I saw a glass counter, computers, metal sculptures, and two stylishly dressed women busily tapping keyboards.

"May I help you?" one of the women asked, standing. She was young, with auburn hair and large, green eyes. She might have been a model. But then, a plastic surgeon had to have beautiful employees, just as much as Natalie Miner's office had to be cozy. If nothing else, I was learning about marketing today.

"I've come about Dr. Killian," I told her.

She grimaced, then tried to smooth her features once more.

"Dr. Killian is no longer available," she informed me. "But I can recommend Doctors Ostrow and Feldman."

"No," I corrected her. "I've come to talk about Reed Killian's death."

That was too much for the young woman.

She sank into her chair with a thud that didn't match her stylish ensemble.

"Who are you?" she asked, her eyes widening.

"I was a member of Reed's deer group," I told her. "I'm trying to find out who murdered him."

Tears rushed to the young woman's eyes. "Reed, he was a

wonderful man. A true gentleman," she mumbled through her tears.

Where had I heard this before? Avis, that's where. Was this woman one of Reed's many lovers?

"I'm married now, but Reed . . ." She swallowed the rest of her words as if swallowing the sorrow his death had brought her.

"I have a list of the deer group members," I told her. "Can you tell me if any of them were patients?"

"We're not allowed to—" she began.

"For Reed," I pressured.

It worked. I recited names and she checked files. Finally, she shook her head. "None of them—"

"Who are you talking to, Cindy?" a voice behind me barked.

The man who owned the voice wasn't a good advertisement for plastic surgery. He was red-faced, with small, close-set eyes that made his face look mean. Or maybe his face just reflected his temperament. For that, he'd need more than plastic surgery.

"Just a friend of Reed's, Doctor," Cindy answered, lowering her eyes.

"You haven't been gossiping, have you?"

"No, Dr. Ostrow," Cindy assured him.

I shook my head in confirmation. She hadn't been gossiping, just sharing confidential information.

"Come with me, Ms. . . . Ms. . . ."

"Jasper," I supplied.

I went with him into a sterile room with comfortable black leather chairs in front of and behind his glass-and-metal desk. I'd barely sunk into my chair before the doctor began to talk.

"Reed Killian has never been anything but trouble. The man cared more about skiing than he did about plastic surgery," Dr. Ostrow began. "Not to mention hang-gliding, traveling, gardening, music, womanizing—anything but his work." And he had prohibited *Cindy* from gossiping?

"Then why was he made a partner?" I asked quietly. I wanted to keep the man on a roll.

"Because of his father," Dr. Ostrow told me. "Man's dead now. Now, *he* was a surgeon and a helluva good one. He put up the money for Reed's partnership before he died. But Reed never took his good luck seriously. He just floated through life, like . . . like, I don't know, a feather or something!"

"Did he have . . . relations with his female patients?" I prodded.

"God, I hope not," Dr. Ostrow said. He sank back into his own chair, his face going from red to a mild green. "Our firm is a professional one, at least now."

If there was someone with a motive for murdering Reed, I was sitting in front of him. But he hadn't been in the deer group.

"Did you happen to know anyone in the Deer-Abused Support Group that Reed was teaching?" I asked hopefully.

"Of course not," Dr. Ostrow retorted. "I'm a busy man. I do not indulge in hobbies."

"Jerry!" another voice burst in from behind me. "Cindy said there was some investigator here . . ."

Then the owner of the voice saw me. He was a short, slender man with matinee-idol features.

"Dr. Feldman," he introduced himself and extended his hand. I shook it. Somehow, a man with those looks shouldn't have had clammy hands, but he did. "And you are?"

"Kate Jasper," I told him. Name, rank, and serial number.

Dr. Feldman sidled up closer to me, and I smelled the distinct scent of marijuana. Apparently Reed Killian hadn't been the only partner causing problems for Dr. Ostrow. Were Dr. Feldman's good looks enough to get him past his all too pungent drug habit?

"Well, Ms. Jasper," Dr. Feldman said, "I'm sure Jerry and Cindy have told you all you need to know about Reed and his association with our firm—"

"Actually, I have a few questions for you," I put in.

"I'm afraid I just don't have time," Feldman told me, glancing at his wristwatch as if he'd just now noticed it.

"Reed loved gardening," I murmured, smiling. "Weed seems more in your line."

Dr. Feldman stiffened, and the scent of perspiration mingled with that of marijuana.

"Just what are you implying?"

"Nothing, just that I'd like a few answers."

I had his attention now. As Dr. Ostrow made blustering noises from across the desk, I recited the names of the deer group members again.

"Do you know any of these people?" I asked sweetly, adding, "I can always check, you know."

"No, I don't!" Dr. Feldman burst out. Then he closed his eyes, opened them again, and smiled, an advertisement for good DNA. Finally, he turned with deliberate grace and swept back out of the office.

On my own way out of Ostrow, Killian and Feldman, I nodded encouragingly at Cindy and reminded myself never to even consider plastic surgery.

But I still didn't know who had killed Dr. Sandstrom or Dr. Killian.

I pulled into my driveway, depressed by the day's interrogative haul. Depressed that Wayne's car wasn't in the driveway. I was walking up the steps to my deck when I saw Maxwell Yang at my door.

I was alone, I realized, alone with a suspect. For some reason, Maxwell Yang's lack of irrational characteristics made him seem all the more dangerous a personality. I stared briefly at his impish face and wondered what all the smiling cost him. My fight or flight indicators pointed toward flight: sweaty hands, dry mouth, nervous belly. But how do you flee your own home?

"Been waiting long?" I asked instead, glancing down to make sure Maxwell wasn't carrying a blunt object, and hoping he wouldn't notice.

"I was just about to ring the bell," Maxwell answered, his smile deepening. He *had* noticed.

"Oh, Wayne should be home soon," I lied brightly.

"Ah," Maxwell replied. "Then we can talk."

So I opened my house to him, a possible murderer.

Before long, we were seated, in opposing swinging chairs. Maxwell didn't want any tea. He wanted information.

"I know you're investigating," he began. His habitual smile wavered. "And so am I."

"Why?" I demanded.

"Dr. Sandstrom . . ." Maxwell sighed. Was he really at a loss for words? A man who made his living with words? "He could be abrasive, but he was a good man—"

There was that word again. "Good."

"And I was once an investigative journalist, a competent one, I hope. I can't just let his death, his and Reed Killian's slide by." He bent forward from his swinging chair. "You, of all people, should understand."

I surrendered to his logic, if it was logic. Because I couldn't let the deaths slide by either.

"What have you learned?" I asked.

Maxwell seemed to relax. He pushed off with his feet and let his chair swing gently back and forth.

"I asked a couple of investigators that work for the show to check out Dr. Sandstrom's patients," he told me. "They'll start on Killian's tomorrow. As far as Sandstrom went, they dug up a few disgruntled patients, people who weren't happy with the doctor's down-to-earth approach. He'd been sued more than once for telling people they were hypochondriacs, for instance."

"Any tie-in with a member of our group?" I prompted eagerly.

Maxwell shook his head. "None that they can uncover, and these investigators are good at their jobs."

"Any significant suits, deaths?" I pushed on.

Maxwell shook his head again. So much for investigators. So much for doctors. So much for Maxwell.

"Why were you at Lisa's today?" I said, changing the subject. "Did she ask you there?"

Maxwell laughed. "No, she didn't," he admitted. "And I

wasn't just in the neighborhood either. The guy at the gate recognized me from my show and let me in. I suppose there was some intelligence to his decision. He knew who I was." He looked me in the eye. "How about you?"

"Lisa invited me to tea," I explained, feeling suddenly defensive.

"Tea," he murmured. "Quaint."

"Lisa is . . ." I struggled for a word.

"Strange," Maxwell supplied.

"Maybe," I conceded. There was something about Lisa's childlike nature that brought out a protective streak in me.

"Well, aren't we all?" he murmured, and was out of his chair before I could ask him any more questions. In fact, he was out of my front door before I even had a chance to say good-bye.

I wasn't sure if I was disappointed or relieved when I heard him drive off. I was still trying to decide a few moments later when the doorbell rang.

I approached my door cautiously, opening it a few inches.

Lieutenant Perez stood on my doorstep, looking in, his beautiful brown eyes desperate.

Twenty-one

I didn't want to disappoint one more person. So I invited Lieutenant Perez in and told him everything I knew. It was only as I spoke that I realized how little that really was.

"Dr. Sandstrom's kids inherit," I began as he sat on the denim couch. I lowered my own, suddenly tired body into a swinging chair. "But his kids don't seem to have motives or any connections to anyone in the deer group."

"We knew that," the lieutenant informed me glumly.

"Oh." I stared down at my hands, unable to look the lieutenant in the eye.

C.C. came galloping into the room with a meow on her little lizard lips. Then she stopped in her tracks to stare at the lieutenant. Was it love?

"Dr. Sandstrom has been sued by patients," I tried again. "But none of them have any apparent connection to anyone in the group either."

"Right," the lieutenant murmured. Now he was staring at *his* hands.

C.C. rubbed up against his ankles.

I sighed. Should I give him the personal stuff I'd learned? Obviously, his men could, and had checked out who inherited, and who was suing, and who had records for murder, and . . . whatever. He wanted something else from me.

"Reed liked women," I offered hesitantly. "He, he . . ."

I couldn't tell him about Avis.

"Your friend Ms. Eldora has disclosed her relationship with Reed Killian," Perez assured me. "Don't worry." That was kind of him.

C.C. looked up at the lieutenant, silently begging to sit in his lap. He ignored her. I could have told him that wasn't enough to stop a cat like C.C., but he'd probably find out soon enough.

"I think Reed's had a lot of affairs, but all the women were happy," I went on. "The receptionist at his office, for one."

"Any connection to the deer group?" Perez asked, his eyes suddenly alive. I felt my own pulse speed up for a moment, till I thought out my answer.

"I doubt she has any connection. And anyway, she's married now."

"Marriage doesn't always stop a woman." Now his eyes were on mine.

I squinted. There was an insinuation in his words, but I couldn't quite make it out. I wasn't—Then I flushed. Right, I *was* a married woman now. That's what he meant.

"Well, *I* certainly wasn't interested in Reed," I fired back. The lieutenant was still looking at me. "Listen, Reed's partner, Dr. Ostrow, didn't like him."

The lieutenant tilted his head. "That's interesting," he said. "Any connection to the—"

But his inevitable question about the deer group was cut off by C.C.'s leap into his lap. She *was* in love. But Lieutenant Perez definitely wasn't. He reached for a gun I hadn't realized he was carrying as she landed, panic in his eyes for a moment.

"She's a cat," I reminded him, hoping he wouldn't shoot.

"Right," he muttered and reholstered his gun while C.C. got down to some serious thigh-clawing. I was surprised he didn't reach for the gun again. I knew what those sharp little claws felt like.

"I don't think Dr. Ostrow was connected to the group," I plodded on. Then I got a little braver. After all, this man was intimidated by my cat. Of course, *I* was intimidated by my cat. "Natalie Miner had a crush on Dr. Sandstrom," I offered.

"So I've noticed." Distaste showed in the lieutenant's handsome face. "She doesn't try to hide it."

"Did you know that Felix Byrne and Maxwell Yang were patients of Dr. Sandstrom's?" I tried.

He only nodded. C.C purred and nuzzled his waistband.

"Maxwell's investigating too," I added.

"Now that I didn't know," the lieutenant murmured. He straightened his shoulders. I pushed off in my chair, swinging back and forth, unaccountably pleased by my one bit of new information. I could feel warmth as I passed in and out of the window's slanting light.

"Why's Yang investigating?" he asked.

I stopped swinging and started squirming. I hadn't meant to get Maxwell into any kind of trouble.

"I think he felt some kind of affection for his doctor," I answered finally.

"Not very many people did."

"No," I argued. "I've talked to a lot of people, and for all the unpleasantness the doctor caused in the deer group, he was well-loved by the people he worked with."

"Hrmphh."

I took that to mean the lieutenant didn't believe me.

"Have you talked to his partner, Dr. Yamoda?" I asked. "She thought he was great."

"So she says."

I opened my mouth to argue again, but gave up. How could I explain the mixed feelings Dr. Sandstrom had provoked?

"All right," I admitted. "A lot of people don't like doctors. A lot of people in the deer group didn't like doctors."

"Who?" the lieutenant asked quickly.

"Oh, Jean Watkins and her granddaughter. And Lisa Orton."

"That doesn't sound like a lot. That sounds like a few."

"Gilda Fitch," I added, remembering her words at the veterinarian's. C.C. mewled as if remembering the place, if not the person.

"But then again," I pointed out, "if you had to classify people who didn't like doctors, you'd probably end up with half the population in that classification."

"That's for sure," Perez agreed. I had a feeling I knew what half of the population he belonged in.

"So what about you guys?" I asked, peering at him sideways. "Did you find out anything?"

"Oh, loads," he answered. Was that sarcasm? "Anyone could have hit either of them. No particular strength was needed. And almost everyone was a gardener. Strong arms. The murderer was right-handed." He paused provocatively. "But then, everyone in your group was right-handed.

"I didn't know that," I whispered, amazed that I had missed something so elementary.

"That reporter friend of yours is a P.I.A.," he added, his olive skin darkening.

"A P.O.W?" I asked, confused.

"No ma'am, a P.I.A., pain in the ass."

"Oh, right." It was my turn to be unsurprised.

"Any reason your friend would kill the two doctors?" he asked.

"Felix?" I don't know why I was astounded, but it was a stretch from P.I.A. to murderer, and one I was sure Felix could never make. "Believe me, Felix could only talk you to death. He doesn't have the stomach for violence. He fainted over both bodies."

"And he was right there on top of both bodies," Perez shot back.

My adrenaline started to pump for Felix's sake.

"Come on, we were all there—"

The doorbell cut off my defense. That was good. I didn't want to get into the habit of defending Felix.

Actually, I didn't want to get in the habit of anything to do with Felix, I decided as I opened my door. Because of course it was Felix on my doorstep.

"Hey, howdy hi," he greeted me, sliding through the doorway with his mouth moving, never noticing I already had a visitor. "So, Sherlock, how's the friggin' sleuth-the-truth going. And don't give me any gonzo excuses. I know you're probably trippin' on the murderer right now. And those potato-heads at the Abierto cop shop are sitting on their duck bottoms, diddlin'—"

Felix stopped as he stared at the man sitting on my couch.

Lieutenant Perez smiled evilly. A chill went down my spine. Or maybe it was just the exhaust from Felix's gasp.

"Mr. Byrne, just the man I wanted to see," Perez announced in a voice out of an Alfred Hitchcock film.

"Hey, yeah, well—" Felix tried.

"Come to confess?" the lieutenant asked conversationally.

Felix's face paled, his luxurious mustache dark against his skin.

"Hey, man," he replied. "You're the friggin' public servant around here. You can't say spooky junk like that."

"I just did," the lieutenant pointed out. "If you confess, it'll go easier on you."

"What is this?" Felix demanded. "A friggin' *Dragnet* episode? I haven't done anything. You some kinda skinny Gestapo or what?"

"What," Perez answered calmly and smiled again.

"Why do you geeks hate me so much anyway?" Felix whined. "Just cause your captain is missing a few bars from his sheet music—"

"The police department doesn't hate anyone, Mr. Byrne. We only investigate . . . and suspect."

"But why me?" Felix's voice was a few octaves above mine now. "I haven't done a friggin'—"

"You live in an apartment, Mr. Byrne," the lieutenant cut in. "Where's your garden?"

"I don't have any stupid garden. I just—"

"Then why were you at the deer group?"

But he didn't even give Felix a chance to answer.

"We've checked the records," he went on. "You've never bought a plant from Eldora Nurseries. Had you ever even been there before the night of the murder?"

"I don't know, man—"

"Did you ever even see a deer before the one that mowed you down in the parking lot?"

"Deer, holy socks! I've seen deer—

"But not in your garden."

"I told you, I don't have a friggin' garden!" Felix's skin wasn't pale anymore, it was red. And his fists were clenched.

"So why were you at the Eldora Nurseries Thursday evening Deer-Abused Support Group?"

A long silence followed. Felix breathed in and out of his nostrils like an asthmatic yoga practitioner. Finally, he spoke.

"Like I said, I don't have a garden." He paused and looked my way. "I just thought that since Kate was there—"

I gave him a warning glance. If he said, "Typhoid Mary of Murder," he was a dead man. He seemed to get the message psychically. Maybe Barbara was rubbing off on him.

"—that it would be fun to be in class with her," he finished off feebly.

Perez shook his head sadly, as if arresting Felix would be a great sorrow to him.

"Or did you want to be in the class with your former doctor?" he demanded once he'd finished the head-shaking.

Felix's skin color returned to paper-white. He groaned. I had a feeling he hadn't told Perez that Dr. Sandstrom had been his personal doctor. I just hoped I hadn't been the one to spill that secret. Hadn't Perez said he'd already known?

"You must remember," the lieutenant plodded on, "Dr. Sandstrom, the doctor you argued with."

Felix's skin went even a shade lighter. I looked at the floor. Was I going to have to catch him if he fainted? I considered interceding on his behalf, but I figured it would just rile the lieutenant.

"Jeez Louise, that was just a little disagreement, you know?" Felix laughed unconvincingly. He sounded like a turkey being choked. "No Titanic thing, man. Just a question of medical approaches. Some of these doctors don't have a friggin' clue, and when you call them on it they get testy. That's all."

"The witnesses said *you* were the one who got 'testy.' "
Perez paused. "In fact, the witnesses said you were screaming
at the doctor. That you had to be escorted out."

I looked at Felix. He hadn't told me about the escort. Dr.
Yamoda?

"Listen, you turnip-brain," Felix challenged. "Two can play
your game. What if I write an article about your looney tunes
boss—?"

"All we have to do is nab you as a suspect," the lieutenant
responded calmly. "And believe me, we could, just on the
evidence we have now. You won't be writing much then. The
only reason I'm holding off is that your friend Ms. Jasper
doesn't believe you could commit murder." He shook his head
sadly again. "But with these nasty insinuations, I just don't
know."

"You can't do that," Felix told him, but it came out as a
whisper.

"Why not?" the lieutenant asked, smiling.

"This is America."

"No kidding."

"Kate," Felix whined

"What?" I asked.

"He's not being fair, Kate. Tell him."

"You're not being fair," I told the lieutenant.

But Lieutenant Perez just smiled and stood, the smile wavering as C.C. tried to retain her place on his pants leg with
her claws. C.C. lost in the end, and turned to leave the room,
her tail high with displeasure.

The lieutenant left too, but not without one last parting shot
at Felix.

"We'll be watching," he warned, and then he marched
through the still open doorway and closed the door carefully
behind him.

"Whoa, Kate, that guy is trippin' gonzo," Felix started in
the moment the door closed. He staggered to the sofa to sit
where Lieutenant Perez had. He was sweating now. And he
had the appropriate scent to go with it. Eau de Terror.

"I told you, they were all flipped," he resumed after he dropped onto the denim surface. "Me, why me?"

"Felix, can't you see he's just goading you?" I replied angrily. I wasn't sure who I was angry at, Felix or the lieutenant. Both, I decided. "You shouldn't have ever said anything about his boss. That's why he hates you."

"But, Kate, you heard him. He'd put me in a cell with some seven-foot-tall rapist who takes his orders from the spirit of Attila the Hun or something and—"

"Felix, stop it!" I ordered.

Felix looked at me, and opened his mouth again.

The phone rang just as I was going to put my hands over my ears.

I picked it up without even waiting for the machine to kick in.

"Maxwell Yang here," a soothing, calm voice greeted me. I could have sang my thanks for the pure contrast to Felix's current bleating. But I didn't have a chance.

"Did your police friend tell you anything relevant?" Maxwell asked before I could even breathe.

"Nothing," I answered. "Except that we're all right-handed." I was glad I could be honest. There was nothing to hold back. "How'd you know Lieutenant Perez was here?" I asked.

"He was driving in as I was driving out," Maxwell told me.

I wondered how he recognized the lieutenant's unmarked car, but I was too tired to ask.

"Perez wasn't there to harass you?" Maxwell inquired smoothly.

Was this gallantry?

"No," I answered briefly. In spite of the lieutenant's handling of Felix, a sense of loyalty kept me from telling Maxwell that a representative of the Abierto Police Department had come to me for help.

Maxwell heard the blankness of my answer. I could feel it in his own silence over the line.

"It's okay," he declared finally. "I don't have to know everything. I just like to."

I laughed. "Me too, I guess."

"Kate, I'm sorry to press."

He sounded so sincere. Too sincere.

"No problem," I assured him and hung up, after promising to call if I had more ideas.

The minute I sat back down in the swinging chair, Felix started in on the Abierto police, specifically Captain Thorton.

"The old looney tunes is totally bonkers, man," he insisted. "It all started when his freakin' house slid off the hill in a mudslide. Right off into the rain, kersplat! Then his spousal unit split and left him in the mud. And then he blew a burglary investigation big time. But the people who work for him are trying to protect his butt, going friggin' Watergate, man. Won't let anyone near him, for fear they'll find out the head of the police department is a nut case."

"I knew that," I said, doing my best to imitate Lieutenant Perez. He scared Felix. I didn't.

"Whaddaya mean, you knew?" Felix objected. "What are you, Barbara?"

"I wish I were Barbara," I whined. It was definitely my turn to complain. "I've talked to everyone, and everyone's partners and receptionists, and I still don't have a clue. Not one!"

"Holy moly, Kate, don't get your wedgie in a twist," Felix ordered. "You're not in trouble. I'm the one that's in friggin' trouble. With a capital friggin' *T*—"

"Felix, do you ever think of anyone but yourself?" I asked. I was truly curious.

"Huh?" he replied.

"Two men are dead. What about them?"

"Um, okay, I'll bite," he tried. "What about them?"

"Felix, this isn't a knock-knock joke!"

"But, Kate—"

It must have been the word "knock." Someone started knocking on the door before Felix could get in any more trouble.

I took a deep, cleansing breath, choked, and answered the door.

Gilda Fitch stood outside, dressed in a post office uniform, carrying my mail and a package.

"Gilda?" I whispered.

"Rather," she replied. "Don't look so thick, old bean. I am a postal carrier, don'cha know?"

"Not mine, you're not," I told her. I knew my postal carrier. I gave him a tip every Christmas. And he had a beard. Gilda didn't.

"I'm not your *regular* carrier," Gilda offered. She grinned. Her expression didn't make me feel any better. "Your regular chap's got the flu. I got you on the overtime list. Dratted nuisance, in the midst of a murder and everything, but there you are."

"I am?"

"What are you doing here?" Felix asked from behind me. Directly behind me. Kate Jasper, human shield.

"Mail delivery service," Gilda answered, handing me my mail and the package. "New thing you have in the States, what?"

"Would you like to sit down or anything?" I finally asked, primordial hostess instincts kicking in.

"No, but thanks, old bean. Neither rain nor sleet nor snow, you know the drill. Well, cheerio."

And then she turned and trotted back down the stairs.

I closed the door slowly behind her. What would she have done if Felix hadn't been with me? She must have known it was my house. My name was on the mail . . . and the package. My regular carrier always brought the packages to the door too, it was true. But—

"How long has friggin' Hail Britannia been delivering your mail?" Felix asked, still behind me.

I turned to him. "Never, as far as I know."

"Whoa," Felix murmured, shaking his head. "Well, it's been real, but I gotta go."

"Afraid she'll come back?" I asked sweetly.

"Kate!" he yelped.

Still, he was out the door within minutes. Two minutes.

Who was Gilda Fitch? I asked myself as I listened to Felix's car roar away. My hairdresser liked her, I remembered. My hairdresser was a good judge of character. I hoped.

I trudged across the entryway to my desk, dumped my mail, and thudded into my office chair, my pulse thudding along with the rest of my body. Work was the thing to do, I reminded myself. Mindless, soothing work. Soon, I was in rhythm. Pay an invoice, wonder about Gilda Fitch. Why had her appearance at my door worried me so? Pay another invoice. And Maxwell Yang. Was he spying on me? Another invoice. Lisa Orton. Why was she angry sometimes and sweet at other times? Another invoice. I thought about the threatening phone call. Another invoice. Another suspect.

An hour later, the rhythm had taken on a sinister beat. What if the murderer was never identified? I reached for my suspect chart. I told myself I could fill it in if I really tried. There was the anger against the doctor that—

The doorbell rang. I almost put my head in my hands and wept. But I was trained like a rat. The doorbell rang, and I had to answer.

I should have wept instead. Kevin and Xanthe pushed through the doorway the moment I opened up.

Kevin had something that looked like a cell phone held up to his head, but it was making funny noises. "Yeah, yeah," I heard. Kevin thumbed a dial on the side of the contraption. A violin played somewhere. He thumbed the dial again. "Oooh, baby," someone moaned.

Kevin's mouth moved. "Mom's in—" But the moan music in the background drowned out the rest of his statement.

"What?" I shouted.

"It's a transistor radio, Katie," Kevin shouted back.

"Turn that thing off," I ordered.

But he couldn't hear me.

"I got it in trade for a pyramid cap," he kept on. "Pretty cool, huh?"

"Turn it off!" I bellowed.

"Anything you say, Katie," he replied as the moaning woman was mercifully silenced.

"Hello, Kevin. Hello Xanthe," I started over. "What did you say about Mom earlier?"

"Mom's in town," Kevin answered cheerfully. "She came to visit, but you weren't home."

TWENTY-TWO

✗

My chest tightened. I tried to swallow. Mom was in town?

"See, Katie," Kevin lectured me, "family is a holistic bond, really cosmic. You can't run away from it. Mom wants to be with you in your time of need—"

"Time of need?" I repeated. Did she know about the murders?

"Your wedding," Xanthe reminded me. "She's all bugged out about your wedding. She'd barely listen to *us* at all—"

"Did you try to sell Mom your pyramid scheme?" I demanded.

"Well, yeah," Kevin conceded, a blush showing around the edges of his dark glasses. "I thought she'd recognize its leading edge potential, but—"

"She didn't," Xanthe finished for him bluntly.

Kevin shrugged. "Older people, you know."

I was going to object to his lumping my mother in a group called "older people." Then I remembered the original point of our conversation. Mom was in town.

I began packing in my mind. Barbara, I'd visit Barbara. Not that I didn't like my mother, but I couldn't bear her accusing eyes, not now. Lieutenant Perez was bad enough. And if Mom was really "bugged out" about my wedding, I didn't want to expose Wayne to her anxiety. Or to expose him to her extended version of her pregnancy at the wedding gone wrong and its obvious warping of my prenatal psyche. My brain was going in circles now. Maybe Kevin was right. Maybe there was no running away from family.

"Hey, Katie, have you checked your answering machine?" Kevin asked. "Maybe Mom left you a message."

I would have applauded Kevin's unprecedented good sense, but I was too busy running to the machine.

There was indeed a message from my mother. Actually, there were quite a few messages. I pressed the button and heard her voice. On the first message, Mom sounded annoyed. She was angry by the second, raving by the third and fourth, and strangely calm by the fifth. Then there was a message from my aunt Mags, asking if I was really married, and a few more from friends with the same question. A call from Jade, my Jest Gifts warehousewoman, followed, enumerating the day's crises. Then a brief request for a return phone call from Avis. And finally, my mother's last message, in a tragic voice that would have done Shakespeare proud.

"I'm afraid I'm just going to have to leave," she told me sadly. "What's the use of waiting if you're never coming home? Call me when you need your mother. And tell Kevin to get a job."

I walked back from the machine, grinning with relief.

Now all I had to do was figure out who killed the two doctors.

Kevin and Xanthe grinned back at me. I should have started worrying then.

"We've come to tell you that we've got you covered on this murder thing—" Kevin began.

"Yeah," Xanthe finished for him. "Slammer's on the case."

I let the grin roll off my face.

"Kevin!" I snapped. "I said No. Did you hear me?"

"But, listen, Katie," Kevin went on. "I did a real good deal for you. And Slammer will only charge you five hundred dollars—"

"For what?" I asked. Then I shook my head. "No, never mind, I don't want to know. Just get him off the case."

"But—"

"I'll tell Mom, Kevin," I threatened. He flinched. How soon he'd forgotten who was in the family doghouse.

"Whoa, Katie, it's no big deal," he shot back. I swiveled around as if to return to the phone. He put up a hand. "I'll tell Slammer to forget it."

"Thank you," I said with all the dignity I could muster, and then I went to call Avis.

Kevin and Xanthe wandered into the kitchen as I punched out her phone number.

No one answered at Avis's house. I looked at my watch. Of course. It was a few minutes short of closing time at the nursery. The refrigerator door slammed in the kitchen as I called the Eldora Nurseries.

And sure enough, Avis was there.

"Kate!" she greeted me. I could almost hear a welcoming hug in her joyful voice. And that sound of joy released the tension I'd been holding in my own body.

"How are you?" I asked her, wanting to ask about Reed, but afraid to.

"Oh, great," she answered, then added more seriously, "I'm fine, really. I just know that Reed is at peace too. I'm trying to remember him positively. He did so many things, loved so many people in his life. It was full, however short."

"Right," I replied, trying to inject an enthusiasm I didn't quite feel into my tone.

"But that's not why I called, Kate," she told me. "I have a surprise for you. Why don't you come down to the nursery?"

I looked at my watch again. It was now just past closing time, and it would be even later by the time I got there. And what surprise could Avis have for me?

"How about tomorrow?" I suggested.

"Tomorrow will be just wonderful," Avis agreed cheerfully.

A chill tickled the hairs on my neck. I didn't like the idea of a surprise during murder season.

"See you then," Avis said and hung up.

I told myself that there was one person I trusted in this

whole thing. Avis. And anyway, she couldn't attack me in daylight—

The doorbell rang before my mind could argue otherwise.

"Doorbell!" Kevin yelled helpfully. The yell had a muffled quality. His mouth was full, I would have bet, full of leftovers from Wayne's recent meals.

So I answered the door.

Howie Damon stood where so many had stood before him, on my doorstep. Suddenly, I was glad that Kevin and Xanthe were munching away in the kitchen. Because Howie Damon was a suspect. And one I knew almost nothing about.

Howie thrust his hands toward me suddenly. I stepped back without thinking and raised my own hands in a defensive tai chi posture.

But then I saw what he was thrusting my way. A stack of neatly photocopied paper. You couldn't kill someone with paper, could you? "I have a copy of my manuscript for Wayne," Howie murmured shyly. He looked down at his feet. "I thought he could look at it. I know he's a writer. And he seems really intuitive."

I lowered my arms and tried to think. Would Wayne want to read Howie's manuscript?

"You know, Wayne only writes fiction," I told Howie gently.

"Oh, but he knows how to write." Howie raised his round face, his small eyes hopeful. "I'm sure of it. He's very sensitive."

I couldn't disagree with that.

Slowly, I extended my arms, and Howie placed the manuscript in them, as if handing over a foundling.

"Well, I'll make sure he sees it," I told Howie.

"Thank you," he murmured, his eyes on his feet again.

"Would you like to come in?" I asked. I can't tell you why. Only that some habits die hard.

"No, I couldn't," Howie answered, shaking his head.

That was a relief.

"Well, see you later, then," I declared, though I was fairly sure he wanted me to talk him into staying. One verbal invitation was enough, though. Habits die hard, but they can still die.

I shifted the manuscript to one arm and reached out my hand, gripping Howie's. His palm was predictably moist, though his handshake was unpredictably athletic. My hand ached when he dropped it.

"Good-bye then," he said wistfully and turned to walk down the front stairs.

I watched until he was actually out of my driveway and into his Honda Civic. When he started his engine and drove away, I closed the door. Manuscript or no manuscript, Howie Damon gave me the creeps. And how did he know where I lived? Then I reminded myself that just about everyone seemed to know where I lived. They probably looked me up in the telephone directory, nothing more sinister than that.

On cue, the phone rang.

I answered, expecting my mother, and was pleased to hear Jean Watkins's voice instead.

"Kate, have you found out anything new?" Now I wasn't so comfortable, especially with an unsolicited manuscript still nestled in one arm.

"Nothing," I told her. At length. My nothingness came out in a stream of complaints about interrupted interrogations, dead ends, and wasted time.

"Darcie talked to Lisa this afternoon," Jean informed me. "Darcie and Lisa are very concerned."

I sighed. We were all concerned. All but the murderer. Or maybe the murderer was the most concerned of anyone.

I was not in a good mood when I set the receiver back in its cradle.

I took Howie Damon's manuscript and set it ceremonially at Wayne's place at the kitchen table.

Kevin and Xanthe had apparently come to the end of their meal, and Kevin was boiling water for tea.

"Want some?" he offered, reaching for another cup.

"Sure, why not?" I agreed and sat at the table across from Xanthe, trying to think things out.

"I don't know why you're so uptight, Kate," Xanthe told me. She popped a pill in her mouth and washed it down with some apple juice. "If you're really scared about this murder thing, hire Slammer."

I didn't ask, For what? this time, because I was fascinated by the pill she'd just taken. Hadn't Reed said something about a pill? But what? I searched my brain, but it was no good. His words had disappeared from my memory banks. But he had said something. I was sure of it.

"Listen, Katie," Kevin said, handing me a steaming cup of peppermint tea. "We're here if you need us for the next few days. You're family, okay?"

And unexpectedly, my eyes moistened.

He reached in his back pocket and pulled out a pyramid cap, then held it out to me. I started to object. "On the house," he told me before I could, and set it on the kitchen table.

"We're gonna stay in town a little longer, but then we're splitting," Xanthe announced, standing up, ignoring her own cup of tea.

I stood too. Were they really leaving?

Xanthe stepped around the table, put her arms around me, and squeezed tentatively. I took a breath that smelled of perfume and squeezed her back.

"We'll probably visit Mom," Kevin murmured.

Lucky you, went through my mind, but I was pretty sure I didn't verbalize it.

Kevin and Xanthe both looked sad from behind as they walked down the front stairs, their tea forgotten and cooling in the kitchen, their respective shoulders slumped.

I put a hand over my mouth to stop from calling them back. My family. Damn.

And then, I really did work on Jest Gifts. Full-tilt boogie, I got down to slinging invoices and ledgers until late that evening when Wayne came home.

"How'd your day go?" he asked.

I settled into his arms, opening my mouth to tell him about each and every suspect. No, I decided, and used my mouth to kiss him instead.

Thursday morning I woke up late. My head ached and my stomach didn't feel so good either. Guilt, anxiety, flu?

By the time I stumbled out of bed, the phone was ringing to match my throbbing temples.

I padded to the phone in my jammies and picked it up, interrupting the answering machine mid-speech.

"Hey, kiddo," Barbara greeted me. "I know you just got up. But I wanted to tell you that you're real close now."

"Real close to what?" I asked blearily. "A nervous breakdown?"

"I'm not sure exactly what you're close to, but you're almost there. I can feel it."

"Barbara!" I bawled. That hurt my head.

"Kate, you have to learn to trust in the unseen—"

"What unseen? What are you talking about?"

"You'll see," she answered. "Love ya, kiddo." And then I heard the dial tone.

After I showered, I checked out my suspect chart one more time. Maybe that's what Barbara had meant about being close. I added, "angry with Dr. S.," in a few columns, "Dr. S.'s patient," in a couple more, and "rosemary" and "pill" under MISCELLANEOUS. Then I looked at it again. Whatever Barbara meant, it clearly was "unseen," at least by me.

Wayne came up behind me as I was staring at the chart. I stuffed it under my desk blotter and turned to him.

He held out the copy of Howie Damon's manuscript in my direction. His eyebrows were low, his jaw set angrily.

"What's this?' he growled.

"Howie's manuscript," I said defensively. "I didn't think you'd mind. He wanted you to read it, and—"

"Did you let him into the house?" Wayne demanded. And then I knew his anger was directed at my possible danger, not the possibility of having to read Howie's manuscript.

"No, I didn't," I shot back. "And Kevin and Xanthe were here, anyway."

"Oh," he said, his voice still tight. "And were they here when you entertained your other visitors?"

How did he know about the other visitors? I decided he was just guessing.

"Wayne, I'm here," I reminded him softly. "I'm alive."

"Be careful, Kate," he pleaded. "I couldn't bear losing you." Then he forced his face into a smile. "Just think of probate now that you're my wife. A mess."

God, I loved the man. A joke, even now.

I laughed, and turned my chair all the way around. He bent down to hug me.

"Wayne," I began when he straightened. "I was going to visit Avis at the nursery today." Had he known his own, personal, good cop, bad cop routine would elicit a confession like this?

He looked up at the clock. "Gotta go into La Fête in half an hour," he muttered, frowning. "Avis asked you?"

I nodded.

"Avis is okay," he declared, and turned to walk off, looking down at the manuscript he held in his hands as he did. He was already reading it before he left my office.

Well, if Wayne wasn't afraid of Avis, I wouldn't be either. I was right the first time. Avis was the one suspect I could trust. Though I hadn't told Wayne about Avis's "surprise."

I left my suspect list under my blotter as I worked. I would forget the whole thing. I just wished Lieutenant Perez could too.

By ten o'clock, I decided it was time to visit Avis and find out what her "surprise" was.

I found Wayne in his back office, his nose buried in Howie Damon's manuscript.

"Time to go?" he asked, looking guiltily at the clock. He jumped up. "Whoops, past time. Howie's story's too good. Three generations of California. I got lost."

"Just don't get lost on the way to work," I told him, with a goodbye kiss.

He returned the kiss, then looked into my eyes.

"Be careful at the nursery, Kate," he said. "If there's a hassle, call me on my cell phone. Or at work."

I nodded.

"I mean it," he growled.

"I love you, too," I growled back.

At least he smiled. And then he ran out of the house, got into his Jaguar, and roared out of the driveway.

I was just about to leave the house myself when the phone rang again.

I made the mistake of picking it up.

My mother had finally caught up with me.

"Where were you yesterday?" she demanded.

"Working," I lied.

"Aren't you married now?" she asked.

I groaned inwardly. Should I try to explain the possibility of the peaceful coexistence of work and marriage? I decided specifics were necessary.

"I still have my business, Mom," I reminded her. "Remember Jest Gifts?" I didn't add how many years of my life had gone into building Jest Gifts.

"Well, Kate," she lectured, "don't forget that men like attention."

"Right, Mom," I conceded. *Everyone* liked attention. I had no problem with that concept.

"And Kate . . ."

I waited impatiently.

"I . . . I miss you," she whispered and hung up.

My heart thunked down with the phone. My mother missed me? I was in a daze as I grabbed my purse and made my way out to the Toyota. Maybe I ought to visit Mom. I turned the key in the ignition. I would visit her. The question was how soon. Hours, days, weeks?

I still didn't know the answer by the time I got to the nursery.

There were only a couple of cars in the lot when I got there: Avis's Saab and a Lexus that looked familiar. Avis wasn't doing much business. But it was still early, and a weekday, probably not the best time for a nursery.

I walked into the main building and found Avis behind the counter. There were no folding metal chairs set out today. And Avis was smiling.

"All right," I prodded, her good mood catching. "What's up?"

"Olive got the job!" she announced with a great flourish of her gloved hands.

"Congratulations," I told her, still waiting for the surprise. "Is she moving out?"

"Yes!" Avis whooped and came around the counter to hug me. "And it was all because of you."

"Me?" Now that *was* a surprise.

"Remember, the clothing wholesaler?"

It was coming back. I'd promised to recommend Olive. But the wholesaler had never called me.

"Eileen O'Brien—"

"Eileen O'Brien—I know her," I interrupted.

"So she said," Avis went on. "She said if Kate Jasper recommended Olive, that was good enough for her."

I put in a short, agnostic prayer that Eileen O'Brien would still be speaking to me the next time we met.

"And this was your surprise?"

"Yes," Avis answered, and gave me another hug. After she released me, she told me to pick the biggest plant in the nursery as my reward.

It was an offer I wasn't going to refuse. I walked out the door of the main building into a paradise of plants. Annuals, perennials, shrubs. Yum. I let the delicious earth and plant smells surround me and fantasized about roses and cherry blossoms. Deer, I reminded myself. I needed something that the deer wouldn't eat. And something that wouldn't break Avis's budget either. I wasn't betting on how long Olive would keep her job. An early-blooming wisteria caught my eye. It was stunning, already trained, its tall stem tied to an even-taller stake, that allowed its clusters of violet-blue buds to stream majestically downward like a waterfall made magically solid. I was in love. I didn't even look at the price tag. I just picked up the pot and lugged it back into the main building to show Avis, panting with exertion.

But once I was back in the building I couldn't see my friend anywhere. I looked down aisles and past the counter.

"Avis?" I called out, setting the wisteria down carefully.

I thought I heard something from behind the counter. Was she hiding? Was she playing a trick on me?

I walked around the counter cautiously, and then I saw her. She was flat out on the cement floor, her hat beside her.

"Avis!" I cried and crouched down beside her. Her eyes seemed to be trying to open. I felt for her pulse and found it. Her skin was warm.

"Avis?" I said again, this time in a whisper, my own body having frozen upon seeing her.

With cold hands, I reached up for the store phone. Time and sound seemed suspended. I remembered what Reed had said about a pill. He'd said there was a green pill, and that Dr. Sandstrom had pocketed it the first time he was hit with the statuette. Suddenly that seemed important. But why?

Lisa Orton. My hand touched the phone ever so slowly and an image flashed in my mind's eye, an image of Lisa lifting something to her mouth and swallowing it that first evening. A simple hand movement, and then she'd swallowed. A pill? It must have been a pill. A green pill? And she'd talked about her abusive father who was a doctor, too. But Lisa? No, I told myself, not Lisa.

That's when I saw the pitchfork coming in my direction.

Twenty-three

✗

It's lucky I'd learned to move from a squatting position in tai chi. And to move fast. I sidestepped and stood at the same time, seeing the pitchfork slam into the counter out of the corner of my eye. Then I turned to face the person holding the important end of the pitchfork and prepared myself to dodge another jab.

But the second jab was verbal, though none the less piercing.

"Lie on the floor next to Avis, or I'll have to kill her," Lisa Orton told me, her voice high and anxious.

Lisa Orton? I looked into her childlike face and was chilled. Because she didn't look any different than before. Her eyes were round. And she sucked in her lower lip, looking her usual vulnerable and waiflike self as she yanked the pitchfork out of the counter. My only clue to her mental state was the perspiration I could see on her vulnerable face.

"And will you have to kill me?" I asked, not quite ready to lie on the floor.

"I don't know!" she shrieked. She raised the pitchfork over Avis's body. "Just do it."

I did it.

I lay down next to Avis like a fellow corpse on a mortuary slab, and then wished that metaphor hadn't occurred to me.

I drew my knees up slowly, and placed my palms on the

floor, ready to spring back up in an instant. The concrete was cold everywhere my body touched it.

Lisa tapped my chest with the prongs of the pitchfork, and the concrete felt even colder. I resisted the urge to close my eyes and waited for the thrust.

But the prongs didn't dig any deeper. Lisa wanted to talk. Or explain. Or rant. Whatever, it was fine with me.

"He caught me at the break and lectured me!" she wailed. "He said I shouldn't be popping pills. He yelled at me, told me to shut up. So I did." She paused, her eyes going even wider. Her pupils seemed to spread like spilled ink across her irises, leaving nothing but black for color. Was she talking about Dr. Sandstrom? I wanted to ask, but decided this wasn't the time.

"The pills," she went on, her voice lower. "I don't know, maybe he was right." She looked down at me and screamed as if I'd disagreed. "No, he couldn't have been right! Anyway, he shouldn't have yelled at me. But then I found the deer statue and hit him with it from behind. I wrapped my scarf around it so I wouldn't leave any fingerprints." She was talking about Dr. Sandstrom, all right. I was beginning to catch the gist of her narrative. "The Goddess must have wanted me to do it."

"But the Goddess is benign," slipped out before I could stop it.

Lisa didn't hear me anyway. She just kept on, the words tumbling from her mouth as fast as my heart was beating.

"I thought he'd never guess it was me. People think I'm a wuss. But my therapist told me I have Goddess energy within me. That I'm strong. I don't know!" She was wailing again. The pitchfork wavered, skidding down to the side of my ribs. All I felt was pressure, no pain under my sweatshirt. "But I did it, I hit him. Only, a pill must have rolled out of my pocket."

Lisa paused for breath. She wasn't really looking at me anymore. Her head was turned to look out the door of the main building. Was she seeing Dr. Sandstrom as she spoke?

I took the chance for a quick glance at Avis. Avis stuck a gloved finger into the air and opened her eyes momentarily. Then she closed them again quickly. So quickly, I wasn't absolutely sure that it had happened.

"When he picked up the pill, I knew he knew, and he'd tell," Lisa whispered. "So the next time, I ran and put on a nursery smock and gloves from the shed, and then I hit him and hit him till I knew he was dead. Nobody even noticed I was gone. They were all watching you and Avis and that little jerky guy. I was brave, wasn't I? It must have been Goddess energy. But his head was so icky. I hid the smock and gloves in the trunk of my car. No one ever checked there." Now she did look at me, and her wide eyes seemed to call out for absolution. "It's all so complicated. I feel like I did before I saw my therapist, so confused. But I had to defend myself. You can't trust anyone."

I nodded. Lisa's hands eased on the pitchfork, color running into her white knuckles.

"And Reed." She kept her eyes on mine now. "Reed guessed from the pill. I could tell. And he was a doctor! My father was a doctor. And there was a hoe right there when I went to talk to Reed. Just like it was left there for me. 'Cause no matter how many times I hit Reed with it, the blood didn't splatter far enough to get on me. And I used the bottom of my shirt to hold the handle. No fingerprints. And no one saw us. I did the right thing." Her voice went quiet, but it was scarier that way. "Doctors should die. Not ones like my therapist, but other doctors."

I nodded again. She pulled the pitchfork over to the concrete floor, away from my body. Was nodding the thing to do?

"Like my father," she explained. "When you're small you can't fight them, but when you're bigger and filled with your true self, you can kill them." Then Lisa actually smiled. I swallowed and smiled back.

"See," she whispered confidentially. "I have a wonderful therapist. She recovered memories for me . . . memories of my father abusing me sexually. I didn't believe it at first—some-

times I still don't—but it doesn't matter. He was mean to me."
Her round eyes narrowed ever so slightly. And I remembered
what Jean Watkins had said about abuse not having to be
sexual to be hurtful. Whether or not Lisa had been sexually
abused, she was obviously deeply wounded emotionally. I just
wished she was receiving therapy right now. In an institution.
"My therapist takes us survivors through cleansing enact-
ments. I got to kill Daddy over and over again. That's what
he deserved. He always told me to shut up."

"Was that how he abused you?" I asked. Even now, I was
curious as to what had actually happened to Lisa Orton to
drive her mad. Because there was no question left in my mind
about her sanity.

"No, it was more," she whispered, but her voice was un-
certain. She shook her head. "It was more . . . my therapist
says so. But, but . . ."

"That's okay," I said as gently as possible. "It doesn't matter."

Lisa's mouth opened wide. "He didn't *love* me!" she
screamed. "What does it matter if he abused me sexually or
not, he didn't love me!" She looked back outside. "So I left
the rosemary sprig."

"For remembrance?" I asked.

She nodded.

"But he wasn't your father," I commented, keeping my
voice light. "Dr. Sandstrom, I mean."

"Oh," Lisa said earnestly, "but he could have been. He was
just the same, so cold and yelling at me. Just the same."

I thought of the other Dr. Sandstrom that I'd come to know
posthumously, and was sorry that Lisa met him on a bad night.

"But how about Reed?" I asked. "Was he like your father?"

"Not exactly, but still, I couldn't trust him. He was a doctor,
wasn't he? At first I thought he was okay anyway. I even
thought I might go out with him. He flirted with me. But I
saw him with Avis. They were kissing! How can you trust
someone like that? And then he started in about the pill I

dropped. He was torturing me, torturing me! He was easy to kill. The hoe was really simple."

As simple as a pitchfork, I thought, but kept the dialogue going.

"Does your therapist know?" I asked.

Tears poured out of those wide eyes then, down Lisa's freckled cheeks. She was still a child. If she hadn't been holding a pitchfork on me, I would have held her.

"I'm afraid to tell her," she sobbed. "I think she'd be proud, but I'm not sure. I trusted her so, but I was afraid she'd turn me in. I miss her. The hypnosis sessions especially."

"Hypnosis?" I repeated.

"Oh, yeah," Lisa murmured, her voice slowing down. "It's so neat. See, first she says, 'Walk down a long green road,' and you do." Lisa's eyes lost focus. I hoped she was seeing that road in her mind.

"And then, when you've walked down the long green road?" I whispered, beginning to hope. Years ago, I'd taken a class in hypnosis with Barbara. She'd said I'd need it someday. Was today the day? And more important, was "long green road" Lisa's trigger phrase?

"She says, 'You see something at the end of the road,' " Lisa replied dreamily.

I felt a gloved hand clasp mine. Avis's. Giving me encouragement. I could have cried. But I didn't have time.

"And what do you see at the end of the road?" I prodded gently.

"It's a little cottage, with roses and ivy and lots of nice things inside."

"Let's walk inside," I suggested. Then I purred, "Oooh, it's beautiful, isn't it?"

"Yes, it is beautiful. There's all kinds of pretty things in here. And my mother is here, and we're having a tea party." The mother who'd died young, I remembered suddenly.

"With porcelain cups?"

"Oh, yes," she murmured, closing her eyes. "Mommy asks me to pour. The tea smells so good."

"Lisa, isn't your arm awfully heavy?" I soothed. "Wouldn't it be nice to lay down that load?"

"Oh, yes." Lisa set the pitchfork down, and then sank to the floor to sit cross-legged at our feet.

Avis rose quietly from the concrete floor at the same time.

"Are there treats?" I asked and pushed myself into a sitting position.

"Oh, yes." Lisa's voice was drowsy now. She extended her legs and torso and lay her own body down on the cold concrete. But she didn't seem to feel it, lost in her ivy-covered cottage.

I heard the door of the main building swing in. I just hoped Lisa didn't. But Lisa was too far gone to hear anything from the outside. I heard a voice, Kevin's, and saw Avis press her finger against her lips urgently, pointing down. Kevin and Xanthe circled around the counter to see Lisa and me. And to hear Lisa.

"And little dogs and kittens," Lisa went on, her voice slurred. "And I have a big flowered hat."

Avis carefully picked up the pitchfork and placed it on top of the counter.

Then Wayne and Felix burst through the door.

Avis lifted her finger to her lips again, but Felix was not to be stopped.

"Holy moly!" he shouted. "What's the friggin' scoop here—"

Wayne clapped a hand across Felix's mouth. I envied him the pleasure. But it was too late. Lisa's eyes had popped open.

"You tricked me," she accused, looking for the pitchfork.

"No," I told her. "No, Lisa. It'll all be all right now."

More softly, Xanthe asked, "What happened, Kate?"

"The Goddess told her to kill two men," I whispered back angrily. I wasn't sure who I was angry with. Lisa? Her therapist? Xanthe? Or their Goddess?

"Oh, Kate, I'm so sorry," Xanthe said, and tears moistened her eyes.

Then Xanthe knelt down and took Lisa into her arms and held her. Lisa clung to her and wept in great racking sobs.

Then I realized. Xanthe understood Lisa. I didn't. I hoped I never would.

Twenty-four

✗

We were all there at Eldora Nurseries on a Sunday afternoon three days later, standing outdoors among the flats of annuals. We, being the survivors of the Deer-Abused Support Group. And Lieutenant Perez, my friend Barbara, Dr. Yamoda, who I'd thought to invite at the last minute, and Kevin and Xanthe, who I hadn't thought to invite, but who came anyway.

I stood in the streaming sunlight, sweating under my turtleneck and listening to the blend of conversation, traffic, and the hum of the countless insects the plants had attracted. No one seemed about to sit on one of the metal folding chairs that Avis had brought outside for the meeting. Or was it a celebration? I breathed in the fragrance of soil and vegetation, felt the sun on my nose, and decided, yes, we were celebrating. I looked up into Wayne's face. His brows were relaxed and a rare public smile tugged at his mouth. I put my arm around his waist, leaned for a moment against his torso, and added his unique scent to the nursery's brew.

Wayne. I felt my own face flowering into a smile. Wayne, who'd had second thoughts when he'd called the nursery from his car phone Thursday morning and received no answer. Wayne, who'd then turned his Jaguar around to come back to Marin after he'd crossed the Golden Gate Bridge. Wayne, who'd even called Felix to meet him at the nursery. I squeezed his waist and glanced over at Kevin and Xanthe, who'd shown up at the nursery too that day. I still didn't know exactly why. Xanthe had only said they'd been "vibed out" by my over-heard decision to visit Avis the day before. They'd come to visit at my house that morning and immediately realized where I was.

Maybe Xanthe was psychic. I swiveled my head Barbara's way and she winked in my direction. An affirmative answer? I didn't really care. I was just thankful I'd been alive and well when the gang of four had arrived at Eldora Nurseries. I could never have forgiven myself if these people who cared for me had found my dead body next to Avis's. "These people" es-pecially being Wayne.

Now, Avis was bragging once again about how I'd saved her life. She straightened her spine and spread her arms wide, perfect in teal today. Teal gloves, hat, hip boots, scarf, and jumpsuit were just the beginning of her outfit.

"I suppose I should have never asked Lisa about the pill," she explained, her voice gentle and clear in the shimmering air. "But it was niggling at me, that pill she'd swallowed. And then Reed mentioning a pill. I didn't mean to get Lisa worked up. In fact, I really didn't think I had at first. She just said 'what pill?' when I asked, and then she was gone. Kate came in and went back out to get her plant. And the next thing I knew, I was reaching to answer the phone, and Lisa ran at me and threw me onto the concrete floor behind the counter like I was a sack of manu . . ." She paused. "Tanbark," she fin-ished. "I must have been unconscious when Kate found me—"

"And Katie talked Lisa out of killing you," Kevin declared proudly. Brothers are good for something.

"I just got her to talk, really," I replied with false modesty. I was still astounded that my hypnosis trick had worked. Hot damn! But then, Lisa had been preconditioned for hypnosis.

"Kate could get a friggin' deer to talk," Felix complained nasally. "I'm supposed to be the whiz-bang journalist, but every time I tried to scoop someone, they just went 'I dunno.' Might as well have been at a friggin agnostic's convention, 'I dunno, I dunno.' Jeez Louise."

"Tell them about Lisa's therapist, tiger-muffin," Barbara ordered.

Ugh. I hated it when Barbara called Felix "tiger-muffin," but at least it got him on another subject.

"Lisa Orton's therapist is gonna lose her ticket," Felix obliged. "She was already under the medico Gestapo-watch, even before Lisa Orton. See, *all* of her patients believed they were molested as children. And none of them believed it before they let her woo-woo them. And get this, they all remembered the same details from their childhoods, every single one. The therapist took each of them through this whole friggin' guided imagery trip, describing an identical, off-the-shelf scene of childhood molestation. And each of them was baked on enough legal drugs to remember anything she suggested, real or not."

"But, hon," Natalie Miner objected, her raspy voice sounding even more Southern today than usual. Maybe it was the sun. "Aren't some of these poor gals really molested?"

Jean Watkins weighed in then.

"That's the very sad thing." Jean shook her head slowly. "With these false memories being implanted, who knows who the real victims are anymore?"

"Yeah, like that old wackhead who wanted me to say I did dirty things with my father," Darcie threw in.

"Precisely," her grandmother agreed. "It wasn't true for Darcie, but how many other unfortunate women have lived through these experiences? And who will believe them now? Now that the whole issue of childhood memories is subject to such scrutiny."

"I did a little undercover for Kate," Xanthe threw in nonchalantly. She lowered her eyes modestly.

"You did?" I asked, stunned. I could feel my mouth hanging open. I shut it. There were too many insects around for open mouths.

"I always thought this Lisa person sounded pretty squirrelly, so I just called her therapist and got an appointment—"

"Wait a minute," I objected. "How'd you even know who Lisa's therapist was?"

"I called Lisa," Xanthe answered simply.

She'd called Lisa. I hadn't thought of that. But I hadn't noticed Lisa was squirrelly either. And Xanthe had just picked it up from conversation.

"Anyway," Xanthe resumed. "the first thing the therapist asked me is whether I'd ever been molested as a child."

"Why didn't you tell me?" I demanded, slapping at a bug who'd landed on my forehead.

"You wouldn't let me, Kate," she snapped. Her mascared eyes opened wide as she put her hands on her hips. Whoa. Cursing time already?

"Oh, Xanthe," I murmured and reached out to touch her shoulder. If only I'd listened to her.

Xanthe dropped her arms and smiled forgivingly. Then she took a deep breath that made the most of her Mae West figure. "See, I went to a therapist like that once. She was the one that taught me to curse people to get it out of my system. I don't think I'll curse people anymore." She paused, frowning for a moment. "At least not as often."

"Did you guess it was Lisa?" Maxwell Yang asked.

"Not really," Xanthe admitted. "But Felix kept talking about Lisa, and I felt like I knew her. No one ever believes I'm psychic."

Barbara chuckled wickedly.

"Maybe we should have you on the force," Lieutenant Perez chimed in, his dark, sexy eyes on Xanthe. Incredibly, I felt a tug of jealousy.

"Maybe," Xanthe purred and winked his way.

The lieutenant blushed and rushed headlong into speech. "We found the green pill in the doctor's pocket, of course, but we just thought that a doctor was likely to carry pills. And no one said anything about Lisa taking a pill." He turned to glare my way.

But the glare went right through me, because I had another piece of the puzzle.

"That's what Dr. Sandstrom meant by 'I'm a doctor,' " I muttered. Then I took a breath and spoke louder. "He meant that he could figure out who hit him if he figured out who took the medication that was on the ground next to him."

"And Lisa knew what he meant," Howie Damon put in, his first words of the day. "I'd wondered about that; in fact I was worried. I never saw Lisa take *her* pill. But I recognized the one the doctor picked up from the ground. I'm on the same medication as Lisa. Antidepressant." He looked at his feet. "I thought the doctor was talking to me. Maybe if Lisa had known, she wouldn't have killed him."

"No," Jean Watkins told him, her hand raised, palm up. "Don't even think that. Lisa was beyond reason."

"Really?" Howie whispered.

Jean nodded her absolution.

Then Howie smiled. "If it weren't such a tragedy, it'd make a great story." His eyes went out of focus.

"Hey, wait a friggin' nanosecond here," Felix jumped in. "This is my story! Sheesh, Lucy, I'm the one who was there—"

"And you know," Wayne cut him off easily, "Lisa was the only one to leave after Dr. Sandstrom. I've thought it out. Kate and Avis were talking and it seemed like everyone was watching. Then Reed and Avis went out, but not till later. So when Lisa went outside, she went alone, alone but for Dr. Sandstrom."

"Lord, the poor man," Natalie murmured.

But Lieutenant Perez reacted differently to Wayne's words. "Why didn't you tell us?" he demanded angrily.

"I didn't put it together in my mind until I was driving back over the bridge," Wayne admitted quietly. "I'd thought everyone had been moving around at random. But it was only the doctor and Lisa who actually left. Maybe it was the adrenaline that triggered the memory. But suddenly I could see it."

I took his hand in mine and caressed it. "Not adrenaline," I whispered in his ear. "Love."

And then I remembered the tea I'd shared with Lisa at her

mini-mansion. My sweat turned cold in the sunlight. I turned to Maxwell Yang, tasting bile.

"Maxwell, did you save my life when I . . ." I began. Then I tried to remember if I'd ever told Wayne about my tea party with Lisa. I looked up at Wayne. He wasn't smiling anymore.

"Perhaps you saved *my* life," Maxwell suggested, with an impish wink. Did he understand what I was trying to hide? "A conversational lag can be the death of my attention." He laughed. I laughed with him, swallowing fear. He *did* understand. I stole another peep at Wayne. He just looked confused now. And then I reminded myself never, never again to have tea alone with a murder suspect.

"By the way m'dear," Gilda broke into my thoughts. "Thought you might want to know I really was working when I delivered your post the other day. Know I got your tail in a twist. When we need a bit of money, we work overtime. Just replaced your regular carrier that day. Dashed sorry if I terrified the wits out of you."

"Too late," I assured her. "My wits were gone long ago."

"Hah-hah, jolly good—"

"Dr. Sandstrom's children are extremely grateful the murderer's been identified," a new voice spoke up. Dr. Yamoda. I swiveled my head and saw her earnest face. "They asked me to thank each of you who were involved. They loved their father."

"Maybe Dr. Sandstrom was a father figure to Lisa too," Avis murmured, then turned and walked into the main building.

"Unfortunately, Lisa despised her father, what?" Gilda added.

Some part of me wanted to laugh hysterically. Because Gilda had it in one. But I kept quiet for Dr. Yamoda's sake.

Then there was a long silence. Everyone seemed to be waiting for something. Perhaps we were waiting to mourn Dr. Searle Sandstrom and Dr. Reed Killian properly. But the sunlight still sparkled with celebration. Even the insect buzzing in my ear seemed to sing with joy.

Avis suddenly appeared in front of me. In each of her gloved hands she held a giant bouquet of flowers. In the quickness of the moment all I could see was color—periwinkle-blue, yellow, lavender, coral, magenta, white, and more, sparkling in the light.

"For the bride and groom," she announced and handed us the bouquets ceremonially.

"Happy honeymoon!" Felix whooped. And he didn't even say "friggin' "

And then Xanthe and Kevin were hugging us, squashing our flowers, and then Barbara, and then everyone else, their identities lost in the deluge of varying squeezes, kisses, textures, and smells.

Wayne and I glanced at each other after the last dizzying hug, linked hands, and ran to our car under the sweet rain of rose blossoms.

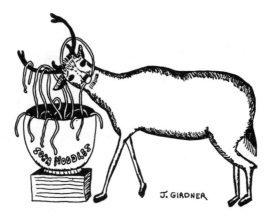

J. GIRDNER

SOBA NOODLE IMBROGLIO

12 ounces soba noodles or linguine
1 pound marinated, diced tofu
1/2 cup shredded carrots
1/4 cup soy sauce
1/4 cup maple syrup
3 tablespoons rice vinegar
1 tablespoon toasted sesame oil
1 tablespoon crushed garlic
1 tablespoon hot mustard
1/4 tablespoon crushed ginger root
4 sliced green onions
venison (extremely optional!)

1. Cook noodles according to package directions. Allow to cool.

2. Combine soy sauce, maple syrup, sesame oil, vinegar, garlic, ginger, and mustard into a smooth dressing.

3. Toss noodles, dressing, onions, tofu, and carrots.

4. Refrigerate, and serve cold as revenge.

4–6 servings as a side dish
2–4 as an entree